Praise for the novels of
#1 *New York Times* bestselling author
Debbie Macomber

"Macomber never disappoints. Tears and laughter abound."

—*Library Journal*

"Debbie Macomber tells women's stories in a way no one else does."

—*BookPage*

"Macomber...knows how to please her audience."
—*Oregon Statesman Journal*

"Popular romance writer Debbie Macomber has a gift for evoking the emotions that are at the heart of the genre's popularity."

—*Publishers Weekly*

"Debbie Macomber is one of the most reliable, versatile romance writers around."
—*Milwaukee Journal Sentinel*

"Virtually guaranteed to please."

—*Publishers Weekly*

"It's impossible not to cheer for Macomber's characters.... When it comes to creating a special place and memorable, honorable characters, nobody does it better than Macomber."

—*BookPage*

DEBBIE MACOMBER

Fairy-Tale Forever

Previously published as
Cindy and the Prince and *Some Kind of Wonderful*

 mira

mira™

Recycling programs for this product may not exist in your area.

ISBN-13: 978-0-7783-3158-2

Fairy-Tale Forever
First published as Fairy Tale Weddings in 2009.
This edition published in 2021.
Copyright © 2009 by Harlequin Books S.A.

Cindy and the Prince
First published in 1987. This edition published in 2021.
Copyright © 1987 by Debbie Macomber

Some Kind of Wonderful
First published in 1988. This edition published in 2021.
Copyright © 1988 by Debbie Macomber

This edition published by arrangement with Harlequin Books S.A.

For questions and comments about the quality of this book, please contact us at CustomerService@Harlequin.com.

Mira
22 Adelaide St. West, 40th Floor
Toronto, Ontario M5H 4E3, Canada
www.Harlequin.com

Printed in Lithuania

MIX
Paper from responsible sources
FSC® C021394

**Also available from #1 *New York Times*
bestselling author Debbie Macomber and MIRA**

CONTENTS

CINDY AND THE PRINCE

One

"Someday your prince will come," Vanessa Wilbur sang in a strained falsetto voice as she ran a feather duster along the top of the bookcase.

Cindy Territo ignored her work partner and vigorously rubbed the thirtieth-story window, removing an imaginary smudge from the glass. The pair were employees of the janitorial company contracted by Oakes-Jenning Financial Services. For four nights a week they were responsible for cleaning the offices of the corporation's top executives. Tedious work, but it supplemented Vanessa's family income so she could pursue her dream of script writing; her hope was to someday see her plays performed on Broadway. And the job paid well enough to keep Cindy in computer classes.

"You have to admit you spend more time cleaning Mr. Prince's office than any of the others," Vanessa said, eyeing her friend suspiciously.

Unable to hide her amusement, Cindy stuffed her cleaning rag in the hip pocket of her coveralls and laughed out loud. "Has anyone told you that you're a hopeless romantic?"

"Of course." Vanessa's eyes shone with laughter. She pointed at Cindy with her feather duster and released an exaggerated sigh. "Sometimes I think you, my friend, could be living a modern-day fairy tale."

"A what?" Cindy might be far more cynical than Vanessa, but one of them had to keep her head out of the clouds.

"A fairy tale."

Cindy ignored her friend and continued window washing—her least favorite task.

"Someday...some way...a handsome prince will come riding into your life on a white stallion and rescue you from all this," Vanessa said.

Cindy shook her head. "You've been spending too much time in dreamland," she scoffed.

"No, I haven't." Vanessa perched on the corner of a large mahogany desk, her legs swinging. "In fact, I believe it's fate. Think about it, girl. Your name is Cindy— as in Cinderella—and you clean the offices of a man named Prince, as in Prince Charming. Now doesn't *that* strike you as fate?"

"Thorndike Prince!" Cindy spewed out his name in a burst of laughter.

"And, as I mentioned, you do spend more time in his office than any of the others!"

"He's the first vice president. His office is largest, for heaven's sake."

"But..."

The idea was so ludicrous that Cindy had to choke back laughter. "Besides, he's got to be at least sixty."

"What makes you think so?"

"First, Oakes-Jenning Financial Services isn't going

to make a thirty-year-old their first vice president, and second—"

"It's been done before," Vanessa interrupted. Folding her arms, she hopped down from the desk to look stubbornly at her friend.

"And second," Cindy continued undaunted, "I clean his office. I know the man. He's staid and stuffy, and that's just the beginning."

"What do you mean?"

"He's so predictable. He eats the same sandwich— pastrami on rye—for lunch nearly every day and orders it from the same deli. He's so set in his ways that he's as predictable as Santa Claus on Christmas Eve. The only thing he knows is business, business, business. Oh, I'm sure he's dedicated and hardworking, but there's a lot more to life than slaving away in some office and making oodles of money." A *whole* lot more—and Cindy doubted the first vice president knew anything about having fun.

"What do you think about the photograph of the gorgeous brunette on his desk?"

Cindy smiled. "Nothing. I'd venture to guess that Mr. Thorndike Prince has been married to the same woman for fifty years."

"The photo," Vanessa reminded her.

"That's probably the old coot's granddaughter."

"Wrong!"

"Wrong?"

"Yup. How'd you like to see a picture of your 'old coot'?"

The twinkle in Vanessa's brown eyes told Cindy she was in for a shock. "And just where did you happen to find a picture of ol' Thorndike?"

"In the financial section of today's paper. Read it and weep, Cindy Territo." She reached inside her cleaning cart and whipped out the folded newspaper, shoving it under Cindy's nose.

One glance at the dark, handsome man in the photograph made Cindy take a surprised breath. She grabbed the paper and held it in both hands as she stared at the picture. "I don't believe it," she murmured. "He's, he's—"

"Gorgeous," Vanessa supplied.

"Young." The word trembled from Cindy's dry throat. He was gorgeous, all right; she admitted that. Rarely had she seen a more strikingly handsome man. He was the type who'd stand out in any crowd. Forceful. Persuasive. Vigorous. His face was square and serious, his chin determined. His eyes gazed back at her and even from the black-and-white image, Cindy could tell they were an intense gray. There wasn't a hint of amusement in those sharp, keen eyes, and Cindy guessed the photographer had been lucky to get the shot. Perhaps most astonishing of all was that Thorndike Prince couldn't be more than thirty-five…if that.

"Well?" Vanessa prodded.

"He isn't exactly how I pictured him."

"You're right about that," Vanessa said with obvious pleasure. "Now all we need to do is to find a way for the two of you to meet."

"What?" Cindy tore her gaze from the paper, assuming she'd misunderstood her friend.

"All we need to do is come up with a way of getting the two of you together," Vanessa repeated. "You're perfect for each other."

Playfully, Cindy placed the back of her hand against her friend's forehead. "How long have you had this raging fever?"

"I'm not sick!"

"Maybe not, but you're talking like a crazy woman."

"Come on, Cindy, dream a little."

"That's no dream—that's a nightmare." Her hand flew to the barely tamed blond curls sneaking out from beneath the red bandana tied at the back of her head. The blue pin-striped coveralls did nothing to emphasize the feminine curves of her hips and breasts.

"Naturally you wouldn't look like this."

"I certainly hope not."

"He'd like you, Cindy," Vanessa continued enthusiastically. "I know he would. You're bright and witty, and ol' Thorndike looks like he could use someone to bring him some love and laughter. You're probably right about him—I bet business is all he thinks about. And you're so pretty with that blond hair and those baby-blue eyes, the minute he sees you, he'll feel as if he's been knocked over the head."

Cindy gave a wistful sigh. She didn't need to close her eyes to imagine her prince—*this* Prince—smiling down at her with a look of such tenderness that it would steal her breath. Just the thought produced a warm, tingling sensation in her stomach.

A frown pinched Vanessa's forehead as her eyes grew serious. "We have one minor problem, though—that woman in the photograph on his desk. I doubt she's his sister. They could be involved."

"Involved," Cindy repeated before she realized what she was saying. She shook her head to dispel the image of Thorndike Prince leaning over to kiss her. In just minutes Vanessa had nearly convinced her that with one look, the first vice president of Oakes-Jenning Financial Services would swoon at her feet. Well, it was easy to dream, but life's realities faced her every day.

"Come on, Neil Simon, we've got work to do."

"Neil Simon?"

"Apparently you've decided to turn your talent toward writing comedies."

"But, Cindy, I'm serious!"

"I'm not. Someone like Thorndike Prince isn't going to be interested in the cleaning woman who vacuums his office."

"You're underestimating the man."

"Stop it! I've got work to do even if you don't."

Although Cindy returned to cleaning and scrubbing with a vigor that had been lacking earlier, her thoughts were far from the tasks at hand. When she left the Financial Center for the dark, windy streets of Manhattan, her mind was still on the tall, dark man in the photograph. It wasn't like her to be so affected by a man simply because he was good-looking. But Thorndike Prince was more than handsome; something deep within her had instantly responded to that picture of him, had innocently, naively, reached out to him. She saw in him the elusive qualities she'd been searching for in a man. He was proud yet honest. Shrewd yet gentle. Demanding yet patient. She couldn't have explained how she knew all this. Call it intuition, but she sensed that he wasn't an ordinary man.

The December wind whistled down the canyon of tall office buildings and Cindy drew her thick wool coat more snugly around her, burying her hands in the pockets. The clock in front of the jeweler's across the street told her Uncle Sal would be there any minute. No sooner had the thought formed than the sleek black limousine came to a stop at the curb. The front door swung open as Cindy approached and she quickly climbed inside, savoring the warmth.

"You been waiting long?"

"Only a couple of minutes." Cindy gave her uncle a reassuring smile.

He removed the black driver's cap and unbuttoned his chauffeur's uniform, letting out a deep breath. "Remind me to talk to your aunt. The cleaners must've shrunk this jacket."

"Right," Cindy said in a mock-serious voice. More than likely it was Aunt Theresa's cooking that was responsible for the tight jacket, but she wasn't about to tell her uncle that.

As the limousine wove through the New York traffic, Cindy stared out the window, too exhausted to talk.

"You're quiet tonight," her uncle commented.

"Count your blessings," she said with a tired laugh. Life in their large Italian family rarely left a moment's peace. Sal and Theresa's home was the hub of the Territo clan. Her aunt and uncle had raised Cindy as their own, nurturing her with all the love they gave their natural child. Cindy's own parents had divorced when she was too young to remember, and her mother had died when Cindy was five. She'd never heard from her father, and when she'd started grade school she'd taken the name Territo to avoid confusion.

Sal chuckled. "Maybe I *should* be grateful for the quiet. When I left the house this afternoon your aunt was blistering the sidewalk with her rant."

"What happened now?"

"She caught Tony and Maria necking on the fire escape again."

At fifteen, Cindy's cousin was already showing the potential for breaking young girls' hearts. "That Tony's just too good-looking."

Sal playfully nudged her with his elbow. "Too much like his old man, huh?"

"Right." Although he'd become a bit portly, her uncle

was still handsome, and the gray streaks at his temples lent him an air of distinction.

They grew silent again, and once more Cindy felt Sal's eyes on her. "You feeling okay?" he asked.

"I'm just tired."

"How many more weeks of school?"

"A couple." Two full weeks and then she could concentrate on the fast-approaching Christmas holidays. Christmas was sneaking up on her this year. Although she'd set aside the money from her last paycheck, she hadn't started her shopping. There hadn't been time and wouldn't be until her computer classes were dismissed.

Her uncle parked the limousine in front of the apartment building in a space unofficially reserved for him. Nothing was posted to claim this curb for Sal's limousine, but the neighborhood, out of love and respect, made sure there was room for him to park every night.

The apartment was quiet. Cindy and her uncle paused in the crowded entryway to remove their coats. Cindy hung hers on the brass coatrack while her uncle reverently placed his jacket inside the hall closet, setting his cap on the shelf above the rack.

"You hungry?" her uncle whispered.

"Not tonight." Aunt Theresa kept plates of food warming in the oven for them, and Cindy and her uncle often sat in front of the TV and enjoyed their late-night dinner.

"You *sure* you're feeling okay?" Sal squinted as he studied her carefully.

"I'm fine. I think I'll take a hot bath and go to bed."

"You do that." Her uncle was already heading for the kitchen, eager for his meal.

Cindy's bedroom was tiny, as were all the bedrooms in the apartment. There was hardly room to walk between the

double bed and the heavy mahogany dresser that had been
her mother's as a child. The closet was little more than an
indentation in the wall, covered by a faded curtain. Cindy
glanced around the room with fresh eyes. Thorndike Prince
definitely wouldn't be interested in a woman who slept in
a room like this. Her thoughts drifted to the dark woman
in the photograph on his desk. No doubt her bedroom was
carpeted with Oriental rugs and decorated with a fancy
brass bedroom set. Perhaps there was even a fireplace....
Cindy sighed and sat on the corner of her bed feeling the
hopelessness of it all. Vanessa had told her it was time to
dream a little, and that was exactly what Cindy planned to
do: she was going to save this special feeling she had for
Thorndike Prince to savor in her dreams.

After luxuriating in a tub filled with hot soapy water,
Cindy fell into a deep, natural sleep.

The following day she managed not to think about Vanessa's crazy schemes during any of her classes. Nor did
she allow thoughts of Prince to invade her mind while
she hurried home from school and changed into her work
clothes. However, the minute she stepped into the Oakes-
Jenning Financial Services building, Cindy was assaulted
on all sides by fantasies she had no right to entertain.

"Hi," Vanessa muttered as she checked the supplies on
her cleaning cart.

"What's wrong with you?" Of the pair, Vanessa was usually the one with the ready smile and quick conversation.

"Traffic was a nightmare."

"Hey, this is New York. What do you expect?"

"A bit of sympathy would come in handy."

"Poor Vanessa. Poor, poor Vanessa." Soothingly, Cindy
stroked her friend's arm. "Did that help?"

"A little," she grumbled, leading the way to the service elevator. They rode it to the main floor, then transferred to the passenger one. Bob Knight, the security officer who guarded the front entrance, waved as they continued through the foyer.

Cindy leaned her weight against the back of the elevator as the door glided silently shut. She was concerned about cleaning Thorndike's office. The room would never be the same to her again. She couldn't empty his garbage without wondering what was happening in his life and knowing she'd never be part of it.

"Hey, did you see that?" Vanessa cried excitedly, making a futile attempt to stop the elevator as it began to rise.

"See what?" Cindy was instantly alert.

The moment the elevator hit the thirtieth floor, Vanessa pushed the button that sent them back down.

"Vanessa, what's going on?"

"Give me a minute and I'll tell you."

"Tell me what?" Cindy chuckled at the way her friend bit her bottom lip. "Have you discovered the secret to peace and goodwill for all mankind?"

As soon as the doors opened, Vanessa grabbed Cindy's arm and jerked her out of the elevator. "Look at this!" she said, shoving her friend toward a large notice board.

"Look at what?" The only thing she could see was information about some type of party.

"Read it out loud," Vanessa said impatiently.

Shrugging, Cindy complied. "The Oakes-Jenning Christmas Ball, 7:30 p.m., Saturday, December 12. Hotel St. Moritz, Grand Ballroom. By invitation only."

"Well?" Vanessa's arched her eyebrows devilishly.

"Well, what?" Gradually the answer seeped into Cindy's perplexed brain. "You're nuts! You couldn't possibly mean I should—"

"It's the perfect chance to get you two together."

"But..." So many objections crowded Cindy's mind that she couldn't express them all. The first one to untwist itself from her tongue was the most obvious. "I don't have an invitation."

"Hey, there are ways—"

"Forget it!" Cindy hoped she'd said it with enough force to cancel all further argument. She stepped back into the elevator and waited for Vanessa to join her.

"I'm not going to forget it and neither are you. It's fate... kismet. I knew it the minute I saw Thorndike Prince's picture in the paper and so did you, so don't try to argue with me."

"I'm not arguing," Cindy told her calmly. "I simply refuse to discuss it."

"But why?"

Faking a yawn, Cindy brought her hand to her mouth, then glanced conspicuously at her watch.

"All right, all right, I get the message," Vanessa said under her breath. "But you aren't kidding me one bit. You're dying to attend that Christmas Ball."

Was she? Cindy asked herself as the night progressed. Dusting Mr. Prince's outer office granted her the solitude to think about the magic of a Christmas ball, and she realized her friend was right once again. Cindy had never thought of herself as transparent, but she would gladly have submitted to the taunts of two ugly stepsisters for the chance to attend such a gala event. Only she didn't have any stepsisters, ugly or not, and she wasn't Cinderella. But a ball... the Christmas Ball... Nowhere else would she have the opportunity to introduce herself to her prince and be accepted as his equal....

She ran her feather duster across his secretary's desk,

and for the first time since she'd been hired by the janitorial company, Cindy wondered about the woman who spent so much of her day with Thorndike Prince. Ms. Hillard rarely let anything go to waste. Even discarded pieces of paper were neatly trimmed into scratch pads, stapled together at the top corners. The woman's theme appeared to be Waste Not, Want Not.

Cindy spent a bare minimum of time in Mr. Prince's office. The room required a dusting now and then and an occasional vacuuming, but other than that, it was surprisingly neat, which was something she couldn't say about the other executives' quarters. Emptying his garbage, she smiled as she noticed the name The Deli Belly, the delicatessen from which Thorndike ordered his lunch. He was apparently a creature of habit, but then they all were, weren't they?

As Cindy moved from one office to the next, she tried to contain her thoughts, but the image of a crystal ball dangling from the ballroom ceiling and the room full of dancing couples kept flitting into her mind. In every image, Cindy and her prince were at the center of the Grand Ballroom, arms entwined around each other.

"Well?" Vanessa said, startling Cindy.

She recovered quickly. "Well, what?"

"Have you been thinking about the ball?"

"It's not going to work." It was a measure of her fascination with Thorndike Prince that she'd even given the matter a second thought. But Vanessa's scheme was impossible from beginning to end.

"It'll work," Vanessa said with blind optimism.

"Then where's my fairy godmother?"

With a saucy grin, Vanessa polished her nails against her cotton shirt. "Hey, you're looking at her."

"And my coach led by two perfectly matched white

horses. And how about turning mice into footmen? Have you got that trick up your sleeve as well?"

For a moment Vanessa looked concerned, then she smiled and flexed her fingers. "I'm working on it."

"Are you working on a gown, too?"

"Sure…"

"If I were a fairy godmother, I'd tackle the invitation business right away."

For the first time Vanessa seemed daunted. "I didn't realize this was going to be so complicated."

"And that's just the beginning." Cindy turned back to her cart, pushing it down the wide hallway, humming as she went. It was nice to dream, but that was all it would ever be—a dream.

Cindy picked up the green metal garbage can of the assistant to the third vice president and dumped its contents into the large plastic bag on the end of her cart. As she did, a flash of gold caught her eye. Out of curiosity, she reached for it, and when she read the gilt print, her heart rushed to her throat.

Holding the paper in both hands, she walked out of the room in a daze. "Vanessa!" she cried. "Vanessa, hurry. I don't believe it…."

Her partner met her in the hallway. "What is it?"

"Look." Reverently, she handed the folded piece of heavy paper to her friend.

"It's an invitation to the ball," Vanessa whispered, raising round, shocked eyes to meet Cindy's. "Wow!" She waved an imaginary wand over Cindy's head. "Did you feel the fairy dust?"

"It's coming down like rain, my friend." Cindy shook her head in wonder.

"Where did you find it?"

"In the garbage."

"You've got to be kidding!"

Cindy shook her head again. "They must've been sent out last week."

"And apparently Ms. Reynolds has decided not to attend, in which case you will humbly accept in her place."

"But—"

"It's fate! Surely you're not going to argue with me *now!*"

"No." Cindy was more than willing to accept this unexpected gift. She'd attend the ball and satisfy her curiosity regarding Thorndike Prince. She'd indulge herself this once—and only this once.

On the evening of December 12, Cindy's stomach was a mass of nerves. Her cousin Tony knocked on her bedroom door and called, "Vanessa's here."

"Okay, tell her I'll be right out." Squaring her shoulders, Cindy forced herself to smile and walked into the living room, where her family and Vanessa were waiting.

Her friend stood as Cindy entered the room. "Oh, Cindy, you're…beautiful."

Cindy's aunt dabbed the corner of one eye and murmured something in Italian. "She looks just like her mother."

Vanessa didn't seem to hear her. "Where did you ever find such an elegant dress?" The floor-length pale blue taffeta gown had an off-the-shoulder neckline and a fitted bodice with a full ruched skirt.

"Do you like it?" Slowly she whirled around, letting Vanessa view the full effect.

"I'm speechless."

For Vanessa, that was saying something. Cindy's gaze rested lovingly on her aunt.

Aunt Theresa lifted her hand in mock salute. "It was nothing...an early Christmas gift."

"She made it?" Vanessa gasped.

"I sewed it," Theresa said, "with loving fingers."

"Where'd you get the purse?"

Cindy lifted the small pearl-beaded clutch. "My aunt Sofia."

"And the combs?"

Cindy's hands flew to her hair, held in place with pearl combs. "Those were my mother's."

"You look more like a fairy tale princess than anyone I've ever seen. I don't know what to say."

"For once," Cindy laughed.

Vanessa walked around her, studying every detail.

"How are you getting to the ball?"

"My uncle's dropping me off and picking me up later."

"Excellent plan."

"Listen." Suddenly Cindy's nerve abandoned her. She was living her dream just as she'd always wanted, but something deep inside her was screaming that she was being a fool—a romantic fool, but a fool nonetheless. "I'm not sure I'm doing the right thing. Sheila will probably be there." On close examination of the brunette in the photograph on Thorndike's desk, Cindy and Vanessa had seen the woman's bold signature across the bottom of the picture.

"She might," Vanessa agreed. "But you'll do fine." She tossed another imaginary sparkling of fairy dust in Cindy's direction. "The enchantment is set, so don't worry."

"What? Me worry?" Cindy said, crossing her eyes and twisting her face.

Everyone laughed, nearly drowning out the honking from the limousine in the street below.

"You ready?" Aunt Theresa asked, draping a warm shawl around Cindy's shoulders.

"Ready as I'll ever be," she said, expelling a deep breath.

Uncle Sal was standing beside the limousine, holding open the back door. "Where to, miss?" he asked in a dignified voice that nearly dissolved Cindy in giggles.

She climbed into the back and realized that this was the first time she'd ever been seated there. "Hey, this is nice," she called, running her hands along the smooth velvet cushion.

"We have one problem," her uncle informed her, meeting her gaze in the rearview mirror.

"What's that?"

"I'm sorry, kiddo, but I've got to have the limo to pick up the Buckhardt party before one."

"That won't be a problem," Cindy returned cheerfully. "Cinderella's supposed to leave the ball before midnight anyway."

Two

Bored, Thorne Prince stood in the farthest corner of the ballroom, a look of studied indifference on his face. He idly held a glass of champagne. He hated these sorts of functions; they were a waste of time. He'd been obligated to attend this Christmas party, but he held out little hope of enjoying it. To complicate matters, Sheila couldn't attend with him. She, at least, would've made the evening tolerable. Hoping he wasn't being too obvious, Thorne glanced at his gold watch and wondered if anyone would notice if he slipped away.

"Prince, old boy, good to see you." Rutherford Hayden stepped toward him and slapped him on the back.

Thorne's response was a grim smile. He had no use for the man who was trying to ingratiate himself by means other than job skills and performance.

"Fine party."

"Yes." If he hoped to engage Thorne in long-winded conversation, he was going to be disappointed.

A moment of awkward silence passed during which Thorne did nothing to ease the tension. Rutherford paused and cleared his throat. "I've been giving some thought to your suggestion regarding the Hughes account, and I—"

"It was an order, not a suggestion." Thorne frowned. Hayden was going to trap him into talking business, and he'd be stuck with this inept bore half the night. Refusing his overtures would only heighten the growing dislike between them. In spite of his incompetence, Hayden had the ear of Paul Jenning, the company president. Apparently they'd been high-school friends and on occasion played golf together.

"I'm back," Cindy said, feigning breathlessness as she approached Thorne. She gazed at him with wide, adoring eyes. "Thank you for holding my champagne." She took the glass from his lifeless hand and turned her attention to Hayden. "It's good to see you again, Ruffie." She deliberately used the nickname she knew he hated. A woman didn't empty a man's wastepaper basket for a year without learning *something* about him. Cindy was a silent witness to the habits, likes and dislikes of all the occupants of the executive offices.

Rutherford Hayden turned from Cindy to Thorne, then back to her again. "I'm afraid I don't recall your name."

"Cindy," she said, offering him her hand. He shook it politely, and Cindy fluttered her lashes to dazzling effect.

"'Ruffie'?" Thorne asked, cocking one eyebrow.

"Yes, well…" Rutherford looked at the couples dancing on the ballroom floor. "I won't keep you. We can discuss this Hughes matter another time."

"Good idea." Thorne knew from the way Hayden's eyes were scanning the crowd that he'd move on to easier prey.

"Good seeing you again, Tami."

"Cindy," she corrected, taking a sip of the champagne. She smiled beguilingly up at the irritating man.

As soon as Hayden was out of earshot, Cindy handed the glass back to Thorne.

"Now," she said, her eyes twinkling. "I won't disturb you any longer," she murmured sweetly. "You can get back to your pouting. But you really shouldn't, you know—it causes age lines."

Thorne's mouth sagged open with complete astonishment. "'Pouting'?"

"It's true," she said without blinking. "You're a disappointment to me, Thorndike Prince."

Thorne hadn't the foggiest notion who this young woman was, but he gave her points for originality. "I'm devastated to hear it."

"I'm sure." She decided that if he didn't have the common sense to recognize her as his Cinderella, there was nothing she could do about it.

"Just who *are* you?"

"If you haven't figured it out yet, then we're in worse shape than I thought."

"Cindy who?" He studied her closely and couldn't recall ever meeting her.

"You should know."

"We've met?"

"Sort of..." Cindy hedged, her nerve flagging. "All right, since you're obviously not who I thought you were, I guess it won't do any harm to tell you. I'm Cinderella, but unfortunately, you're not my prince—you're much too cynical."

"Cinderella?" Thorne felt laughter expand his chest and would have let it escape if she'd shown the least bit of amusement, but she was dead serious.

"You needn't worry," Cindy said. "I won't trouble you anymore. You can go back to your brooding." With that, she sashayed off, leaving him without even glancing over her shoulder.

Pouting! Brooding! Of all the nerve! No one spoke to him like that! A Prince neither pouted nor brooded!

Gradually the anger wore away. A hint of a smile hovered at the edges of his mouth, and before he knew it, Thorne found himself grinning. He forced back the desire to laugh outright. He didn't recall that the fairy-tale Cinderella had such grit. This one did, and almost against his will he sought her out in the crowded room. He saw her standing against the wall opposite his own. Her eyes met his, and she raised her champagne glass in a silent toast. Her eyes were a brilliant, bottomless shade of blue, and even from this distance he could see them sparkling at him. *Alluring.* That was the word that flashed into Thorne's mind. She was the most appealing woman he'd seen in ages.

From the way her gaze held his, he saw she was interested—and interesting. It wasn't unusual for a woman to approach him; he was intelligent enough to know he was considered a "good catch," and many a debutante would like to sink her claws into him. He knew that in time this woman, too, would return to his side to strike up another conversation. He'd play it cool, but given sufficient incentive he'd forgive her for insulting his pride. Although she was right; he *had* been pouting. But brooding—now that was going too far.

For her part, Cindy was acutely disappointed in Thorndike Prince. He was everything she'd expected and nothing she'd hoped. A contradiction in terms, she realized, but she could find no other way to describe her feelings. He was so cynical—as though the beauty of this lovely evening and the Christmas season left him untouched. For hours she'd been studying him. At first she'd been captivated. Only later did her fascination begin to dim. Whimsically, she'd built him up in her mind, and he'd fallen far short of her expectations. He was her prince. Her hero. The man of her dreams. She'd imagined him gallant and exciting and had found him bored and cynical. Twice he'd looked at his watch and once...once, he'd even had the audacity to *yawn*. Life seemed so predictable and mundane to Thorndike Prince.

In spite of her disappointment, she refused to waste this precious evening. She'd announced who she was. Mission accomplished. She'd better forget about her prince, but there wasn't any reason not to enjoy the ball. Cindy intended to have a marvelous time and not surprisingly she did just that as she mingled with the guests, matching names to faces. Feeling a bit smug because she knew their secrets and they knew none of hers, she danced, nibbled on the hors d'oeuvres and tapped the toe of her high-heeled shoe to the beat of the orchestra music.

An hour. Thorne had been waiting an hour for the mysterious Cinderella to return, but she'd stayed on the other side of the ballroom. Except for the silent toast she'd given him earlier, she'd granted him little more than a disinterested glance now and then. Once, she'd danced with James Barney, a young executive, and Thorne had been hard-pressed not to cross the room and inform her that Barney was no prince! But the thought of taking that kind of action was so utterly irrational, Thorne was stunned that he'd ever entertained it.

At one point, the sound of her laughter drifted over to

him, and Thorne was sure he'd never heard anything more musical. She intrigued him. He discovered he couldn't stop watching her. An unreasonable anger began to build inside him when she danced with two other men.

Finally, when he could tolerate it no longer, Thorne reached for a glass of champagne and marched across the room.

"I think you should explain yourself," he said without preamble.

At first Cindy seemed too shocked to speak. "I beg your pardon?"

"I'll have you know, I never brood." Her blue eyes gleamed like sapphire as a smile raised her mouth in the most sensuous movement he'd ever witnessed. "And this business about being Cinderella—that's going a bit overboard, don't you think?"

"No, but please call me Cindy. Cinderella's such an outdated name."

She laughed then, the sweet, musical laugh that had fascinated him earlier. He stared at her, unable to look away. It took all his restraint not to pull her into his arms. He didn't completely understand his reaction—he hadn't drunk *that* much champagne. "Would you like to dance?" he asked.

She nodded, and Thorne escorted her onto the floor, his hand at the small of her back. Then he turned her into his embrace, holding her at arm's length, almost afraid of what would happen if he brought her body against his. Maybe she'd disappear, vanish into thin air. He half expected to wake up from this trance and find the entire company staring at him while he whirled around the room all alone.

Although Thorne maintained the pretense of dancing, all his concentration was focused on merely looking at his intriguing partner. On closer inspection he found her to be truly lovely; she was more than pretty, she was beautiful. Innocent yet enticing. Her skin looked as soft as silk and felt as warm as a summer's day. He didn't dare think about what that marvelous mouth would taste like. He resisted the instinct to bring her closer, although their movements were awkward and strangely out of sync.

Finally Cindy stopped dancing and dropped her arms. She shook her head. In the space of a few hours, her prince had managed to shatter every illusion she'd dared to form about him. "Not only are you a terrible disappointment to me, but you can't dance worth a darn." She stared at him, defying him to disagree with her.

Thorne didn't—she was right. Without saying a word, he brought her back into his arms, but this time he held her the way he'd wanted to from the first, pressing her body intimately to his.

Cindy slipped her arms around his neck and laid her head along the line of his jaw. The music was a favorite Christmas melody, and her eyes drifted shut as she wrapped herself in the enchantment of the song.

They moved as though they'd spent a lifetime practicing together for this one night. No man had ever seemed more in command as Thorne led Cindy from one end of the dance floor to the other without missing a step, guiding, leading, dictating every action.

"Do you always hum along with the music?" Thorne asked unexpectedly.

Cindy's eyes flew open and she nearly stumbled over his feet as her step faltered. "I'm sorry... I didn't realize."

Thorne chuckled; he cradled the back of her head and urged her temple to its former position against his jaw. "You were only slightly off-key," he murmured.

Cindy could feel him smile and she relaxed, not wanting to disturb the wonder of the moment.

Maybe she'd been wrong. Maybe, just maybe, he could be her prince after all. Thorne was holding her just as she'd dreamed and judging by the way his arms tightened around her at the end of the song, it felt as though he didn't want to let her go.

"Would it be selfish to request another dance?"

"Cinderella's prince did," Cindy whispered.

"Then I should, don't you think?"

It was all Cindy could do to nod. They danced again and again and again, neither speaking, each savoring the delight of being held. The only thought in Thorne's mind was the woman in his arms.

The only thought in Cindy's was that fairy tales could come true; she was living one.

"You say I'm a disappointment?" he ventured as the dance ended and the orchestra took a break. He had to discover everything he could about her.

Cindy lifted her head. "Not anymore."

Thorne felt the full dazzling impact of her blue eyes. "Not anymore?" he repeated, smiling despite his effort not to. "Have we met before tonight?" He was sure they hadn't; he wouldn't have forgotten her or those incredible eyes.

"Never," she confirmed.

"But you know me?"

Cindy lowered her gaze. "Yes and no."

"You *are* an employee of Oakes-Jenning?"

The corners of her mouth quivered as she tried to hold back a smile. "Did you think I'd crashed your precious party?" That was so close to the truth she quickly averted her eyes.

Thorne ignored her obvious enjoyment of this one-sided

conversation. "How did you know Rutherford Hayden's nickname is Ruffie?"

"The same way I know you hate tuna salad." Cindy turned to look at the tables loaded with a spectacular assortment of salads, meats and cheeses. "Now, if you'll excuse me, I'd like something to eat."

"Would you mind if I joined you?"

"Not at all," she said.

"My mother sent you, didn't she?" Thorne breathed a sigh of relief; he had it all figured out. His mother had been trying to match him up for years. She must have searched extra-hard to find someone as perfect as Cindy.

"Your mother? No."

The honesty in her eyes couldn't be doubted. But even if his mother *had* put Cindy up to this, he felt an instant, overwhelming attraction.

Bemused, Thorne followed her through the long line that had formed at the buffet tables, heaping his plate with a wide variety of the offerings.

"What? No pastrami?" Cindy teased after they'd found a table in the crowded room.

Thorne paused, his napkin only half unfolded. "I had a pastrami sandwich for lunch. You couldn't have known that, could you?"

"No. It was an educated guess." Cindy focused her attention on buttering her dinner roll.

"An educated guess? Such as my not liking tuna?"

"No." Deliberately she took a bite of her seafood salad.

Thorne waited patiently until she'd finished chewing. "But you know me?"

"A little." Not nearly as well as she wanted to.

"How?"

"I *do* work at Oakes-Jenning," she said and pointed to the

huge green olives he'd removed from the top of the dainty sandwiches. "Are you going to eat those?"

"The green olives? Good grief, no."

"Can I have them?"

Without ceremony, Thorne placed three of them on her plate, then fastidiously wiped his hands on the linen napkin.

Cindy eagerly picked up an olive and held it between her lips, luxuriously sucking out the pimento, then popping the entire thing in her mouth. She paused to lick the tips of her fingers. Thorne's scowl stopped her when she reached for another. The lines at the side of his mouth had deepened, and she noted the vein pulsing in his temple. Alarm filled her. Her worst fear had been realized: unwittingly, she'd committed some terrible faux pas.

"What did I do wrong?" she whispered. She clutched the napkin in her lap.

For a long moment, their eyes locked. Thorne had been mesmerized, watching her eat the olive. Such a small, simple pleasure, but she'd made it appear highly sensuous. He couldn't seem to take his eyes off her—or off the tempting shape of her mouth. Again he felt the overwhelming urge to kiss her. Her eyes, her mouth, the curve of her cheek. Everything about her intrigued him. For years women had used their bodies and their wits to entice him. But no woman had ever had the effect on him that this one did with the simple act of eating an olive.

"What did you do wrong?" Thorne repeated, shaking his head to clear his befuddled thoughts. "What makes you think you did anything wrong?"

"You were looking at me...oddly."

He smiled. "Then I apologize."

Cindy picked up the second olive. Thorne's eyes widened and he groaned inwardly, setting his fork beside his plate.

The music started again long before they'd finished their meal and Cindy tapped her toe to the beat. Christmas was her favorite time of year, and the orchestra seemed to be playing all the carols she loved best.

"Would you like to dance again?" Thorne asked.

Cindy nodded. She couldn't refuse the opportunity to be in her prince's arms. This was her night, a night for enchantment, and she wanted to remember and relive every moment of it for the rest of her life. Tomorrow she'd go back to being plain Cindy Territo, the girl who cleaned his office. But tonight...tonight she was the alluring woman he held in his arms.

By unspoken agreement they stood together and walked to the center of the dance floor. Thorne brought Cindy into his arms, holding her close, savoring the way she felt, inhaling her fresh, delicate scent, reveling in the warmth of her nearness. He felt as if he were a hundred years old in ways she knew nothing about and, conversely, that he'd just turned twenty-one. She did this to him and he didn't have an inkling why.

Thorne's arms tightened around her, anchoring her against him. His hands clasped her waist and he laid his cheek next to hers and closed his eyes. To think that only a few hours earlier he'd contemplated sneaking away from this party. Now he dreaded the time it would end, praying that each minute would stretch out forever...

Cindy pressed her cheek to his and prayed she'd always remember every minute of this night. She planned to store each detail in her heart. She couldn't possibly hope to explain it to anyone; this magical, mystical night was hers and hers alone. She would have a lifetime to treasure these precious hours and relive them over and over.

Even when the music grew lively, Thorne held her as if

it were the slowest dance of the night. He wanted to kiss her so badly he was forced to inhale deep breaths to restrain his desire. Thorndike Prince did not make a spectacle of himself on the dance floor for any reason. However he soon discovered that the temptation was too strong. Her nearness was more than any man could resist and he turned his head ever so slightly and ran his mouth along her ear.

Cindy sighed with pleasure and moved her hands to the back of Thorne's neck, drawing her fingers through his thick dark hair. When his lips sought the hollow of her throat, she groaned.

Unexpectedly Thorne dropped his arms and reached for her hand. "Let's get out of here," he said in a voice that sounded unlike his own.

He led her off the ballroom floor as though he couldn't leave fast enough. "Did you bring a coat?"

"A shawl."

Irritably he held out his hand. "Give me your ticket."

Her fingers shook as she opened the beaded clutch and retrieved the small tab. "Where...where are we going?"

He sounded almost angry, certainly impatient. "Anywhere but here," he mumbled.

He left her then and Cindy stood alone, pondering the strangeness of his actions. She wanted to ask him more, longed to know why he'd insisted on leaving so abruptly. But when he returned she said nothing, following him silently as he escorted her out of the ballroom and into the hallway, where the elevators were.

A male voice called out to them. "Thorne, you're not going, are you?"

Cindy turned around, but Thorne applied pressure to her back, directing her forward.

"That man was talking to you."

"I have no desire to talk to anyone," he said stiffly, guiding her into the crowded elevator. They stepped off at the ground floor and Thorne took her to the entrance of the hotel.

The doorman came forward. "Taxi, sir?"

Thorne glanced at Cindy. "No, thanks." He grabbed her hand and they hurried across the busy street to the paved pathway that led to the interior of Central Park.

"Thorne," Cindy whispered. "Why are you so angry?"

"Angry?" He paused in front of the large fish pond.

The moon beamed silvery rays all around them, and Cindy could see that his face was intent, his mouth bracketed with harsh lines. His gray eyes were narrowed and hard, yet when they rested on her she saw them soften.

"I'm not angry," he said at last, his breathing labored. "I'm..." He rammed his hands into his pockets. "You're right, I am angry, but not at you."

"Then who?"

He shook his head and his eyes grew warm as he studied her upturned face. Almost as if he were in a trance, Thorne pulled one hand from his pocket and cupped her chin, staring at her with a thoroughness that brought a rush of color to her cheeks. "You're so beautiful," he whispered with a reverence that made his voice tremble.

Cindy lowered her eyes.

His grip tightened almost imperceptibly. "It's true," he continued. "I've never known anyone as lovely."

"Why did you bring me here?"

Thorne expelled his breath, and his words were an odd mixture of anger and wonder. "For the most selfish of reasons. I wanted to kiss you."

Cindy's questioning gaze sought his. "Then why haven't you? Cinderella's waiting."

He smiled then. "You're taking this prince stuff seriously, aren't you?"

"Very."

He slid his thumb across her bottom lip, his eyes pensive. "I've never experienced anything like this."

"Me neither." It was important that he know these feelings were as much a shock to her. Despite her fantasy, despite her hopes, she hadn't expected this to happen, hadn't believed it ever would. When she'd first seen him, her disappointment had been acute. But all of that had changed the moment he'd come to her and asked her to dance. From that time forward he'd been magically transformed into the prince who'd dominated her dreams for weeks. He was everything she'd imagined and a thousand things more.

"I haven't any right," he said, but his mouth inched toward hers as though he wanted her to stop him.

She couldn't—not when she longed for his kiss the way she did; not when every part of her was crying out for the taste of his mouth on hers.

The ragged beat of his heart echoed her own as Cindy flattened her hands against his chest and slowly, deliberately, tilted her face to receive his kiss. They were so close their breath mingled. Cindy stood on tiptoe as Thorne gently lowered his lips to hers. His mouth was firm and so tender that Cindy felt a tear form at the corner of her eye. Their mouths clung, and Cindy's hands crept up to rest on his shoulders.

"So sweet, so very sweet," Thorne groaned and buried his face in the slope of her neck. "I knew it would be like this. I knew it would be this sweet." His breathing was uneven.

Cindy felt shocked into speechlessness. Her whole body went numb, tingling with wonder. As difficult as it was, she resisted the urge to raise her fingers to her lips. Thorne looked equally shaken. They broke apart and Cindy teetered for a moment until she found her balance.

Their eyes met for a timeless second. When Thorne reached for her, Cindy walked willingly into his arms. Then his mouth was on hers, twisting, turning, tasting, testing as if he had to reexperience these sensations. As if he hadn't believed they could be real.

When he released her, Cindy was weak and trembling. She looked up at Thorne and saw that he was unnaturally pale.

Thorne took a step back and removed his heavy coat. Gently, he draped it over her shoulders, his hands lingering there. "You're cold," he whispered.

"No," she murmured, shaking her head. "It's not the cold. It's you—you make me tremble."

"Feel what you do to me." He took her hand and placed it over his pounding heart. A frown drove his dark brows together. "I'm no inexperienced schoolboy. What's happening to me—to us?"

Cindy smiled and pressed a soft kiss to the corner of his mouth. "Magic, I think."

"Black magic?" He regarded her suspiciously, but his eyes were smiling.

"No, this is the very best kind."

He agreed. Nothing that felt this good could be wrong. He slipped his arm around her shoulders and led her to one of the many benches that faced the pond.

Silently they sat together, neither speaking, neither needing words. Thorne continued to hold her, simply because letting her go was unthinkable. His mind spun with a hundred questions. He prayed she was a secretary so he could make her *his* secretary. He didn't care what strings he had to pull; he wanted her working with him. Ms. Hillard was planning to retire, and the thought of greeting each day with Cindy was enough to— He *was* going crazy. The cardinal rule in any office was never to become romantically involved with a colleague or an employee.

He must have given her a startled look because Cindy's eyes softened with such compassion that Thorne could barely breathe.

"It's all right," she whispered.

"But…"

"No," she said and brought her fingers to his lips, silencing him.

He frowned at her. Could she read his thoughts? Was she clairvoyant? She couldn't possibly have known what he'd been thinking, yet she showed him in a glance that she understood.

"You don't need to tell me," Cindy said after a long moment. "I already know about Sheila."

Three

"Sheila." The name seared his mind. He was practically engaged to Sheila, and here he was sitting beside Cindy, madly plotting to keep her in his life. He thrust his face toward her, his mouth gaping as one thought stumbled over another. He had to explain—only he wasn't sure how to unscramble his own feelings, let alone reassure *her*. It was as though Sheila meant nothing to him. Nothing. Yet a few days before, he'd contemplated giving her an engagement ring for Christmas. He'd actually been entertaining the idea of marriage and starting a family.

His confusion must have been visible in his eyes, because Cindy smiled with such sweetness that the panic gripping him was instantly quelled.

He looked so astonished that Cindy placed her index finger on his lips. "Shh. You don't need to tell me anything. I understand."

If she did he wished she'd explain it to him. Thorne felt like a scheming hypocrite. He was nearly engaged to one woman and so attracted to another he could hardly take his eyes off her. Even now that she'd brought Sheila's name between them, he couldn't force himself to leave. He knew he should stand up and walk away. He should escape before whatever was happening on this enchanted evening could affect him. His gut reaction was that Cindy's imprint on him could well be indelible. It was crazy, the things he was thinking. Insane to want her working with him. Absurd to seriously consider getting involved with an employee. His mother would be horrified, his father amused. They'd been after him for years to settle down, but they'd made it abundantly clear that they expected him to marry the "right type" of woman.

"You're angry again," Cindy said, studying the dark emotion that crossed his face.

"Not angry," he told her. "Confused."

"Don't be."

He took her hand in his, weaving their fingers together. She had beautiful hands. Each finger was narrow and tapered, and intuitively Thorne felt the comfort she would be capable of granting with a mere touch. The nails were a reasonable length, neither too long nor too short. He supposed she had to keep them like that in order to type properly.

"Who are you?" he asked, surprised that even her fingers could entice him.

Cindy felt the magic slowly dissipating. "I... I already told you."

"Cinderella?"

"Yes."

"And I'm your prince?"

"Yes." She nodded vigorously. "I've dreamed of you so often, and then I met you, and I knew you were everything my fantasies had promised."

He made her gaze meet his by slipping his index finger beneath her chin. Studying her intense blue eyes was like looking into the crystal-clear water of a mountain lake. She was incapable of deception. Completely innocent. She was everything he'd ever hoped to find in a woman—yet had never believed he would. She was unexpected sunshine and warmth on a winter day. Laughter and excitement. Love when he least expected it and was least prepared to deal with it. "You said I disappointed you."

"That was before. Now I know who you really are."

"Oh, Cindy." He couldn't stop himself. He lowered his mouth to hers and kissed her again, wrapping his arms around her, holding her tight. She tasted exquisite, and her lips promised him paradise. "Cindy," he whispered against her mouth. Never had a name been lovelier. He kissed her again.

Cindy leaned into him, afraid she'd wake up any minute and discover this had all been a dream.

Thorne heaved a sigh that came from deep inside him and held her so close his arms ached.

"Thorne…"

"I'm hurting you?" He relaxed the pressure instantly and ran his hands down her back and up again to rest on the curve of her shoulders. His thumb stroked the pulse that was rapidly pounding near the hollow of her throat. Reluctantly he eased her away from him. "Tell me about yourself. I want to know everything."

Cindy dropped her gaze and laughed lightly to hide her uneasiness. She couldn't tell him anything. "There isn't much…."

She rested her hands on the sides of his face and slowly stroked his jaw. "I see so much pride in you. Stubborn pride," she said. "And determination. Were you always like this?"

Thorne smiled in response. "Always, I think. My mother claims that when I was fourteen months old, I threw my bottle against the wall and refused to drink out of anything but a cup from then on. When other children were riding tricycles, I wanted a two-wheeler. I was reading by age five and not because I was gifted. My older sisters read, and I was hell-bent to do anything they could."

"Whereas I refused to give up my blankie until I was six," Cindy admitted sheepishly. It had been her only comfort after her mother had died, and she'd clung to it feverishly, initially refusing to accept the love her aunt and uncle had offered.

"You must have been a beautiful little girl."

"I had buckteeth and freckles."

"I wore braces and corrective shoes."

Cindy laughed. "You were always athletic, though, weren't you?"

Thorne's eyes clouded momentarily. "Yes."

"Something happened." Cindy could see it—a flash of memory that came so briefly another person might have missed it.

His heart hammered relentlessly. He hadn't thought about the accident in years. He'd only been a child. Ten years old.

Cindy saw the pain in his eyes and although she didn't understand it, she knew she had to comfort him. She lifted her hand and touched his face. "Tell me," she whispered in a low, coaxing tone. "Tell me what happened."

Sensation raced through Thorne. He caught her hand, raised it to his mouth and kissed her palm. "I fell off my horse. I thought I was dead, then I realized that death couldn't hurt that much. I was barely conscious. Every breath I took was like inhaling fire."

Cindy bit her lip. The thought of Thorne in pain, even pain he'd suffered years before, was intolerable. "Broken ribs?"

"Six, and a bruised kidney."

Her fingers tightened over his. He was remembering more than the physical pain—something far deeper, far more intense. "What else happened?"

He gave her a long, hard look. "I already told you. I fell off the horse."

"No. Afterward."

"Afterward," he repeated. He remembered lying in bed in his darkened room hours later. The pain hadn't lessened. If anything, it had grown so much worse he wished he had died just so he wouldn't have to bear the agony any longer. One eye had been so severely bruised it had swollen shut. The side of his face was badly scraped, and the ache in his jaw wouldn't go away. Two days later, the doctor discovered that it, too, had been broken in the fall.

When Thorne was a child, his father was away much of the time, traveling for business, but he'd come to see his son the afternoon of the accident. Thorne had looked up at him, grateful he was there. Tears had welled in Thorne's eyes, but instead of offering comfort, his father had spoken of what it meant to be a man and how a true man never revealed his emotions and certainly never cried.

"Thorne?" Cindy prompted.

"My father forced me out of bed and back into the saddle." He'd never told anyone about that incident. It made his father sound heartless and cruel. Thorndike Sr. was neither—only proud and stubborn like his son. And a man whose beliefs had been formed by an uncompromising father of his own. Thorne paused, his eyes narrowed. "Why am I telling you this?"

"You needed to," she answered simply.

Thorne felt startled. She was right. He *had* needed to tell someone about it, but he hadn't recognized that himself. Until tonight with Cindy.

"Let's walk," he said, getting to his feet.

Cindy joined him and he tucked her hand into the crook of his elbow. "This really is an enchanted evening, isn't it?"

"Magical," she returned, her eyes smiling softly into his.

They strolled along the walkway around the pond. Thorne felt like singing, which of course was ridiculous. He didn't sing. Ever. Not even in the shower. "Do you have any deep, dark secrets?"

"Plenty," she answered, swallowing a laugh.

"Tell me just one so I won't feel like such a fool."

"Okay." She felt an overwhelming urge to throw back her head and laugh. "No one knows this."

"Good."

She hesitated. "You'll probably find this silly...."

"I won't laugh," he promised.

She regarded him steadily, unsure she could trust him. "I still have my blankie."

"Do you sleep with it?"

"Of course not!" She was a little offended when she realized he was amused by her admission. She bit back an annoyed response. He'd shared something profound with her, while her threadbare blankie was a minor thing. "It's hidden in a bottom drawer."

His eyes sparkled.

"Thorndike Prince, you're laughing at me!"

"I swear I'm not." He gave her a look of innocence. "Tell me something else."

"No way," she vowed, a chuckle punctuating her words.

Thorne slung his arm over her shoulder. He lifted his eyes to the clear night sky. Stars filled the heavens, glimmering, glinting, glistening above the skyscrapers. "It's a beautiful night."

Cindy's gaze followed his. "Shall we make a wish?"

He turned to face her. "A wish?"

"Upon a star." She moved to stand directly in front of him. "You haven't done this in a long time, have you?"

"No." He'd seldom played childish games. In some ways, Thorne had never been allowed to be a boy. Responsibilities had come to him early; he was the only son, and great things were expected of him.

"Then do it now," she urged, throwing back her head to stare up at the heavens. She picked the brightest star, closed her eyes and wished with all her heart that this night would never end. "Okay," she whispered. "It's your turn."

He looked at her blankly. "You're sure you want me to do this?"

"Yes," she said.

Like Cindy, he raised his head and studied the heavens. "You don't honestly believe in this, do you?"

"You're asking Cinderella something like that? Of course, I believe. It's required of every princess in a fairy tale."

"What should I ask for?"

It took Cindy a moment to realize that whatever Thorne wanted in life he purchased without a second thought. He probably had every material possession he could possibly desire.

"Ask for something you never expected to receive," she told him softly.

Thorne looked at Cindy. He'd never expected to meet

anyone like her. Someone so pure and good, so honest and forthright. A woman who stirred his mind as well as his heart. A woman of insight and laughter. He felt like a teen-ager, yearning to find a way to please her—to thank her for giving him this priceless gift of joy.

She felt as though his eyes were melting her soul. He was looking at her as she'd always imagined the great he-roes of literature viewed the loves of their lives. The way Heathcliff regarded Catherine or Mr. Rochester saw Jane Eyre. The bored, cynical look that tightened his features when she'd first arrived at the party had been replaced with one of tenderness.

"Close your eyes," she told him when she found her voice. "You have to close your eyes to make your wish come true."

Reluctantly he did. But he didn't need any stars or wishes to be granted his one request. Without his even asking, it had already come true: everything he'd ever wanted was standing a few inches away from him. And if he doubted, all he had to do was reach out and touch her. Cindy was his, and he'd found her just in time. To think that only a few hours before, he'd dreaded attending this party. Now he'd thank God every day of his life that he'd been there to meet Cindy.

"Have you finished?" she whispered.

Slowly Thorne opened his eyes. "Are you going to tell me your wish?" he asked, bringing her against his side. He had to keep touching her to believe she was real.

"I might as well," she said softly. "There's no possibil-ity it'll ever come true."

"Don't be so sure. I thought we agreed this night is filled with magic."

"It *couldn't* come true." Her footsteps matched his as they continued strolling. "I asked that this night never end."

"Ah." Thorne nodded. "But in some ways it never will."

"How's that?" Cindy turned her head to study his expression. When she'd first conceived of this plan, she'd counted on the magic of the night to work for her. Now that she saw how much Thorne had been affected by her schemes, she marveled at the power of a wish.

"This night *will* last forever," Thorne said thoughtfully.

"But how?" Cindy didn't understand because midnight loomed and she knew she had to leave him. There was no staying at the ball for Cinderella.

"It will live in our hearts."

Tears sprang to Cindy's eyes, and she hurriedly turned her head in an effort to hide her emotion from Thorne. She hadn't dared to hope he'd be so romantic.

"That's beautiful," she said in a choked whisper. "Prince Charming himself couldn't have said it any better."

"Only Cinderella would know that."

Cindy smiled, letting the wonder of the night dispel all doubts.

"So you're still claiming to be Cinderella?"

"Oh, yes, it's quite true."

His steps slowed. "Do you have two ugly stepsisters?"

"No," she answered, grateful he'd steered the conversation to lighter subjects.

"What about a fairy godmother?"

"A wonderful but quite ordinary godmother," she answered, convinced her aunt would appreciate the compliment. "But that doesn't mean she lacks magical abilities."

"Did she turn the mice into horses for your carriage?"

Cindy frowned. "I don't exactly have a carriage."

"Yes, you do," Thorne said, leading her onto the sidewalk along Central Park South. Horse-drawn carriages lined the streets, as though waiting for her command. "Your carriage, my lady," Thorne told her with a bow.

As if reading Thorne's mind, the middle-aged driver, who wore a black top hat, stepped forward and opened the carriage door. Cindy accepted his hand and climbed onto the black leather cushion. She tucked her dress around her, still wearing Thorne's overcoat. She wondered guiltily if he felt chilled, but the warmth of the look he gave her chased away her concerns.

Sitting beside Cindy, Thorne slipped his arm around her shoulders. "I've lived in Manhattan for the past six years and I've never done this."

"Me neither," Cindy admitted, feeling as excited as a child.

"I may have confused the driver, however," Thorne said, his eyes twinkling with merriment. "I told him we wanted to survey our kingdom."

Cindy laughed. "Oh, dear, the poor man. He must think we're both crazy."

"We are, but I don't care. Do you?"

"Not in the least."

The driver jumped into the carriage box and urged the horse onto the street. The giant wheels at Cindy's side drowned out the clopping of the horse's hooves against the pavement.

"I've always wanted to do this," Cindy said. "Thank you, Thorne." She laid her head on his shoulder and drew in a deep breath. She yearned to hold on to this moment for as long as she could....

Thorne intertwined his fingers with hers and raised her hand to his mouth. "I know so little about you."

"You know everything that's important."

"I feel like I do," he said. "I know this seems impossible, but it's as if I've known you all my life."

"In some ways, I think I might've been born for this night," Cindy told him.

"I feel like I've been born for *you*."

She went still. She couldn't swallow. They had only tonight, only these few hours, and when midnight came, she'd have to go back to being the girl who cleaned his office. A nobody. Certainly no one who'd ever interest Thorndike Prince, first vice president. Her mind whirled with countless dreams and visions, but they all ended with the same shattering reality. She couldn't change who she was, and he couldn't change the man he'd become. There could be no middle ground for them.

"You're very quiet all of a sudden," Thorne observed. He liked having her close to him. He loved holding her and kissing her. But the fascination he felt for her wasn't merely physical. It was more than that. Something buried deep within him had reached out and touched something deep within her, something profound. His inner self had connected with hers. With Cindy, he experienced a wholeness, a rightness that had been missing from his life.

"Let's not think beyond anything except tonight," Cindy said. She was trying to conjure up ways in which she could meet him again, but she quickly realized the hopelessness of it all. A sadness surrounded her heart.

"We'll share every night for the rest of our lives," Thorne promised. He knew he was rushing her. They'd only met a few hours before, and here he was, practically asking her what names she wanted to give their children. The thought stunned him. He'd always been described as an unemotional, hard-hearted cynic, but he was talking like a lovesick teenager. And everything he'd said made sense. He'd been ignorant before meeting Cindy. Stupid. Now that he'd met her, he understood what drove men to impossible feats in the name of love. He'd walk over hot coals to get to Cindy. He'd wade through a raging river. Nothing would stop him now that he'd discovered her.

"I want you to meet my family." He shocked himself by making the suggestion.

"Your...family?" Cindy repeated.

"Yes." He'd talk to his mother and father first. They'd be surprised, of course, since they'd been expecting him to announce that he was marrying Sheila. Sheila. He nearly laughed aloud. He couldn't even remember what the other woman looked like.

His parents could be his and Cindy's biggest hurdle. But once they met her they wouldn't question his actions. After the initial displeasure his mother would love her, Thorne was certain of that. His father was another matter, but given time, he'd respect Thorne's decision. Things could get a bit sticky with Sheila, but she was a reasonable woman. She always said she wanted what was best for Thorne, and as soon as he explained, Thorne was convinced that she, too, would understand.

Within a matter of hours a young woman with a saucy grin had turned his life upside down. And Thorne loved it.

"I...can't meet your family." Cindy's mind was in turmoil.

"Of course you can. They're going to fall for you just like I have."

"Thorne—"

"Stop." He pressed his finger to her lips, as she'd done to him earlier. "Here," he said, and placed her hand over his heart. "Feel how excited and happy I am. I feel alive for the first time in years. You've done that for me. I want to laugh and sing and dance, and I never do any of those things."

"But I can't—"

"I know I'm probably going a thousand times too fast. I realize it all sounds crazy, but I've been waiting *years* for you. Years." He framed her face with his hands and he kissed her with infinite gentleness. His mouth lingered on hers as if he couldn't get his fill. "What took you so long, Cindy? What took my Cinderella so long?"

Cindy swallowed a sob at the tenderness she saw in his eyes. "Thorne, please...don't..."

His mouth stopped her. He was kissing her again until her senses spun at breakneck speed. There was no question of refusing herself the luxury of his touch. Nor was there any question of disillusioning him. Soon enough he'd learn the truth. Soon enough he'd know she wasn't who she pretended to be. She was no princess. Her family name wasn't going to gladden any banker's heart.

"I'd be honored to meet your family," she finally said.

"Tomorrow, then."

"Whenever you wish." She couldn't meet his eyes, knowing there'd be no tomorrows for them.

They had so little time together. She couldn't ruin everything now. Maybe it was wrong not to tell him she was the janitorial worker who cleaned his office and that she had no intention of embarrassing him in front of his family. But it couldn't be any more wrong than crashing the party and seeking out Thorndike Prince in the first place.

The carriage driver cleared his throat. Irritated, Thorne broke away from Cindy and saw that they'd completed the circle and were back.

"Shall we go around again?" On this trip, he'd gotten her to agree to meet his family. He'd seen the fear in her eyes and realized how much the thought had intimidated her. Yet she'd agreed. He yearned to hold her and assure her that he'd never leave her, that with a little time and patience his family would be as impressed with her as he was.

Somewhere in the distance church bells began to chime. Cindy paused, counting the tones. "Midnight!" she cried, her heart beating frantically. "It's midnight. I've… I've got to go. I'm sorry…so sorry." She stood, and with the driver's help climbed down from the carriage.

"Cindy." Thorne reached out for her, but she was already rushing away. He ran after her. "I'll take you home. Don't worry about missing your ride—I'll see you safely home."

Tears filled her eyes as she handed him his coat and paused to throw her arms around him, hugging him fiercely. "You don't understand."

She was right about that, Thorne mused. She looked stricken—frightened and so unhappy that he longed to ease whatever pain she was suffering.

"It was the most wonderful night of my life. I'll…remember it, and I'll always…always remember you."

"You won't get a chance to forget me." He tried to keep her with him, but she whirled around and picked up her skirts, racing off as though there were demons in wild pursuit.

Bewildered, Thorne watched her race into traffic. She'd crossed the busy street and was halfway down the sidewalk, when she turned abruptly. "Thank you," she yelled, raising her hand to wave. "Thank you for making my dreams come true." She covered her mouth with her hand and even from this far away Thorne could see that she was weeping. She ran in earnest then, sprinting to the corner. The instant she reached it a long black limousine pulled up. As if by magic, the door opened and Cindy slid inside. The limo was gone before Thorne could react.

"Sir."

For a moment Thorne didn't respond.

"She dropped this." The carriage driver handed Thorne a pearl comb.

The older man in the black top hat stared at Thorne. "Had to be home by midnight, did she?"

"Yes," Thorne answered without looking at him.

"Sounds like Cinderella."

"That's who she said she was."

The driver chuckled. "Then you must be Prince Charming."

Thorne still didn't move. "I am."

Apparently the carriage driver found that even more amusing. "Sure, fella. And I'm Donald Trump."

Four

The first thing Thorne thought about when he woke early Sunday morning was Cindy. He'd drifted into a deep, restful sleep, picturing her lovely face, and he woke cursing himself for not getting her phone number. Being forced to wait a whole day to see her again was nearly intolerable, but she'd left in such a rush that he hadn't managed to ask her for it. Now he was paying the price for his own lack of forethought.

After he'd showered, he stood, wearing a thick robe, in front of his fourteenth-floor window. Lower Manhattan stretched out before him. He couldn't believe how much he felt like singing. In fact, he'd been astonished to find himself humming in the shower. He gripped the towel around his neck with both hands and expelled a long sigh. It was almost as if…as if he'd been reborn. The world below seethed with activity. Yellow cabs crowded the streets. A tourist boat cruised around the island. Funny, he hadn't paid much attention to the Hudson River or the seaport or any other

New York sights in a long while. Now they sparkled with new freshness, like a thousand facets in a flawless diamond. It seemed ridiculous to be so sure he was in love, but he felt breathless with excitement just thinking about Cindy.

The phone rang and Thorne reached for it immediately. It was unrealistic to hope the call was from Cindy, yet he nearly sighed with disappointment when his mother's voice greeted him.

"Good morning, Thorne."

"Good morning, Mother."

"You certainly sound cheerful. How was the Christmas Ball?"

"Fabulous."

"Did Sheila go with you?"

"No, she couldn't get away." His mother liked to keep close tabs on her children. Thorne tolerated her frequent calls because she was his mother, and her motivations were benign, but he'd made it clear that his personal life was his own. She wanted him settled, sedately married and producing enough grandchildren to keep her occupied. His sisters had done their part and now it was his turn.

He spoke again, remembering that he'd asked Cindy to meet his family. "Mother, listen, I'm glad you phoned. There's someone I'd like to bring to the house. Would it be possible to have her to dinner soon?"

"Her?"

"Yes, if it's not inconvenient, perhaps we could set it up for Christmas week."

"Do you have exciting news for us, darling?"

Thorne weighed his words. "I suppose you could say that." He'd met the woman he planned to share his life with. It didn't get much more exciting than that, but he wasn't about to announce it to his family. After all, he'd just met

Cindy. His parents would scoff at him, and even Thorne had to admit that, on the surface, anyway, he was behaving like a romantic fool.

"I believe your father and I have already guessed your news." His mother's voice rose with excitement.

"It's not what you think, Mother." Thorne paused and chuckled. "Or *who* you think. I met someone wonderful…someone very special. I suppose it's a bit presumptuous of me, but I invited her over to meet you and Dad." The invitation alone must have astounded his mother, since he rarely introduced his girlfriends to his family.

A short silence followed. "This someone you met… she isn't by chance… Sheila?" his mother asked, her voice tinged with unlikely hope.

"Her name is Cindy, and we met at the Christmas Ball." His mother would assume he'd lost his mind if he were to tell her that the minute he'd held Cindy, he'd known she was going to be the most important person in his life.

"Cindy." His mother repeated it slowly. "What's her last name?"

Thorne knew she was really inquiring about Cindy's family. He hated to admit it, but his mother was a terrible snob.

"Surely this girl has a surname?" She was obviously displeased with this unexpected turn of events.

Thorne hesitated, realizing he didn't know Cindy's surname any more than he did her phone number. "I…don't believe she told me."

"You don't know her last name?"

"I just told you that, Mother. But it's no problem. I'll see her again Monday morning." Even as he said it, two days felt like an eternity, and Thorne wasn't convinced he could wait that long. "She's an employee of Oakes-Jenning."

Another lengthy pause followed. "You haven't said anything to Sheila?"

"Of course not, I only met Cindy last night. Listen, Mother, I'm probably making a mistake even mentioning her to you, but—"

"It's just a shock, that's all," his mother responded calmly, having regained her composure. "Do me a favor, Thorne, and don't say anything to Sheila yet."

"But, Mother—"

"I wouldn't want you to mislead the poor girl, but you might save yourself considerable heartache until you and... What was her name again?"

"Cindy."

"Ah, yes, Cindy. It would be better if you sorted out your feelings for Cindy before you said something to Sheila that you might regret later."

"Cindy knows all about Sheila."

"Yes, but Sheila doesn't know about Cindy, and my guess is you should let this new...relationship simmer until you're sure of your feelings."

Thorne's jaw tightened. He'd been foolish to say anything to his mother. It was too soon. Later, when they saw how much he'd changed, they'd want to know the reason; he could tell them all about Cindy then.

"Thorne?" His mother prompted. "Do you agree?"

For a moment he had to stop and figure out what she wanted him to agree to. "I won't tell Sheila," he promised.

"Good." She sighed loudly, her relief evident.

"You must have called for some reason, Mother."

"Oh, yes," she said and laughed nervously. "It was about Christmas Day. I was wondering if you minded...if I invited Sheila."

"Perhaps it would be best if you didn't." Although

Christmas was only a week and a half away, Thorne had hoped to share this special day with Cindy. Christmas and every day before and every day after.

The pause that followed told Thorne his objection had come too late.

"I'm afraid… I happened to run into her yesterday when I was shopping…and, oh, dear, this is going to be a bit messy."

"Sheila's already been invited," Thorne finished for his mother. He closed his eyes to the anger that rained over him, but quickly forgave her interfering ways. She hadn't meant to cause a problem. It must've seemed natural to extend the invitation when he'd recently indicated he'd probably be marrying Sheila.

"Will that be too uncomfortable, darling?"

"Don't worry about it, Mother. I'm sure everything will work out fine." Cindy would understand, Thorne thought confidently. She was a generous person who revealed no tendencies toward unreasonable jealousy.

"I do apologize, but your father and I both thought Sheila would be joining our family.…"

"I know, Mother. My change of heart was rather unpredictable."

The conversation with his mother ended soon, and Thorne hung up the phone, more certain than ever about his feelings for Cindy. Remembering the way she'd strolled up to him at the ball and announced that she was Cinderella brought a quivering smile to his mouth. And then she'd told him what a disappointment he was. Thorne laughed out loud. Monday morning couldn't come soon enough.

Cindy woke late the next morning, feeling both exhilaration and regret.

The evening with Thorne had been so much more than she'd dared to dream. She hadn't been able to sleep for hours after Uncle Sal had taken her home. She'd lain in bed, reliving every part of the evening. The night had been perfect—after their awkward beginning when she'd introduced herself. Remembering the tenderness she'd seen in his gaze when he looked down at her in the carriage, she felt an aching sob in her chest.

She'd been wrong to play the role of Cinderella. It would've been so much easier if she'd never met Thorne Prince. Now she was forever doomed to feel this ache within her for having so flippantly tempted fate.

When she'd arrived home, even before she'd undressed, Cindy had sat on the end of her bed and tried to picture Thorne in her home. The image was so discordant that she'd cast the thought from her mind. If Thorne were to see this apartment and the earthy family she loved, he'd be embarrassed. Thorne Prince didn't know what it meant to live from paycheck to paycheck or to "make do" when money was tight. He might as well be from another planet in a neighboring solar system, he was so far removed from her way of life.

"Cindy." Her aunt knocked at the bedroom door. "Are you awake?"

Cindy sat up awkwardly and leaned against her headboard. "I'm up...come on in."

Slowly, her aunt opened the door. Her eyes met Cindy's. "It's nearly noon. Are you feeling ill?"

It was unusual for Cindy to stay in bed for any reason. "A headache."

Aunt Theresa sat on the edge of the bed and brushed the hair away from Cindy's forehead. "Did you have a good time last night?" she asked.

Cindy's gaze dropped to the patchwork quilt that served as her bedspread. "I had a wonderful time."

"Did Cinderella meet her prince?"

Cindy's eyes glistened at the memory. "I spent most of the evening with him."

"Was he everything Cinderella expected?"

Cindy nodded because speaking was impossible. She leaned forward enough to rest her head on her aunt's shoulder.

"And now?" The older woman probed.

"And now Cinderella realizes what a terrible fool she was because at midnight she turned back into plain, simple Cindy Territo." A tear scorched her cheek and her arms circled her aunt's neck. Just as she had as a child, Cindy needed the warmth and security of her aunt's love.

"My darling girl, you are neither plain nor simple."

Cindy sniffled and sadly shook her head. "Compared to other women he knows, I am."

"But he liked you."

"He probably thought I was a secretary."

"Nevertheless, he must've been impressed to have spent the evening in your company. Does it matter so much if you're a secretary or a cleaning woman?"

"Unfortunately, it does."

"It seems to me that you're selling your prince short," her aunt said soothingly, stroking Cindy's hair. "If he's everything you said, it wouldn't matter in the least."

Cindy said nothing. She couldn't answer her aunt's questions. Her own doubts were overwhelming.

"Do you plan to see him again?" Theresa asked, after a thoughtful moment.

Cindy closed her eyes. "Never," she whispered.

* * *

Monday morning Thorne walked into his office fifteen minutes before he usually did. Ms. Hillard, his secretary, looked up from her desk, revealing mild surprise that her boss was early.

"Good morning, Ms. Hillard. It's a beautiful day, isn't it?"

His secretary's mouth dropped open. "It's barely above freezing and they're forecasting a snowstorm by midafternoon."

"I love snow," Thorne continued, undaunted.

Ms. Hillard rolled out her chair and stood. "Are you feeling all right, sir?"

"I'm feeling absolutely wonderful."

"Can I get you some coffee?"

"Please." Thorne strolled toward his desk. "And contact Wells in Human Resources, would you?"

"Right away." A minute later she delivered his coffee. The red light on his phone was lit, and Thorne sat down and reached for the receiver.

"This is Thorndike Prince," he began in clipped tones. "Would you kindly check your files for the name *Cindy*. She works on the executive floor. I'd like her full name and the office number."

"Cindy?" the director repeated.

"Unfortunately, I don't have her surname."

"This may take some time, Mr. Prince. I'll have to call you back."

Thorne thumped his fingers against his desk in an effort to disguise his impatience. "I'll wait to hear from you." He replaced the receiver and leaned back in his chair, holding his mug of coffee in both hands. He gazed out the window and noted for the first time the dark, angry clouds that threatened the sky. A snowstorm, Ms. Hillard had said. Terrific! He'd take Cindy for a walk in the falling snow and warm her with kisses. They'd go back to the park and feed the pigeons and squirrels, then head over to his apartment and drink mulled wine. He'd spent one restless day without her and he wasn't about to waste another. His head was bursting with things he wanted to tell her, things he found vitally important to share. Today he'd learn everything he could about her. Once he knew everything, he'd take her in his arms and tell her the magic hadn't stopped working. The spell she'd cast on him hadn't faded and it wouldn't. If anything, it had grown stronger.

The phone rang, and he jerked the receiver off its cradle. "Prince here."

"This is Jeff Wells from HR."

"Yes?"

"Sir—" he paused and cleared his throat "—I've checked all our records and I can't find anyone named Cindy or Cynthia employed on the executive floor."

"Then look again," Thorne said urgently.

"Sir, I've checked the files three times."

"Then please do so again." Thorne hung up the phone. He wondered grimly if he'd have to go down there and locate Cindy's name himself.

A half hour later, Thorne had to agree with Wells. There wasn't a secretary or assistant in the entire company named Cindy. Thorne slammed the filing-cabinet drawer shut with unnecessary force.

"Who was in charge of the Christmas Ball?" he demanded.

Jeffrey Wells, a diminutive man who wore a bow tie and glasses, bowed his head. "I was, Mr. Prince."

"The ball was by invitation only. Is that correct?"

"Yes, sir, I received my instructions from—"

"I want the list."

"The list?" He pulled out a file and handed Thorne several sheets of paper. "The name of every employee who received an invitation is here, except one, and—"

"Who?" Thorne whirled around to face the other man.

"Me," Wells said in a startled voice.

Thorne scanned the list, then again more slowly, carefully examining each name. No Cindy.

"How many extra invitations were sent to outside guests?"

"A dozen—I have the list here." Wells pulled a sheet of paper from the file and Thorne took it and counted the names. Exactly twelve. But again, no Cindy.

"Sir...perhaps this Cindy crashed the party.... There are ways," he stammered. "The hotel staff do all they can to assure that only those with an invitation are granted admission, but...it's been known to happen."

"Crashed the ball..." Thorne repeated, stunned. He rubbed a hand over his face. That was what had happened. The instant he heard Wells say it, he'd recognized the truth. "Thank you for your trouble, Mr. Wells."

"It was no problem, Mr. Prince. Perhaps if you could describe the girl, I could go through our files and locate pictures. Perhaps she's employed by Oakes-Jenning, but was assuming another name."

Thorne shook his head. "That won't be necessary." He turned and left the office, reaching his own without remembering how he got there.

Ms. Hillard stood when he entered the room, her hands filled with the mail. Thorne gave her a look that told her he'd deal with his correspondence later, and she sat down again.

For two days he'd been living in a dreamworld, acting like an idiotic, romantic fool. The joy drained out of him and was replaced by a grim determination not to allow such folly to overtake him a second time. He'd put Cindy out of his mind and his heart as easily as he'd instilled her there. She was a fraud who'd taken delight in duping him. Well, her plans had worked beyond her expectations. He slumped into his chair and turned to look at the sky. Ms. Hillard was right. The weather was terrible, but then so was the day.

Five

Thorne's violent sneeze tore the tissue in half. He reached for another in the nick of time. His eyes were running, he was so congested he could barely breathe and he had a fever. He felt thoroughly miserable, and it wasn't *all* due to this wretched cold. He'd gotten it the night he'd given Cindy his coat. Cindy. Despite his resolve, she haunted his dreams and filled his every waking thought. He wanted to hate her, shout at her and...and take her in his arms and hold her. There were moments he despised her, and then there were other times, usually late at night, when he'd welcome the memories. That was when she came to him, in those quiet hours. He'd be on the ballroom floor with her in his arms; a second later he'd recall with vivid clarity the agony in her eyes as she tearfully told him goodbye. When she told him how sorry she was, the words seemed to echo over and over in his mind.

Thorne picked up the pearl comb and fingered it for the thousandth time in the past five days. He'd kept it with him constantly, seeking some clue from it, some solace. He found neither. He'd taken it to a jeweler and learned it was a fairly inexpensive comb that was perhaps twenty-five years old—certainly of little value beyond the sentimental. Too bad she hadn't left a glass slipper behind like the real Cinderella. Then he could take it around the executive floor and try it on women's feet to see if it would fit. Instead, his Cinderella had left him something useless. He couldn't trace her with a common pearl comb.

Other than that, Thorne had nothing with which to find Cindy. The crazy part was that he wasn't completely sure he *wanted* to see her again. She'd lied to him, played him for a fool and mercilessly shattered his dreams—serious crimes for a woman he'd known less than five hours—and yet he couldn't stop thinking about her. Every minute. Every day. He wanted to cast her from his mind; then and only then could he finally escape her.

Thorne's thoughts were followed by another thunderous sneeze. He pressed the intercom button and summoned Ms. Hillard. "Did you get that orange juice?" he asked.

"It's on its way," she informed him.

"Thank you." Thorne pulled open the top desk drawer and grabbed the aspirin bottle. He felt miserable, in body *and* spirit.

Cindy inhaled a deep breath and forced herself to enter Thorne's office. It was torture to be inside the room where he spent so much of his time. She could feel his presence so strongly that she kept looking over her shoulder, convinced he was there, standing behind her. She wondered what he'd say to her—if he hated her or if he even thought about her—then decided she'd rather not know. Her heart was weighed down with regrets.

Pushing Thorne out of her mind, she ran the feather duster over his desk. Something small and white fell onto the carpet. Cindy bent over and picked it up. A pearl. She held it in the palm of her hand and stared at it. Thorne had her mother's missing comb! Cindy had thought it was lost to her forever. Not until she was home did she realize one of them had fallen from her hair, and she'd been devastated over its loss. She had so few of her mother's personal possessions that losing even one was monumental.

"What's that?" Vanessa asked, standing in the open doorway, her feather duster in her hip pocket.

Cindy's hand closed over the pearl. Knowing that Thorne had the comb gave her an oddly secure feeling. "A pearl," she said, tucking it inside the pocket of her coveralls.

Vanessa studied her closely. "Do you think it might be from your mother's comb?"

"I'm sure it is."

"Then your prince must have it."

Cindy nodded, comforted immeasurably by this fact.

"How do you plan to get it back?"

"I don't," Cindy said. She continued dusting, praying Vanessa would return to her own tasks.

"You aren't going to get it from him? That's crazy. You were sick about losing that comb."

"I know."

"Well, good grief, Cindy, here's the perfect opportunity for you to see your prince again. Grab it, for heaven's sake!"

Cindy's mouth quivered. "I don't want to see him again."

"You might be able to fool your family, but you won't have such an easy time with me." Vanessa's expression was grim and her eyes revealed her disapproval. "You told me the ball was the happiest, most exciting night of your life."

Cindy's back stiffened. The warm, fairy-tale sensations

the ball had aroused were supposed to last a lifetime, and instead the evening had left her yearning for many, many more. "The night was everything I dreamed, but don't you see? I was playing a role... I was glamorous and sophisticated and someone totally different from the Cindy you see now. The show closed, the part's cancelled and I've gone back to being just plain me—Cindy Territo, janitorial worker, part-time student."

"And Cindy Territo, woman in love."

"Stop it, Vanessa!" she cried and whirled around to face her friend. "Adults don't fall in love after one night. Not true love—it just doesn't happen!"

Vanessa crossed her arms and leaned against the side of Thorne's rosewood desk. "That's not what I hear."

Cindy snorted softly. "What you're talking about isn't love...it's infatuation. It wasn't like that with Thorne and me. I don't think I can explain or define it—I've never felt anything like this with any other man."

"And yet you're convinced it can't be love?" Vanessa taunted.

"It's impossible," she insisted, although she didn't believe it. "I don't want to talk about him or that night again. I—we have to put it out of our minds." She reached for Thorne's wastebasket and unceremoniously emptied it inside her cart. When she saw the contents her eyes widened. "Vanessa, look." She picked up a discarded aspirin box and another for a cold remedy. "Thorne's sick."

"He must've gone through a whole box of tissues."

"Oh, no." Cindy sagged into his chair, lovingly stroking the arm as though it were his fevered brow. She longed to be with him. "The night of the ball," she began, her voice strained with regret, "when we went into the park, he gave me his coat so I wouldn't catch cold."

"At a price, it seems."

Cindy's face went pale, and she gazed distractedly at her friend before turning her head and closing her eyes. "It's all my fault. Christmas is only a few days away.... Oh, dear, I did this to him."

"What do you plan to do about it?"

"What can I do?" If Cindy was miserable before, it was nothing compared to the guilt she suffered now, knowing her prince was ill because of her. He'd grown chilled, which had made him vulnerable to the viruses so abundant this time of year.

"Make some chicken soup and take it to him," Vanessa suggested.

Cindy's eyes widened. "I couldn't."

"This is the same woman who sauntered up to Thorndike Prince and announced he was a disappointment to her?"

"One and the same," Cindy muttered.

Vanessa shook her head. "You could've fooled me."

If anybody was a fool, Cindy determined the following afternoon, she was the one. She'd spent the morning chopping vegetables into precise, even pieces and adding them to a steaming pot of chicken broth and stewing chicken while her aunt made a batch of homemade noodles.

"Maybe I should have Tony deliver it for me," Cindy said, eyeing her aunt speculatively.

"Tony and Maria are going to a movie, and you can bet that your prince isn't going to hand over that comb to my son without getting information out of him." The way she was regarding Cindy implied that Thorne would use fair means or foul to find out whatever he could.

"Thorne wouldn't hurt anyone." Cindy defended him righteously, and from the smile that lit up the older woman's face, Cindy realized she'd fallen neatly into her aunt's trap.

"Then you shouldn't have any qualms about visiting him. It's not Tony or anyone else he wants to see—it's you."

Cindy raised questioning eyes to her. "I'm not convinced he does want to see me."

"He kept the comb, didn't he?"

"Yes, but that doesn't mean anything."

"No man is going to carry around a woman's hair ornament without a reason."

"Oh, Aunt Theresa, I feel like such an idiot. What if he hates me? What if—"

"Will you stop with the *what ifs!* The soup's finished. Take it to him and go from there."

"But…" She strove to keep the emotion from her voice. But she couldn't hide her nervousness. If she saw Thorne today, there'd be no fancy gown or dimmed lights to create an illusion of beauty and worldliness. No moonlight and magic to entice him. Her plaid wool skirt, hand-knit sweater and leather pumps would tell him everything.

Theresa caught her by the shoulders. "Stop being so nervous! It's not like you."

Cindy smiled weakly. She'd go to him because she had to. Her actions were mapped out in her mind. She'd already looked up his address. She'd arrive at his apartment, present him with the soup and tell him how sorry she was that he'd gotten a cold. Then, depending on how he responded, she'd ask for her mother's comb. But only if he showed signs of being pleased to see her. Somehow she doubted he would.

The television droned in the background, but Thorne couldn't manage any interest in the silly game shows that ran one after the other. They, however, were only slightly less boring than the soap operas and talk shows on the other channels. He felt hot, then chilled. Sick and uncomfortable. Sleepy from the medication and yet wide-awake. It was only three days until Christmas and he had all the love and goodwill of an ill-tempered, cantankerous grinch.

The small tree in the corner of his living room was testament to his own folly. He'd enthusiastically put it up the day after meeting Cindy, and now it sat there taunting him, reminding him what a fool he was to believe in romantic dreams. In three days' time he'd be obligated to show up at his parents' home and face them—and Sheila. The thought was not pleasant. All he wanted to do was hide in his condo and insist the world leave him alone.

He sighed and reached for a glass of grapefruit juice and another cold tablet. Discarded cold remedies crowded his glass coffee table. He'd taken one pillow plus the quilt from his bed, trying to get comfortable in the living room.

The doorbell chimed and he ignored it.

Seemingly undaunted, the bell rang a second time. "Go away," he shouted rudely. The last thing he wanted was company.

The ring was followed by loud knocking.

Furious, he shoved his quilt aside and stormed to the front door. He jerked it open and glared angrily at the young woman who stood before him. "I said go away!" he shouted, in no mood to be civil. "I don't want any..." His voice faded to a croak. "Cindy?" He was too shocked to do anything, even breathe. The first thing that came to mind was to haul her into his arms and not let her leave until she told him who she was. But that impulse was immediately followed by an all-consuming anger. He glared at her with contempt.

Cindy stood there, unable to move or to manage a coherent word. A rush of color heated her face. This was a hundred times worse than she'd imagined. Thorne hated her. Dismayed and disheartened, she handed him the large paper sack. "I...heard you were sick."

"What's this?"

"Chicken soup."

Thorne's eyes lit up with sardonic amusement. She resembled a frightened rabbit standing in front of a hungry wolf. He wondered how anyone could look so innocent and completely guileless when he knew her to be a liar and a cheat. "You might as well come in," he said gruffly, stepping aside.

"I can only stay a minute," she said shakily.

"I wouldn't dream of inviting you to stay longer," he answered, willfully cruel. He was rewarded when he saw the color drain from her face. Good. He wanted her to experience just a taste of the hell she'd put him through.

She caught her breath and nodded, saying without words that she understood.

He set the soup on the coffee table and slumped onto the white leather sofa. "I won't apologize for the mess, but as you've heard, I haven't been feeling well." He motioned toward the matching chair across from him. "I know what you want."

Surprise widened her deep blue eyes. "You do?"

"It's the comb, isn't it?"

Cindy nodded and sat on the edge of the cushion, folding her hands primly in her lap. She clasped her fingers tightly together. "It was my mother's... You have it?"

"Yes."

She sighed with relief. "I thought I'd lost it."

"You knew very well that I had it."

Cindy opened her mouth to argue with him but quickly closed it. He couldn't believe anything but the worst, and she couldn't blame him.

"What? No heated defense?"

"None. You have the right to hate me. I lied to you, but not in the way you think."

"You're no secretary."

"No, but if you'll remember, I never said I was."

"But you didn't stop me from thinking that."

Cindy dropped her eyes to her clenched hands. "As I said before, you have every right to be angry, but if it's any consolation to you—I am deeply and truly sorry."

His gaze narrowed, condemning her. "Such innocent eyes. Who would have guessed that such deception lay just below the surface?"

Cindy clamped her teeth together with such force that her jaw ached. Every word was a slap in the face and it hurt. His eyes were so cold and full of contempt. "If I could have the comb... I'll be on my way."

"Not quite yet." He stood and joined her, pulling her to her feet. "You owe me something for all the lies you told... for deceiving me into thinking you were kind and good." For filling his head with dreams and breaking her unspoken promises...

Cindy drew back sharply.

His eyes narrowed on her flushed face and his hands tightened around her upper arms. He pulled her against him and slanted his mouth over hers.

Cindy went still but didn't resist.

Thorne felt her submission and he loosened his grip, drawing slowly back. She'd gone deathly pale, and he instantly felt overwhelming regret. He dropped his hands and watched as she took a stumbling step away from him.

"I apologize for that," he said hoarsely. He was wrong about her. She wasn't cold and calculating, but warm and generous. It was all there for him to read in her clear, blue eyes. Her chin shook slightly and those magical eyes stared up at him, glimmering with hurt. He longed to soothe away the pain he'd inflicted. Utterly defeated, he turned and walked away. "I'll get the comb."

Thorne stumbled halfway down the hall that led to his bedroom. The floor seemed to pitch and heave under him, and he sagged against the wall to keep from falling. He knew it was the medication—the doctor had warned him about the dizzying effect.

"Thorne…" Cindy was at his side, wrapping an arm around his waist.

"I'll be fine in a minute."

Her hold tightened. "You're sick."

His breathless chuckle revealed his amusement. "Are you always so perceptive?"

"No." She tried to support him. "Let me get you into bed."

"Those are misleading words, Cinderella. I'm sure your fairy godmother would be shocked."

"Quit joking, I'm serious."

He turned his head and his gaze pinned hers. "So am I."

"Thorne!" Her face heated. As best she could, Cindy directed him into the bedroom. The huge king-size bed dominated the middle of the room and was a mess of tangled sheets and blankets. She left him long enough to pull back the covers and fluff up the pillows.

Because he felt so weak, Thorne sat on the edge of the bed and ran a weary hand over his face. Under normal circumstances he would've been humiliated to have a woman fuss over him like this, but nothing about his relationship with Cindy was conventional.

"Here, let me help you," she insisted, urging him to lie down. She held the back of one hand to his forehead.

"No." He brushed her hand away.

"You need to rest."

"No," he repeated.

"Thorne, please, you're running a fever."

"If I fall asleep," he said, holding her gaze, "you'll be gone when I wake up." His mouth curved into a sad smile. "Will you promise to stay?"

Cindy hesitated.

"I'll stay until you wake," she finally said.

"Do you promise?"

She nodded.

"Say it, Cindy."

"I'll be here," she cried, angry that he couldn't trust her. "I wouldn't dream of leaving you like this."

He fell against the pillow and released a long sigh. "Good," he said and closed his eyes. For the first time in days he felt right. From the moment Cindy had left him standing in the park, it was as though a part of him had been missing. Now she was here, so close that all he had to do was reach out and touch her.

Standing at his side, Cindy pulled the covers over his shoulders and lingered beside the bed. She wouldn't leave the room until she was sure he was asleep. He appeared almost childlike, lying on his side, his brow relaxed and smooth. The harsh lines around his mouth were gone, as were the ones that fanned out beside his eyes.

A minute later, his lashes fluttered open and he looked around, startled.

"I'm here," she whispered and stroked his forehead to reassure him.

"Lie down with me," he pleaded, shifting to the far side of the bed, leaving more than ample room for her.

"Thorne, I can't."

"Please." His voice was barely discernible, hardly more than a whisper.

No one word could be more seductive. "I shouldn't."

He answered her by gently patting the bed, his eyes still closed. "I need you," he said softly.

"Oh, Thorne." She pressed her lips together and slipped off her shoes. He was manipulating her and she didn't like it one bit. As soon as he was well she'd tell him in no uncertain terms what she thought of his underhanded methods.

Keeping as close to edge of the bed as possible without falling off, Cindy lay stiff and tense at his side. Thorne was under the covers while she remained on top, but that did little to diminish her misgivings.

Gradually, so gradually she was hardly aware of what he was doing, Thorne eased himself closer to her so he could feel the warmth of her body against his. Sleep was so wonderfully inviting. He draped his arm over her ribs and brought her next to him. He felt the tension leave her limbs, and for the first time since the Monday after the Christmas Ball, Thorne Prince smiled.

Cindy woke two hours later, astonished that she'd slept. The room was dark and she lay watching the shadows on the bedroom walls, thinking. Her mind was crowded with conflicting thoughts. She should leave him while she could, with her heart intact—but she'd promised she wouldn't. No matter what the consequences, she wouldn't lie to him again.

As gently as possible, Cindy slipped from his arms and tiptoed across the plush carpet. Clothes littered the floor and she automatically picked them up as she made her way out of the room. She collected towels from the bathroom and threw everything in the washing machine, which she found in its own alcove.

Dirty dishes were piled in the kitchen sink, and Cindy placed them in the dishwasher and turned it on. The pots and pans she scrubbed by hand. She'd finished those when she turned around and discovered Thorne standing in the middle of the kitchen, watching her.

"I thought you'd left," he murmured. He'd woken to find her gone and momentary terror had gripped his heart. It wasn't until he'd realized she was in the other room that he'd been able to breathe again.

"No, I'm here," she said unnecessarily.

"I don't need you cleaning for me. I've got a woman who comes in for that."

"What's her name?"

He stared at her blankly, surprised by the inane conversation they were having. "She's sent by an agency. I wouldn't know her if I met her on the street. Does it matter?"

Cindy turned to face the sink and bit her bottom lip at the pain. With deliberate movements, she rinsed out the dishrag and wrung it dry, then folded it over the faucet. She dried her hands on the kitchen towel.

"Cindy." He touched her shoulder, but she ignored him.

"I promised you I wouldn't leave while you were sleeping," she said, her eyes avoiding his. "But I have to go now. Could I please have the comb?"

"No."

"No? But...it's part of a matching set."

"You told me they belonged to your mother, didn't you?"

Cindy nodded.

"They obviously mean a great deal to you."

"Yes...of course." She didn't understand where he was going with this.

"Then I'll keep it until I find out why you need to disappear from my life."

"That's blackmail!"

"I know." He looked pleased with himself. "I'll feel a whole lot better once I shower and shave. When I'm finished, we'll talk."

Cindy's fingers gripped the counter behind her. "Okay," she murmured. She hated lying to him—again—but she had no intention of staying. She couldn't. She'd kept her promise—she hadn't left while he slept. Now he was awake and so was she. Wide-awake.

The minute she heard the shower running, Cindy sneaked into the bedroom and retrieved her shoes. She'd reached the front door before she hesitated. A note. He deserved that much.

She found paper and a pen in the kitchen and wrote as fast as her fingers could move. She told him he was right in assuming the combs meant a lot to her. So much so that she wanted him to keep the comb he'd found—keep it in memory of the night they'd met. She told him she'd always remember him, her own dashing prince, and that their time together was the most special of her life. Tears fell from her eyes and her lips trembled as she signed her name.

She left the paper on top of the television. Soundlessly she hurried to the front door, where she paused again, blinded by tears. Her fingers curled around the knob. Everything within her told her to walk out that door and not look back. Everything except her heart. Cindy felt as if it was dissolving with every breath she took. She pressed her forehead against the polished mahogany door, fighting to strengthen her resolve.

Then she heard his voice behind her.

"I didn't think I could trust you," he said bitterly.

Six

Thorne's harsh words cut her savagely. With tears streaming down her cheeks, she turned toward him, all the pent-up emotion in her eyes there for him to read. He had to see that it was killing her to walk away.

One look at the pain etched so plainly on her tormented face, and Thorne's anger evaporated. He moved across the room. "Oh, Cindy," he groaned and reached for her, folding her in his arms. At first she resisted his comfort, standing stiff and unyielding against him, but he held her because he couldn't bear to let her go. His hands cupped her face and he directed her mouth to his, kissing her again and again until she relaxed and wound her arms around his neck. Thorne could feel her breath quicken and he knew he'd reached her.

Cindy's heart seemed to stop and then surged again with hurried beats. Being held and kissed by Thorne only made leaving him more difficult. She could hardly breathe past the wild pounding of her heart. She shouldn't have come to him, shouldn't have asked for the return of her missing comb. But she had—seeking some common ground, hoping to bridge the gap between their lives. But it couldn't be done. His words about his cleaning woman had proven how unfeasible any relationship between them would be.

"No." She eased herself away from him. "Please, don't try to stop me.... I have to go."

"Why?"

She pinched her lips together and refused to answer.

Thorne caressed her thick blond hair. He drew in a calming breath and released it, repeating the action several times until he could think clearly.

"You're married, aren't you?" he asked in a stark voice.

"No!"

"Then why do you insist on playing hide-and-seek?"

She dropped her head and closed her eyes, unable to look at him any longer. "Trust me, it's for the best that we never see each other again."

"That's ridiculous. We're perfect together." He was nearly shouting at her. He lowered his voice, wanting to reason with her calmly. "I *need* to be with you. That night was the most wonderful of my life. It was like…like I'd suddenly woken up from a coma. The whole world came alive for me the minute you arrived. At least give us a chance. That isn't so much to ask, is it?"

A tear slipped from the corner of her eye.

"Cindy, don't you realize I'm crazy about you?"

"You don't know me," she cried.

"I know enough."

"It was *one* night, don't you see? One magical night. Another night would never be the same. It's better to leave things as they are rather than disillusion ourselves by trying to live a fantasy."

"Cindy." He stopped her, bringing his lips hungrily to

hers, kissing her until she was weak and clinging. "The magic is stronger than ever. I feel it and so do you."

She leaned her forehead against his chest, battling the resistance in her heart. But she couldn't deny the truth any more than she could stop her heart from racing at his slightest touch.

"One more night," Thorne said softly, enticingly, "to test our feelings. Then we'll know."

Cindy nodded silently, unable to refuse him anything when he was holding her as if she were an enchanted princess and he her sworn love. When she did speak, her voice was hardly above a whisper. "One more night," she repeated. "But only once."

Thorne felt the tightness in his chest subside and the tension seep out of him. He wanted to argue with her; he wanted a lot more than one night—but she looked so confused and uncertain that he didn't dare press her. For now he'd be satisfied with the time she could freely give him.

He grinned. "Where would you like to go? A play? A jazz club? Dinner?"

"Thorne." She placed her hand on his arm. "You're ill."

"I feel a thousand times better." And he did.

"We'll stay right here," she countered, and breaking out of his arms, she returned to the kitchen. Catching him by the hand, she took him with her. She sat him down at the table and proceeded to inspect his freezer and cupboards.

Thorne watched as she organized their meal. Before he knew what was happening, Cindy had him at the counter, ripping apart lettuce leaves for a salad. It was as though she'd worked in his kitchen all her life. She located frozen chicken breasts, thawed them in the microwave and set them in the oven with potatoes wrapped in aluminum foil.

Then she searched his cupboards, gathering the ingredients for a mushroom sauce.

Thorne paused long enough in his task to choose a CD. Soon music surrounded them as they worked; once everything was prepared they moved to the living room. As they sat on the couch, Thorne's arm went around her shoulders and she bent her arm to connect her fingers with his. Her head rested on his shoulder. The moment was serene, peaceful. Thorne had never known a time like this with a woman. All the women he'd met wanted parties and excitement, attention and approval. He hadn't married, hadn't even thought of it until recently. He'd given up looking for that special woman, the one who'd fill his days with happiness and love. With Sheila, he'd been willing to accept "close enough," never expecting to feel what Cindy made so simple. Yet here she was in his arms, and he was willing to do everything humanly possible to keep her there.

Cindy gave a contented sigh. These few minutes together were as close to paradise as she ever hoped to come in this lifetime. She found it astonishing that they didn't need to speak. The communication between them didn't require words, and when they did talk, they discovered their tastes were surprisingly similar. Cindy loved old movies; so did Thorne. They'd both read everything John LeCarré had ever written and devotedly watched reruns of *Seinfeld*. Both Cindy and Thorne were so familiar with the television comedy that they exchanged lines of dialogue. Excited and happy, they laughed and hugged each other.

Cindy couldn't believe this was happening and held him to her, breathless with an inexplicable joy. Somehow she'd known they'd discover that the night of the Christmas Ball hadn't been a fluke.

Thorne couldn't believe how *right* they were together.

They enjoyed the same things, shared the same interests. He'd never thought he'd find a woman who could make him laugh the way Cindy did.

When dinner was ready, Thorne lit candles, set them in the center of the dining-room table and dimmed the overhead lighting. The mood was wildly romantic.

"The fairy dust is so thick in here I can barely see," Cindy teased as she carried their plates to the table.

"That's not fairy dust."

"No?"

"No," he said, and his eyes smiled into hers. "This is undiluted romance." He pulled out her chair and playfully nuzzled her neck when she was seated.

"I should've recognized what this is. You'll have to pardon me, but I've been so busy with school that I haven't dated much in the past and—" She stopped abruptly, realizing what she'd said.

Thorne sat down across from her and unfolded the linen napkin. "You go to school?" He'd been so careful not to question her, afraid she'd freeze up if he bombarded her with his need to find answers. From the moment she'd arrived, he'd longed to discover how she'd known he was ill. Cindy was like a complex puzzle. Every bit of information he'd learned about her was a tiny interlocking piece that would help him reveal the complete picture of who and what she was—and why she felt she had to hide from him.

"I attend classes," she admitted, feeling awkward. Without being obvious, she tried to study his reaction, but his face was an unreadable mask. He'd been in business too long to show his feelings.

"What are you studying?"

"Various things." Her stomach fluttered and she sent

him a reproving glance before returning her attention to her meal.

Thorne's grip on his fork tightened as he saw her visibly withdraw from him. Her eyes avoiding his, she sat uneasily in the chair; her mouth was pinched as though she was attempting to disguise her pain. Intuitively he knew that if he pressed her for answers, he'd lose her completely. "I won't ask you anything else," he promised.

She smiled then and his heart squeezed with an unfamiliar emotion. The ache caught him by surprise. He didn't care who Cindy was. She could be an escaped convict and it wouldn't matter. He wanted to tell her that regardless of what troubled her, he could fix it. He'd stand between her and the world if that was what it took. Forging rivers, climbing mountains, anything—he'd do it gladly.

After they'd finished eating, Cindy cleared the table. Thorne moved across the living room to change the music.

Blinded by tears, Cindy reached for her coat and purse.

"Do you like classical?" Thorne asked without turning. "How about jazz?"

"Anything is fine." Cindy prayed he didn't hear the quaver in her voice. She shot him one last look, thanking him with her eyes for the second most magnificent night of her life. Then, silently, she slipped out the front door and out of her dreams.

"I've got the music to several Broadway shows if you'd prefer that."

His statement was met with silence.

"Cindy?"

He walked into the kitchen. She was gone.

"Cindy?" His voice was hardly audible. He didn't need to look any further. He knew. She'd run away. Vanished into thin air. He found the note propped on the television and read it, then read it again. She asked him to forgive her. He stared at the words coldly.

Thorne folded the paper in half and ripped it viciously, folded it a second time, tore it and crumpled the pieces. His face was rigid and a muscle worked convulsively in his jaw as he threw her note in the garbage. He stood, furious with her, furious with himself for being caught in this trap again.

He slammed his fist against the counter and closed his eyes in an effort to control his anger. Fine, he told himself. If this was how she wanted it, he'd stay out of her life. Thorndike Prince didn't crawl for any woman—they came to him. His face hardened. He didn't need her; he'd get along perfectly well without her and the silly games she wanted to play. He was more determined than ever to put her out of his mind.

Christmas Day was a nightmare for Cindy. She smiled and responded appropriately to what was going on around her, but she was miserable. She couldn't stop thinking about Thorne. She wondered who he was with and whether he thought of her.... After the sneaky way she'd left him, Cindy believed he probably hated her. She couldn't blame him if he did.

"Cindy, Cindy..." Her four-year-old cousin crawled into her lap. "Will you read to me?"

Carla had always been special to Cindy. The little girl had been born to Cindy's aunt Sofia when she was in her early forties. Sofia's other three children were in their teens and Sofia had been shocked and unhappy about this unexpected pregnancy. But Carla had become the delight of the Territo family.

"Mama's busy and all Tony wants to do is talk to Maria."

"Of course I'll read to you." She hugged Carla tightly.

"You're my favorite cousin," Carla whispered close to Cindy's ear.

"I'm glad, because you're my favorite cousin, too," Cindy whispered back. "Now, do you have a book or do you want me to choose one?"

"Santa brought me a new story."

"Well, good for Santa." Her eye caught Aunt Sofia's and they exchanged knowing glances. The little girl might be only four, but she was well aware that Santa looked just like her dad, Cindy's uncle Carl, after whom Carla had been named.

"I'll get it." Carla scrambled off Cindy's lap, raced across the room and returned with a large picture book. "Here," she said, handing it to Cindy. "Read me this one. Read me *Cinderella.*"

Cindy's breath jammed in her lungs and tears stung her eyes. *"Cinderella?"* she repeated as the numbing sensation worked its way through her whole body. She prayed it would anesthetize her from the trauma that gripped her heart.

"Cindy?" Carla's chubby little hands clasped Cindy's knee. "Aren't you going to read to me?"

"Of course, sweetheart." Somehow she managed to pick up the book and flip open the front cover. Carla positioned herself comfortably in her cousin's lap, leaned back and promptly inserted her thumb in her mouth.

It took all of Cindy's energy to start reading. Her throat felt incredibly dry. "'Once upon a time…'"

"…in a land far, far away," Mary Susan Clark told her five-year-old son, who sat on the brocade cushion at her feet.

Thorne gazed at his sister, who was reciting the fairy tale to her son, and his heart slowed with anger and resentment.

"Do you think it's a good idea to be filling a young boy's head with that kind of garbage?" Thorne demanded gruffly.

Mary Susan's gray eyes widened with surprise. "But it's only a fairy tale."

"Thorne." His mother studied him, her expression puzzled. "It's not like you to snap."

"I apologize," he said with a weak smile. "I guess I've been a bit short-tempered lately."

"You've been ill." Sheila, with her dark brown eyes and pixie face, automatically defended him. She placed her hand in his and gave his fingers a gentle squeeze.

He liked Sheila well enough; she was unfailingly pleasant and loyal. One day she'd make some man an excellent wife. Maybe even him. Thorne was through playing Cindy's games. Through believing in fairy tales. He couldn't live like this. Cindy didn't want anything to do with him, and he had no choice but to accept her wishes. Sheila loved him—at least she claimed she did. Thorne didn't know what love felt like anymore. At one time he'd thought he was in love with Sheila. Maybe not *completely,* but he'd expected that to happen eventually. Then he'd met Cindy, and he was head over heels in love for the first time in his thirty-three years. Crazy in love. And with a woman who'd turned her back on him and walked away without a second thought. It didn't make sense. Nothing did anymore. Nothing at all. Not business. Not life. Not women.

Thorne and Sheila had been seeing each other for nearly six months and she'd hardly been able to conceal her disappointment when an engagement ring hadn't been secretly tucked under the Christmas tree. But she hadn't questioned him. He wished she wasn't so understanding; he would've preferred it if she'd gotten angry, demanded an explanation.

Thorne noticed his mother still studying him and he

made an attempt to disguise his unhappiness. Smiling required a monumental effort. He managed it, but he doubted he'd fooled his mother.

"Thorne, could you help me in the kitchen?"

The whole family turned to him. That was code for talking privately, and it wasn't the least bit original.

"Of course, Mother," he said with the faintest sardonic inflection. He disentangled his fingers from Sheila's and stood, obediently following Gwendolyn Prince out of the room.

"What in heaven's name is the matter with you?" she snapped the minute they were out of earshot. "It isn't that... that girl you mentioned, is it?"

"What girl?" Feigning ignorance seemed the best response.

"You haven't been yourself..."

"...since the night of that Christmas Ball," Aunt Theresa said softly.

"I know," Cindy whispered. "You see, there's something I didn't realize.... Fairy tales don't always come true."

"But, Cindy, you're so unhappy over him."

"We said goodbye," she said, her eyes pleading with her aunt to drop this disturbing subject. Accepting that she'd live without Thorne was difficult enough; discussing it with her aunt was like tearing open a half-healed wound.

"You haven't stopped thinking about him."

"No, but I will."

"Will you, Cindy?" Theresa's deep brown eyes showed her doubt.

Cindy's gaze pleaded with her. "Yes," she said and the words were a vow to herself. She had no choice now. When she'd left Thorne's apartment it had been forever.

Although the pain had been nearly unbearable, it was better to sever the ties quickly than to bleed slowly to death.

"Mother and I are planning a shopping expedition to Paris in March," Sheila said enthusiastically, sitting across the table from Thorne.

They were at one of Thorne's favorite lunch spots. Sheila made it a habit to visit the office at least once a week so they could have lunch. In the past, Thorne had looked forward to their get-togethers. Not today. He wasn't in the mood. But before he'd been able to say anything to Ms. Hillard, she'd sent Sheila into his office, and now he was stuck.

"Paris sounds interesting."

"So does the chicken," Sheila commented, glancing over the menu. "I hear the mushroom sauce here is fabulous."

Thorne's stomach turned. "Baked chicken breast served with mushroom sauce," he read, remembering all too well his last evening with Cindy and the meal she'd prepared for him.

"I hope you'll try it with me," Sheila urged, gazing at him adoringly.

His mouth thinned. "I hate mushrooms."

Sheila stared down at the menu and she pressed her lips tightly together. "I didn't know that," she said after a long moment.

"You do now," Thorne muttered, detesting himself for treating her this way. Sheila deserved better.

The waiter came to the table, hands behind his back. "Are you ready to order?"

"I believe so," Thorne said, closing his menu and handing it back. "The lady will have the chicken special and I'll have a mushroom omelet."

Sheila gave him an odd look, but said nothing.

During lunch Thorne made a sincere effort to be pleasant. He honestly tried to appear interested when Sheila told him about the latest fashion trends in France. He even managed to stifle a yawn when she hinted at the possibility of buying several yards of exclusive French lace. It wasn't until they'd left the restaurant and were walking toward his office that Thorne understood the implication. French lace—wedding gown.

Suddenly something caught his attention.

There. The blonde, half a block ahead of him. *Cindy.* It was Cindy.

"And I was thinking…"

Sheila's voice faded and Thorne quickened his pace.

"Thorne," Sheila said breathlessly. "You're walking so fast I can't keep up with you."

Without thought, he removed her hand from his arm. "Excuse me a minute." He didn't take his eyes off Cindy, fearing he'd lose her in the heavy holiday crowds.

"Thorne?"

He ignored Sheila and took off running, weaving in and around the people filling the sidewalk on Sixth Avenue.

"Cindy!" He yelled her name, but either she didn't hear or she was trying to escape him. Again. He wouldn't let her. He'd found her now. Relief flowed through him and he savored the sweet taste of it. He'd dreamed this would happen. Somehow, some way, he'd miraculously stumble upon her. Every time he stepped outside, he found himself studying faces, looking. Searching for her in a silent quest that dominated his every waking thought. And now she was only a few feet away, her brisk pace no match for his easy sprint. Her shoulder-length blond hair swayed back and forth, and her navy wool coat was wrapped securely around her.

Thorne raced around two couples, cutting abruptly in front of them. He didn't know what he'd do first—kiss her or shake her. Kiss her, he decided.

"Cindy." He finally caught up with her and put his hand on her shoulder.

"I beg your pardon." The woman, maybe fifty, slapped his hand away. She didn't even resemble Cindy. She was older, plain, and embarrassed by his attention.

Thorne blinked back the disbelief. "I thought you were someone else."

"Obviously. Mind your manners, young man, or I'll report you to the police."

"I apologize." He couldn't move. His feet felt rooted to the sidewalk and his arms hung lifelessly at his sides. Cindy was driving him mad; he was slowly but surely losing his sanity.

"Decent women aren't safe in this city anymore," the woman grumbled and quickly stepped away.

"Thorne! Thorne!" Sheila joined him, her hands gripping his arm. "Who was she?"

"No one." He couldn't stop looking at the blonde as she made her way down the street. He would've sworn it was Cindy. He would've wagered a year's salary that the woman who couldn't escape him fast enough had been Cindy. His Cindy. His love.

"Thorne," Sheila droned, patting his hand. "You've been working too hard. I'm worried about you."

"I'm fine," he said absently.

The pinched look returned to Sheila's face, but she didn't argue. "March gives you plenty of time to arrange a vacation. We'll enjoy Paris. I'll take you shopping with me and let you pick out my trousseau."

"I'm not going to Paris," he snapped.

Sheila continued to pat his hand. "I do wish you'd consider it. You haven't been yourself, Thorne. Not at all."

He couldn't agree more.

Two hours later Thorne sat at his desk reading financial statements the accounting department had sent up for him to approve.

"Mr. Williams is here," Ms. Hillard informed him.

Thorne closed the folder. "Send him in."

"Right away," Ms. Hillard returned crisply.

Thorne stood to greet the balding man who wore a suit that looked as if it hadn't been dry-cleaned since it came off the rack at Sears ten years before. His potbelly gave credence to his reputation as the best private detective in the business; from the looks of it, he ate well enough.

"Mr. Williams," Thorne said, extending his hand to the other man.

"Call me Mike."

They exchanged brisk handshakes. The man's grip was solid. Thorne approved.

"What can I do for you?" Mike asked as he sat down.

"I want you to find someone for me," Thorne said, without preamble.

Mike nodded. "It's what I do. What's the name?"

Thorne reclaimed his chair and his hands clutched the armrest as he leaned back, giving an impression of indifference. This wasn't going to be easy. "Cindy."

"Last name?" The detective reached for his pencil and pad.

"I don't know." He paused. "I'm not actually sure Cindy's her first name. It could've been made up." Thorne was braced to accept anything where Cindy was concerned. Everything and anything.

"Where did you meet her?"

"At a party. The one put on by this company. She doesn't work here. I've already checked."

Williams nodded.

"She did leave this behind." Thorne leaned forward to hand the detective the comb. It was missing one pearl, he saw to his dismay. "I've had it appraised and the comb isn't uncommon. She has two, and she claims they belonged to her mother. There are no markings that would distinguish this one from ten thousand other identical combs."

Again Williams nodded, but he examined the comb carefully. "Can I take this?" he asked and stuck it in his pocket.

Thorne agreed with a swift nod of his head. "I'll want it back."

"Of course."

They spoke for an additional fifteen minutes and Thorne recalled with as much clarity as possible each of the two meetings he'd had with Cindy.

Williams stopped him only once. "A limo, you said."

"Yes." Thorne slid forward in his chair. He'd forgotten that. Cindy had gotten into a limousine that first night when she'd escaped from him. She'd handed him his coat, run across the street and been met by a long black limousine.

"You wouldn't happen to remember the license plate, would you?"

"No." Thorne shook his head disgustedly. "I'm afraid I can't."

"Don't worry about it. I have enough." Williams scanned the details he'd listed and flipped the pad shut. He got to his feet.

Thorne stood, too. "Can you find her?" he asked.

"I'll give it my best shot."

"Good." Thorne hoped the man couldn't see how desperate he'd become.

* * *

A cold northern wind chilled Cindy's arms as she waited on the sidewalk outside the Oakes-Jenning building. It was well past midnight. She was exhausted—physically and mentally. She hadn't been sleeping well and the paper she should be writing during the holiday break just wouldn't come, although she'd done all the research. It was because of Thorne. No matter what she did, she couldn't stop thinking about him.

Uncle Sal pulled to a stop at the curb. Cindy stepped away from the building and climbed into the front seat beside him.

"Hi," she said, forcing a smile. Her family was worried about her and Cindy did her best to ease their fears.

"A private detective was poking around the house today," her uncle announced, starting into the traffic.

Cindy felt her heart go cold. "What did he want?"

"He was asking about you."

Seven

"Asking about me... What did you tell him?"

"Not a thing."

"But..."

"He wanted to look at my appointment schedule for December 12, but I wouldn't let him."

The chilly sensation that had settled over Cindy dropped below freezing. Her uncle's refusal would only create suspicion. The detective would be back, and there'd be more questions Sal would refuse to answer. The detective wouldn't accept that, and he'd return again and again until he had the information he wanted. This stranger would make trouble for her family. In a hundred years, she never would've guessed that Thorne would go to such lengths to locate her. She had to find a way to stop him...a way to make him understand and leave things as they were.

Cindy went to bed still thinking about the whole mess and got up even more tired and troubled than she'd been before. She'd repeatedly examined her own role in this situation. Playing the part of Cinderella for one night had seemed so innocent, so adventurous, so exciting. She'd slipped into the fantasy with ease, but the night had ended with the stroke of midnight and she could never go back to being a fairy-tale character again. She'd let go of the illusion and yes, it had been painful, but she'd had no choice. The consequences of that one foolhardy night would follow her for the rest of her life.

She'd never dreamed it would be possible to feel as strongly about a man in so short a time as she did about Thorne. But her emotion wasn't based on any of the usual prerequisites for love. It couldn't be. They'd only seen each other twice.

Thorne might believe he felt as strongly about her, Cindy realized, but that wasn't real either. She was a challenge—the mystery woman who'd briefly touched his life. Once he learned the truth and recognized that she'd made a fool of him, it would be over. Given no alternative, Cindy knew she'd have to tell Thorne who she really was.

"He could get me fired," she said aloud several soul-searching hours later. Her hands clutched her purse protectively as she waited outside the Oakes-Jenning Financial Services building. Employees streamed out in a steady flow. Cindy stood against the side of the building, just far enough back to examine their faces as they made their way out. They all looked so serious. Cindy didn't know much about the business world, but it certainly seemed to employ dour people, Thorne included.

For most of the afternoon, Cindy had weighed the possible consequences of telling Thorne the truth. Losing her job was only one of several unpleasant options that had entered her mind. And ultimately he could hate her, which would be so much worse than anything else he could do.

She wanted to scream at him for being so obstinate, so willful, so determined to be part of her life. He had to know she didn't want to be found, and yet he'd ignored her wishes and driven her to this. He'd forced her into doing the one thing she dreaded most—telling him the truth.

Her tenacity hardened as she watched Thorne step out of the building, his face as sober as everyone else's. He carried a briefcase in one hand and walked briskly past her. Unseeing. Uncaring. As oblivious to her then as he was every morning when he walked into his clean office.

"Thorne." She didn't shout; her voice was little more than a whisper.

He stopped abruptly, almost in midstride, and turned around. "Cindy?" His gaze scanned the sea of faces that swam before him. "Cindy?" he repeated, louder this time, unsure if this was real. He'd been half out of his mind for days on end. Nothing shocked him anymore. He'd known her voice instantly, but that too could be part of his deep yearning to find her. She was here and she'd called out to him, and he wouldn't let her escape him again.

"Here." She took a step closer, her hands clenched in fists at her sides. "Call off the detective. I'll tell you—" She wasn't allowed to finish.

Thorne dropped the briefcase onto the sidewalk, grabbed her shoulders and hauled her into his arms. His mouth came down on hers with such intensity that he drove the breath from her lungs. His hand dug into her hair as he tangled it with his fingers, as though binding her to him. His mouth on hers left her in no doubt regarding the strength of his emotions.

Cindy's first reaction was stunned surprise. She'd expected him to be furious, to shout at her and demand an explanation. But not this. Never this.

Once the initial shock of his kiss faded, she surrendered to the sheer pleasure of simply being in his arms. She held on to him, throwing her arms around him, relishing the rush of sensations that sprang up within her. She couldn't have pushed him away had her life depended on it. The resolution to end their relationship had melted the minute he'd touched her.

"This had better not be a dream," Thorne said, moving his lips against her temple. "You taste so unbelievably real."

Cindy flattened her palms against his chest in an attempt to break away, but he held on to her. "Thorne, please, people are looking."

"Let them." He kissed her again, with such hunger that she was left breathless and disoriented. She made a weak effort to break loose again.

"Thorne," she pleaded. Every second he continued to hold her weakened her determination to explain everything. He felt so warm and vital…so wonderful. "Please…don't," she begged as he covered her face with kisses. Even as she spoke, pleading with him to stop, she was turning her head one way and then another, allowing him to do as he wished.

"I'm starving for you," he murmured, kissing her again.

She was so weak-willed with Thorne. She could start out with the firmest of resolves but after being with him for ten seconds she had no fortitude left at all.

"Cindy—" his arms tightened "—I've been going crazy without you."

It hadn't been any less traumatic for Cindy. "You hired a detective?"

"He found you?"

"No… I heard you were looking." Her hands lovingly framed his face. "Thorne, please call him off." She didn't want the private detective harassing or intimidating those she loved most. "I'll tell you everything you want to know…only, please, please, don't hate me."

"Hate you?" His look was incredulous. "I'm not capable of feeling any different toward you than the night we met." For the first time he seemed to notice the stares they were generating. "Let's get out of here." He reached for her hand and led her purposefully away.

"Thorne," she cried with a surprised glance over her shoulder. "Your briefcase."

He seemed so utterly astonished that he could have forgotten it, Cindy laughed outright.

Without hesitating, he turned and went back to retrieve it, dragging her with him. "See what you do to me?" His words were distressed.

"Do you know what you do to me?" she responded with equal consternation.

"I must have quite an effect on you, all right. You can't seem to get away from me fast enough. You sneak off like a thief in the night and turn up when I least expect it. I don't sleep well, my appetite's gone and I'm convinced you're playing me for a fool."

"Oh, Thorne, you don't honestly believe that, do you?" She came to an abrupt stop. People had to walk around them, but Cindy didn't care. She couldn't bear it if Thorne believed anything less than what she truly felt for him. "I think I'd rather die than let you assume for even a minute that I didn't care for you."

"You have one heck of a way of showing it."

"But, Thorne, if you'd give me a chance to—"

Undaunted by the traffic, Thorne paraded them halfway into the street, his arm raised. "Taxi!"

"Where are we going?"

A Yellow cab pulled up in front of them. Thorne ignored

her question; he opened the car door and climbed in beside her a second later.

Before Cindy could say another word, Thorne spoke to the driver. When he'd finished he leaned back and stared at her as though he still wasn't completely sure she was really there.

Cindy hadn't thought about *where* she'd talk to Thorne, only that she would. Over and over she'd rehearsed what she wanted to say. But she hadn't counted on him hauling her across Manhattan to some unknown destination. From the looks he was giving her now, he didn't appear any too pleased with her.

Thorne finally relaxed and expelled a long sigh. "Do you realize we've been to bed together and I don't even know your name?"

Cindy felt more than saw the driver's interest perk up. Color exploded into her cheeks as she glared hotly at Thorne. "Would you stop it?" she hissed. He was doing this on purpose, to punish her.

"I don't think I can." He regarded her levelly. "You've got me so twisted up inside, I don't know what's real and what's not anymore. My parents think I need to see a shrink and I'm beginning to agree with them!"

Cindy covered his hand with her own. "I'm certainly nothing like the Cinderella you met that night." Her voice was a raw whisper, filled with pain. "I thought I could pretend to be something I'm not for one glamorous night, but it all backfired. I've hated deceiving you—you deserve better than me."

"Is your name really Cindy?"

She nodded. "That's what started it all. Now I wish I'd been named Hermione or Frieda—anything but Cindy. If

I had, then maybe I wouldn't have believed in that night and decided to do something so stupid."

"No matter who you are and what you've done," Thorne told her solemnly, "I'll never regret the Christmas Ball."

"That's the problem—I can't either. I'll treasure it always. But Thorne, don't you see? I'm *not* Cinderella. I'm only me."

"In case you haven't noticed, I'm not exactly Prince Charming."

"But you are," Cindy argued.

"No. And that's been our problem all along—we each seemed to think the other wanted to continue the fantasy." He put his arm around her and drew her close to his side. "That evening was marvelous, but it was one night in a million. If we're going to develop a relationship, it has to be between the people we are now."

Cindy leaned against him, sighed inwardly and closed her eyes as he rested his chin on her head.

"I want to be with Cindy," he said tenderly, "not the imaginary Cinderella."

"But Cindy will disappoint you."

"If you're looking for Prince Charming in me, then you're in for a sad awakening as well."

"You don't even know who I am!"

"It doesn't matter." Her lovely face commanded all his attention. He sensed that something deep inside her was insecure and frightened. She'd bolted and run away from him twice, her doubts overtaking her. No more. Whatever Williams had dug up about her had brought her back. She was here because Mike had gotten close to her, had begun to uncover her secrets.

Thorne had found his Cindy again and could on go with his life. The restless feeling that had worn away at him was dissipating. He was a man who liked his privacy, but overnight he'd discovered he was lonely and could no longer adjust to the solitude. Not when he'd met the one woman he wanted to share his world with. All he had to do was persuade *her* of that. Only this time, he'd be more cautious. He wouldn't make demands of her. She could tell him whatever was troubling her when she was ready. Every time he started questioning her, it ended in disaster.

Cindy sat upright, her back stiff as she turned her head and glanced out the side window. She knew he was right; they couldn't go back to the night of the Christmas Ball. But she wasn't completely convinced they could form a lasting relationship as Thorne and Cindy.

"You say it doesn't matter," she said thoughtfully, "but when I tell you I'm the girl who—"

"Stop." His hand reached for hers, squeezing her fingers tightly. "Are you married, engaged or currently involved with another man?"

She glared at him for even suggesting such a thing. "No, of course not!"

"Involved in any illegal activity?"

She moved several inches away from him and sat starchly erect, shocked at his questions. "Is *that* what you think?"

"Just answer me."

"No!" She had difficulty saying it. She tucked a strand of hair behind her ear in nervous agitation. "I don't cheat, rarely lie and am thoroughly law-abiding—I don't even jaywalk, and in New York that's something!"

Thorne's warm smile chased the chill from her bones. "Then, who and what you are is of no importance. You're the one who has all the objections. What I feel is apparently of little consequence to you."

"That's not true. I'm only trying to save you from embarrassment."

"Embarrassment?"

"My family name isn't linked with three generations of banking."

"I wouldn't care if it was linked with generations of garbage collecting."

"You say that now," she snapped.

"I mean that. I'm falling in love with a girl named Cindy, not a fairy-tale figure who magically appeared in my life. She's bright and funny and loving."

Falling in love with her! Cindy's heart felt like it was going to burst with happiness. Then she realized—once again—the impossibility of an enduring relationship between them. Dejectedly she lowered her gaze. "Please don't say that."

"What? That I'm falling in love with you?"

"Yes."

"It's true."

"But you hardly know me," she said. Yet that hadn't deterred *her* from falling head over heels for him.

The taxi came to a stop in the heavy traffic, and the driver told them, "Central Park is on your left."

"Central Park?" Cindy echoed, pleased at his choice of locations to do their talking. She hadn't paid attention to where they were going.

"I thought we should return here and start over again."

She got out as Thorne paid the driver. A moment later, he joined Cindy on the sidewalk. He placed her hand in the crook of his arm and smiled seductively down on her.

Her returning smile was feeble at best.

"Hello, there," he said softly. "I'm Thorne, which is short

for Thorndike, which was my father's name and his father's before him."

"I'm a first-generation Cindy."

"Well, Cindy, now that we've been properly introduced, will you have dinner with me tonight?"

"I...can't." She hated to refuse, but she couldn't spend time with him when she was paid to clean his office. As it was, she was due there within half an hour.

His face tightened briefly. "Can't or won't?"

"Can't."

"Tomorrow, then."

"But it's New Year's Eve." Surely he had other places to go and more important people to spend the evening with. Arguments clustered in her mind and were dispelled with one enticing look from Thorne.

"New Year's Eve or not, I'll pick you up and we'll paint the town." He felt Cindy tense and guessed why. Quickly he amended his suggestion. "I'll meet you somewhere. Any-place you say."

"In front of Oakes-Jenning." Although it was a holiday, she'd be working; she couldn't afford to turn down time and a half. "I...won't be available until after eleven-thirty."

"Fine, I'll be there."

"You're late," Vanessa said unnecessarily when Cindy ran breathlessly into the basement supply room.

"I know."

"Where were you?"

"Central Park." She made busy work filling her cart with the needed supplies. She'd left after promising Thorne she'd meet him the following night. His gaze had pleaded with her to give him something to hold on to—a phone number, a name, anything. But Cindy had given him something of far greater value—her word. Letting her go had been a measure of his trust. She could see that he wasn't pleased, but he hadn't drilled her with questions or made any other demands.

What he'd said was true. Neither of them could continue playing the role of someone they weren't. Cinderella was now Cindy and Prince Charming had gone back to being Thorne. They'd been a bit awkward with each other at first, but gradually that unease had evaporated.

Cindy was beginning to believe that although there were many obstacles blocking their path, together they might be able to overcome them. There hadn't been time to say the things she needed to say because she'd had to rush to work. She hadn't explained that to Thorne and saw jealousy appear on his face.

"What are you thinking?" Vanessa asked, studying her.

"Nothing."

"Nothing?" her friend complained. "Give me a break! Are we back to that?"

Cindy relented. "I'm seeing Thorne tomorrow night."

"You are?" Even Vanessa sounded shocked. "But it's New Year's Eve...oh, heavens, did you forget we have to work?"

"No... I told him I wouldn't be ready until after eleven-thirty."

"And he didn't ask for any explanation?"

"Not really." The questions had been there, in his eyes, but he hadn't voiced a single one. Cindy felt her friend regarding her thoughtfully and busied herself with the cart, making sure she had everything she needed before heading for the upper floor.

She only hoped she was doing the right thing. Thorne kept insisting that who she was didn't matter to him. She was going to test that and in the process wager her heart and her future happiness.

"Thorne, I've been trying to reach you."

Thorne frowned at the telephone receiver. He could tell by the slight edge to his mother's voice that she was going to bring up an unpleasant subject—Sheila. The other woman was quickly becoming a thorn in his side. No pun intended.

"Yes, Mother," he returned obediently, throwing his magazine on the coffee table. This conversation would require his full attention.

"Your father and I are having a New Year's Eve party tomorrow night and we'd like you to attend."

He'd never enjoyed parties, which was one reason his mother had been so keen on Sheila, who loved to socialize. Sheila would be good for his career, his father had once told him. At the time, Thorne had considered that an important factor in choosing a wife. Not anymore.

"I apologize, Mother, but I'll have to decline, I've already made plans."

"But Sheila said—"

"I won't be with Sheila," he responded shortly.

"Oh, dear, is it that Cheryl woman again? I'd thought that was over."

"Cindy," he corrected, swallowing a laugh. He knew his mother—she remembered Cindy's name as well as she did her own.

"I see," his mother said, her voice sharpening with disapproval. "Then you haven't said anything to Sheila."

"As I recall, you advised me against it," he reminded her.

"But, Thorne, the dear girl is beside herself with worry.

And what's this about you chasing a strange woman down some sidewalk? Really, Thorne, what's gotten into you?"

"I'm in love."

The horrified silence that followed his announcement nearly made him laugh into the phone. His parents had been waiting years for him to announce that he'd chosen a wife, and now that he was in love, they acted as if he'd committed a terrible crime. However, Thorne was positive that once his parents met Cindy, they'd understand, and love her, too.

"Are you claiming to love a woman you hardly know?"

"That's right, Mother."

"What about her family?"

"What about them?"

"Thorne!"

His mother sounded aghast, which only increased Thorne's amusement. "Would you feel better if you could meet her?"

"I'm not sure… I suppose it would help."

"Dinner, then, the first part of next week. I'll clear it with Cindy and get back to you."

"Fine." But she didn't seem enthusiastic. "In the meantime, would you talk to Sheila? She hasn't heard from you all week."

"What do you suggest I say to her?"

"Tell her…tell her you need a few days to think things over. That should appease her for now. Once I've had a chance to…meet your Cheryl, I'll have a better sense of the situation."

"Yes, Mother," he said obediently and replaced the receiver. Family had always been important to Thorne, but he wouldn't allow his mother or anyone else to rule his life.

Leaning back, Thorne folded his arms behind his head. He felt good, wonderful. He'd never looked forward to anything more than tomorrow night. New Year's Eve with Cindy. And with it, the promise of spending every year together for the rest of his life.

The following day, Thorne worked until noon. He did some errands, ate a light dinner around six, showered and dressed casually. The television killed several hours, but he found himself glancing at his watch every few minutes. He'd leave around eleven, he figured. That would give him plenty of time to get to Oakes-Jenning, and from there he'd take Cindy to Times Square. It was something he'd always wanted to do, but had never had the chance. They could lose themselves in the crowd and he'd have every excuse to keep her close.

The doorbell chimed around eight, and Thorne hurried to answer, convinced it was Cindy. Somehow, some way, she'd come to him early. His excitement died when he saw Sheila standing in the hallway.

"Sheila."

"Hello, Thorne." She peered up at him through seductively thick lashes. "May I come in?"

He stepped aside. "Sure."

"You're looking very casual." She entered the apartment, removed her coat and sat on the sofa. Wearing a slinky, low-cut black dress, she looked anything *but* casual.

"This is a surprise." He stood awkwardly in the center of the room, hands buried in his pockets.

"I haven't heard from you since our luncheon date and thought I'd stop in unannounced. I hope you don't mind?"

Thorne would have preferred her to choose another day, but since she'd come, he might as well use the opportunity to tell her about Cindy. "I'm glad you did." At the happiness that flashed in her eyes, Thorne regretted his poor choice of words.

She folded her hands in her lap and regarded him with such adoration that Thorne felt his stomach knot.

"Sometimes I do such a terrible job of explaining my feelings," she said softly, lowering her gaze to her hands. "I want you to know how much you mean to me."

The knot in Thorne's stomach worked its way up to his chest. "I treasure your friendship, as well."

She arched her brows. "I thought we were more than simply friends. Much more."

Thorne sat on the ottoman and rolled it toward Sheila so that he sat directly in front of her. "This isn't easy."

"Don't." She shook her head. "I already know what you're going to say.... You've met someone else."

"I don't want to hurt you." They'd been seeing each other steadily for months, and although he'd come to realize how mismatched they were, Sheila hadn't seen it yet, and he honestly wished to spare her any pain.

"But, darling, you don't need to. I understand about these things."

"You do?" Thorne hadn't the foggiest notion what there was for her to understand.

"A woman has to accept this sort of thing from her husband. I know Daddy's had his women on the side. Mother's aware of it, too."

Thorne surged to his feet. "You're saying you expect me to have an *affair?*"

"Just to get her out of your system. I want you to know I understand."

Years of discipline tempered Thorne's response. He was so furious that it took all his restraint to continue being civil after Sheila's announcement. He marched to the plate-glass window and looked out, afraid to speak for fear of what he'd say. Instead he analyzed his anger.

"Thorne, you look upset."

"I am." He realized he was so outraged because Sheila's seeming generosity had insulted Cindy by suggesting she belonged on some back street.

"But why?"

"Cindy isn't that kind of woman," he said, and turned around. "And neither are you."

A gush of feminine tears followed. Embarrassed, Thorne retrieved a box of tissues and held Sheila gently in his arms until she'd finished weeping.

Dabbing her eyes, Sheila said she needed something to drink and nodded approvingly when Thorne brought out a bottle of expensive French wine he knew she liked. He had plenty of time to soothe her wounded ego. Cindy wouldn't be available until almost midnight.

Once Sheila had dried her eyes, she was good company, chatting about the fun times they'd shared over the months they'd been seeing each other and getting slightly tipsy in the process.

Slowly, Thorne felt his anger evaporate. Sheila did most of the talking, and when she suggested they have a cocktail at the Carlyle, Thorne agreed. It was still two hours before he could meet Cindy.

The Carlyle was crowded, as were two of Sheila's other favorite hangouts where they stopped for drinks.

"Let's drop in at your parents'," she said casually, swirling the ice in her empty glass.

"I can't. I'm meeting Cindy." He raised his arm to look at his watch and the air left his lungs in one disbelieving gasp. "I'm late."

"But, Thorne…"

It was already eleven forty-five and he was at least another fifteen minutes from Oakes-Jenning. And his cell phone was useless—he had no number for her, no surname, nothing. The regret seared through him.

"You can't just leave me here!" Sheila cried, trotting after him.

He handed their ticket to the coatcheck girl and paced restlessly until she returned. When she did, Thorne thrust her a generous tip.

"Thorne." Sheila gave him a forlorn look, her eyes damp with tears. "Don't leave me."

Eight

All of New York seemed alive with activity to Cindy. New Year's Eve, and it could've been noon for all the people milling in the streets. Times Square would be a madhouse, filled with anxious spectators waiting for the magical hour when the New Year's Eve ball would descend, marking the beginning of another year.

Cindy felt wonderful. Free. Thorne might have claimed not to be Prince Charming, but he'd demonstrated some truly princely qualities. Judging by the way he'd searched for her, he seemed to feel genuine affection. Surely he wouldn't have hired a private detective to find her if he didn't care. Nor would he have been willing to overlook the secrecy she wore like a heavy shroud. He didn't like it, but he accepted it. He claimed it didn't matter who or what she was, and to prove his point he'd refused to listen when she'd tried to explain. He didn't insist on answers even though the questions were clearly written in his eyes, nor did he make unreasonable demands. She'd told him she couldn't meet him until eleven-thirty, and without voicing any qualms he'd agreed to that.

A police car, with its siren screaming, raced down the street and Cindy watched its progress. A glance at her watch told her Thorne was fifteen minutes late. After months of cleaning his office, Cindy could confidently say that he was rarely late for anything. He was too much of a businessman to be unaware of the clock.

Remembering the police car, Cindy stepped to the curb and looked up and down the street. Unexpectedly, she felt alarmed. Perhaps something had happened to Thorne. Perhaps he was lying somewhere hurt and bleeding—or maybe he'd suffered a relapse and was ill again.

Cindy couldn't bear to think of him in pain. She'd rather endure it herself than have him suffer. It took her another five minutes to reason things out. Thorne was perfectly capable of looking after himself, and she was worrying needlessly. He'd gotten tied up in traffic and would arrive any minute. If he was hurt, she told herself, she'd know. Somehow, her heart would know. Thorne would come to her, regardless of the circumstances. All she had to do was be patient and wait. He couldn't look at her the way he did and ask her to spend this special night with him and then leave her standing in the cold. She'd stake her life on it.

Thirty minutes later, Cindy's confidence was dying a slow, painful death. She was cold. Her face felt frozen and her toes were numb. She'd been silly enough to wear open-toed pumps and was paying the price of her own folly. She hunched her shoulders against the wind that whipped her hair back and forth across her face. Resentfully she thought of how hard she'd worked, rushing from one office to another to finish early, and how quickly she'd showered and changed clothes—all so she could spend extra time on her hair and makeup. She'd wanted this night to be perfect for Thorne. But after forty-five minutes of standing in the wind, her hair was a lost cause and her makeup couldn't have fared any better.

Another fifteen minutes, Cindy decided. That was all she'd give him.

And then fifteen intolerable, interminable minutes passed.

Five more, she vowed, and that was it. She'd walk away. Thorne would have a logical explanation, she was sure of it, but she couldn't stand in the cold all night.

Dejected and discouraged, Cindy waited out the allotted five minutes and decided there was nothing she could do but leave. Drawing her coat more tightly around her, she walked to the corner and paused. Not yet. She couldn't leave yet. What if Thorne arrived and they just missed each other? She couldn't bear for him to find her gone. He'd be frantic. Even if she'd had a cell phone, she wouldn't have known how to reach him.

She pulled her hand from her pocket and studied her watch one last time. Maybe she should wait another minute or two—it wouldn't hurt. Her toes were beyond feeling and a few more minutes wouldn't matter.

A niggling voice in the back of her mind tried to convince her that Thorne had left her waiting in the cold as punishment for disrupting his staid, regimented life.

Forcefully, Cindy shook her head. She refused to believe it. The voice returned a moment later, suggesting that he was with another woman. Sheila. This possibility seemed far more feasible. Sheila's photograph remained on prominent display in his office. A hundred doubts crowded each other in her troubled thoughts. Sheila. He was with Sheila!

Determined now to leave, Cindy buried her hands deeper in the pockets of her wool coat. It was too late to ring in the New Year with Thorne. Too late to believe that a relationship between them could work. Too late to demand her heart back!

Hunched against the piercing wind, her collar as close to her face as she could arrange it, Cindy turned and walked away.

The sound of tires screeching to a halt and a car door slamming startled her.

"Cindy!"

She turned to find Thorne racing toward her.

Breathless, he caught her in his arms and held her to him. He pushed the hair from her face as though he needed to read her expression and see for himself that she was safe and secure. "Oh, Cindy, I'm sorry, so sorry."

Every wild suspicion died the minute Thorne reached for her. He was so warm and he held her as though he planned to do it for a good long while. "You came," she murmured, laughing with pure relief. "You came." She slid her arms around his middle and tucked her head beneath his chin. She noticed there was something different about his usually distinctive masculine scent, as if it were mingled with some other fragrance.... But she was too deliriously happy at being in his arms to puzzle it out right now.

"You must be half-frozen," Thorne moaned, nuzzling her hair.

"Three-quarters," she joked. "But it was worth every second just to be with you now."

He kissed her then, his mouth cherishing hers. Cindy absorbed his warmth, focusing on him like a flower turning toward the sun, seeking its nourishing rays as the source of all life.

Thorne lifted his head, cradled her chilled face in both hands and released a sigh that came from deep within him. He'd been overwrought, checking his watch every ten seconds, half crazed with fear that she'd walk out of his life and he'd never find her again. The traffic had been a nightmare, the streets crammed with cars and people. He hadn't dreamed she'd still be there waiting, although he prayed she was. An *hour* she'd stood and waited in the freezing cold. He cursed Sheila and then himself.

"Let's get out of here," he said breathlessly. Slipping his arm around her waist, he led her back to the taxi and helped her inside. He paused long enough to ask the driver to take them to a nearby restaurant.

Inside the cab, Cindy removed her shoes and started to rub feeling back into her numb toes.

"Let me do that," Thorne insisted, holding her nylon-covered feet between his large hands and rubbing vigorously.

Cindy sighed, relaxed and leaned against the back of the seat.

"Better?"

She nodded, content just to be with Thorne. "Where are we going?"

"Someplace where I can get some Irish coffee into you."

"I'm Italian," she said with a smile.

"Italian?" He eyed her curiously. "But you're blond."

"There are plenty of us, trust me."

They arrived at the restaurant, but it wasn't one that Cindy recognized. Thorne helped her climb out of the taxi, then paid the driver and escorted her inside the lounge. They were given a table immediately, although the place was crowded. Cindy realized the large bill Thorne passed the maître d' had something to do with the waiting table.

Once they were seated, Thorne expelled his breath in a deep sigh. "I feel like I've been running a marathon," he said.

"What happened?"

The waitress arrived and Thorne ordered their drinks, glad of the interruption. He was going to lie to Cindy. It was only a lie of omission, but it bothered him. He expected her to be honest, and it felt wrong to be less so with her. "I miscalculated the time and got caught in traffic. I didn't dare hope you'd still be there. I don't know what I would've done if you'd left."

"I'd already decided to contact you in the morning."

He closed his eyes. "Thank God for that."

"You wanted to give us the unprincely Thorne and the unadorned Cinderella—a chance, and I agreed, didn't I?"

"Yes."

He looked at her, his eyes tender and loving. "We didn't ring in the New Year together." His words revealed his regret.

"I know." She dropped her gaze because looking at him was too intense, like staring into the sun for too long. She was becoming blind to the facts that surrounded their unusual relationship, ignoring the overwhelming potential for emotional pain.

The waitress brought their drinks and Cindy sipped the liquor-laced coffee. It was hot, sweet and potent, instantly spreading its warmth. The tingling sensation left her toes and fingers almost immediately.

"Next year we'll make it to Times Square?" Thorne suggested, his voice lifting slightly at the end of the statement.

"Next year," she agreed, desperately wanting to believe they'd be together twelve months from now. It was safer not to look ahead with Thorne, to live for the moment, but she couldn't help herself.

"Are you hungry?" he asked next.

"Famished." She hadn't eaten anything since early afternoon.

"Good. Do you want to order dinner now or would you rather have another drink?"

"Dinner," Cindy told him. "But if you want another drink, don't let me stop you."

He picked up the menu and shook his head. "I had wine and a couple of cocktails before I caught up with you."

Cindy raised her menu and mulled over the information he'd let slip. He'd lost track of the time, he'd claimed. That would be easy enough to do if he'd been having a good time in the company of a beautiful woman. Her earlier suspicions resurrected themselves. Thorne had been with Sheila. He'd brought in the New Year with the other woman when he'd asked to share the moment with her. He hadn't been with Cindy, but with Sheila, the woman whose picture still sat on his desk. She suddenly knew with certainty that the faint scent she'd noted on Thorne's jacket earlier was perfume. *Sheila's* perfume.

All the special excitement she experienced every time she was with Thorne rushed out of her like air from a punctured balloon. She felt wounded. The commotion and noise in the restaurant seemed to fade into nothingness.

"Have you decided?" Thorne asked.

She stared at him blankly, not understanding what he meant until she realized he was inquiring about her dinner selection. "No. What do you suggest?" It astonished her that she could speak coherently. There would be no next year for them—probably not even a next week. She'd be surprised if they made it through dinner.

You're overreacting, she told herself. *He had a drink with another woman. Big deal.* Thorne wasn't her exclusive property. But he'd obviously held Sheila, held her in his arms…even kissed her. He must have, or the cloying scent of expensive perfume wouldn't be on his clothes.

Deliberately she set the menu aside and glared at him.

"Cindy?"

"Yes?" She made a conscious effort to look attentive.

"What's wrong?"

"I'm fine," she lied. How could she be anything close to fine when all her hopes and expectations were crumbling at her feet? When her dreams had become ashes? Again she told herself she was making too much of it. She had little to go on but conjecture, but in her heart she *knew.* Thorne had left her standing in the miserable cold, alone, while he toasted the New Year with Sheila.

"If you'll excuse me a minute, I think I'd like to freshen up." Somehow she managed to keep her voice level, revealing none of the emotion she felt.

"Of course." He stood when she did, but as she moved to turn away, his hand reached for her, stopping her. "There are tears in your eyes."

She hadn't been aware that she was crying. She rubbed her face. "What would I have to cry about?" The words sounded as if she were riding on a roller coaster, heaving in pitch, squeezing through the tightness that gripped her throat.

"You tell me."

Cindy reached for her coat and purse, the tears flowing in earnest now. That one drink on an empty stomach had gone to her head and she swayed slightly. "I suddenly figured everything out. I lost the feeling in my toes waiting for you."

Thorne blinked. She wasn't making any sense. "What do your toes have to do with the fact that you're crying?"

She jabbed a finger in his direction. "You...were... with... Sheila, weren't you?"

He gently pushed her down and took his chair again. He wouldn't back down from the fierce anger in her gaze. Thorne realized his mistake—he should've leveled with her earlier. He would have if he hadn't feared exactly this reaction. "Yes, I was with Sheila."

She leaned across the small table, her eyes spitting fire. "For more than an hour I waited in the cold and wind. You let me stand there while you...entertained another woman. You're right, Thorne, you're no Prince Charming."

"At the moment there isn't the faintest resemblance between you and Cinderella, either."

She ignored that. "If I had any magic left in me, I'd turn you into a frog."

"Then I'd make you kiss me." He loved her. They were actually arguing, laying their feelings on the table, being honest—even if they were talking the language of fairy tales.

"I don't think it would do any good," Cindy said hotly. "Me kissing you, I mean. You'd still be a frog."

"Possibly," he told her with a grin, "but I doubt it."

Cindy bit her lip. Thorne seemed to think this witty exchange was fun while she was devastated. He was so casual about it, and that hurt.

Thorne immediately sensed the change in Cindy. "I didn't want to be with Sheila," he said, his eyes dark and serious. "I begrudged every minute I wasn't with you."

Cindy didn't know what to believe anymore.

"Then why..."

"I was trapped," he said, and his eyes pleaded for understanding. "I would've given anything to welcome the New Year with you. God willing, I will next year."

Hours later, when she crawled into bed, she wasn't any more confident than she'd been in the restaurant. They'd both ordered lobster and talked for hours, their earlier dispute shelved because their time together was too precious to waste. Cindy was astonished by the way they could talk. They liked the same things, shared the same interests, exchanged ideas and lingered over coffee so long that the waitress grew restless. Only then had Cindy and Thorne noticed that they were the only couple left in the restaurant.

"When can I see you again?" he'd asked.

"Soon," she'd promised, buttoning her coat. "I'll contact you."

He hadn't liked that, Cindy could tell. Before they parted, he'd made her promise that she'd get in touch with him. She would.

Now, as early-morning shadows flitted across the walls, Cindy lay in her bed undecided. Because she'd given Thorne her word, she would meet him, but this had to be the end of it. Oh, heavens, how often had she said that? Too often. And each time, walking away from him had become more difficult. Despite their feelings, despite their similarities of preferences and opinions, their worlds were simply too different.

He was so wonderfully good for her and so disastrously bad for her. She didn't know what she should do anymore. Desire was at war with common sense.

Thorne stood on the dock as large sea gulls circled overhead. The Staten Island ferry, filled with crowds of tourists who'd wanted a closer view of the Statue of Liberty, was slowly advancing toward the pier.

Cindy had said she'd meet him here. She hadn't shown up yet, but it was still too early to be worried. It had been a week since he'd seen her. His fault, not hers. He'd been out of town on business and had returned home to find a note taped to his apartment door. She'd set the time and place for this meeting. How she'd known he'd be free this afternoon was beyond him. But where she got her information no longer concerned him. Seeing her, being with her—that was what mattered. Nothing else did.

He had to find a way to assure her that she was the most important person in his life. The incident with Sheila had been left unsettled between them. Thorne could tell from Cindy's taut features that she wanted to believe that whatever he'd shared with Sheila was over. But he knew she had her doubts, and he couldn't blame her.

Briefly he thought about the large diamond he kept in the safe at his office. He wanted it on her finger, wanted her promise to be his wife, but he couldn't ask her yet. The timing had to be right. When she completely trusted him, when she opened up to him and told him everything about her life, then he could offer her his.

For now, all he could do was love her and dispel her doubts, one at a time. Today he'd come up with a way of doing that.

"Hi." Cindy joined him on the dock. Her hands were in her pockets as she stood there, looking out at the water.

Slow, grateful relief poured over Thorne. She'd come to him. He could relax and smile again.

"Hi, yourself," he responded with a smile, resisting the urge to take her in his arms.

"How was Kansas City?"

He smiled, because she'd surprised him again. She'd

known where he'd been and for how long. "Dull. I wanted to get back to you. Did you miss me?"

Cindy nodded, although she'd rather not admit it. The week they'd spent apart had seemed like a lifetime. For seven days she'd told herself she'd better get used to living without him as the focal point of her existence. "School started again, so I've been busy."

"But you still thought about me?"

Every minute of every day. "Yes," she answered.

The ferry docked and they stood and watched silently as the passengers disembarked.

"I haven't been to the Statue of Liberty in years," he said. "Have you?" It was obvious that something was troubling her. Cindy wasn't this quiet this long, unless she felt anxious or upset.

"No." The wind swirled her hair around her face and she lifted a strand from her cheek.

Thorne studied her. She looked so troubled, so uncertain that he gently pulled her into his embrace, holding her close.

She sighed and leaned against him, relishing his touch after seven long days without him. She wouldn't be the same after Thorne. She'd go on with her life, but she'd never be the same.

"Are you ready to talk?" he asked, raising her chin so she'd meet his eyes.

At one time she had been, but not anymore. They seemed to take one step forward, then quickly retreat two. Just when she was beginning to feel secure about loving him, he'd left her waiting while he was with Sheila. Although he'd repeatedly claimed the other woman meant nothing to him, he continued to keep her picture on his desk. And recently, quite by accident, she'd discovered a receipt from

Tiffany's for a diamond ring. If she'd been insecure about her position in Thorne's life before, now she was paranoid.

"Cindy?" he prompted.

Sadly she shook her head, then brightened. "Shall we walk along the water to get in line for the ferry?"

"No."

"You don't want to go?"

"I have a surprise for you."

"A surprise?" Her heart rocketed to her throat.

He reached for her hand. "We're going someplace special today."

"Where?"

"That's the surprise." He smiled at her and tightened his hand on hers. "My car's down the street."

"Your car?"

"We can't get to...this place by subway."

Despite her reservations, Cindy laughed. "I don't really like surprises."

"This one you will." His fingers tightened around hers. "I promise." After today, Cindy would be sure of her position in his life.

"Is this...someplace I want to go?"

"Now, that may be in question, but you've already agreed."

"I did? When?"

Thorne kissed the tip of her nose. "The night we met."

Cindy shuffled through her memories and came up blank. "I don't recall agreeing to anything."

Thorne pretended shock, then shook his head in mock despair. "How quickly they forget."

"Thorne!" He led her up the street.

"This isn't anyplace fancy, is it?" She wore jeans, a pink turtleneck sweater and loafers with hot pink socks.

"You're perfect no matter what you wear."

"I suppose this is some fancy restaurant where everyone else will be dressed up."

"No restaurant."

"But we are eating?" She hoped they were. As usual, she was starving.

She walked trustfully beside him, despite her reservations about his "surprise." Why, oh, why did it always happen like this? She'd be so uneasy, so certain nothing would ever work between them, and after ten minutes with Thorne, she'd gladly hand over her soul. The thought of being separated from him was unthinkable. She was crazy in love with this man.

"Are you worried about your stomach again?"

"Don't worry, it's something lobster will cure," she joked and was rewarded with a smile.

Cindy would've bet Thorne drove a Mercedes in a subdued shade of gray or steely blue. She was wrong—his car was a Corvette, bright red and so uncharacteristic of him that she stood with her hands on her hips and shook her head.

"I bought it on impulse," he said a bit sheepishly, holding open the passenger door.

She climbed inside, and when she had trouble with the seat belt, Thorne leaned over and snapped it in place. He teased her unmercifully about her lack of mechanical ability, then kissed her soundly when she blushed.

Once they were on the Jersey turnpike, Cindy grew all the more curious. "Just how many days will we be traveling?"

"Forty-five minutes," he answered.

"That long, huh? Aren't you going to give me any clues?"

"Nope. Not any more than I already have."

He was in such a good mood that it was impossible to be serious. Soon they were both laughing, and Cindy didn't notice when he exited the freeway. He drove confidently through a neighborhood of luxurious homes.

"This must be quite some place."

"Oh, it is," he said.

When he turned into a long circular driveway that curved around a huge water fountain, Cindy's curiosity was even sharper. She'd never seen a more opulent home. Huge white pillars dominated the entrance. It looked like something out of *Architectural Digest*.

"Wow." She couldn't find any other word to describe it.

The front door opened and a lovely gray-haired woman came out to greet Thorne. The older woman's gaze rested on Cindy, and although she revealed little emotion, Cindy had the impression the woman disapproved of her.

Thorne got out of the car and hurried over to kiss the woman on the cheek.

A rock settled in the pit of Cindy's stomach as Thorne opened her door and offered his hand to help her out.

"Cindy," he said, "I'd like you to meet my mother."

Nine

Cindy's introduction to Thorne's parents was strained at best. She was enraged that he'd bring her to his family home without any warning or preparation. Even worse, he'd informed her that what she was wearing was perfectly fine. He couldn't have been more wrong. Jeans and a turtleneck sweater weren't acceptable if Gwendolyn Prince's frown told Cindy anything. Cindy would've been more comfortable being granted an unexpected audience with the pope.

Seated beside Thorne in the extravagant living room, Cindy held the stem of a crystal wineglass between her fingers. Although Thorne's mother was subtle about it, Cindy could feel the other woman studying her. His father's gray eyes sparkled with undisguised delight. He, at least, seemed to be enjoying this farce.

"Where was it you said you met?" the elder Thorne asked.

"The company Christmas party."

Cindy let Thorne answer for her. Her mouth was dry,

and she wasn't sure her tongue would cooperate if she tried to speak.

"So you're employed by Oakes-Jenning?"

This time the question was shot directly at Cindy.

"Dad," Thorne interrupted smoothly. "I think I'd like a refill." He held out his glass to his father, who stood and poured the wine.

The elder Prince held the bottle out to Cindy, but she refused with a shake of her head. If there was ever a time she needed to keep her wits about her, it was now. The minute she was alone with Thorne, she'd let him know what she thought of his "surprise."

"I don't believe I caught your last name," his mother said smoothly.

"Territo. Cindy Territo." Her voice came out more like a croak.

"That sounds ethnic," Thorne's mother commented.

"It's…" Cindy began.

"Italian," Thorne finished.

"I see." His mother obviously didn't.

Cindy watched as the older woman downed the remainder of her wine. She appeared to be as uneasy as Cindy.

"Thorne tells me you're a student?" His father continued the inquisition.

"Yes, I'm studying computer programming."

This, too, was news to Thorne. He knew Cindy was uncomfortable answering all these questions. He'd asked his parents to make her feel welcome, but he should've known better than to suggest they not intimidate her with rounds of inquiries. His father was too cagey to let the opportunity pass. Thorne reached for Cindy's hand and was astonished to discover that her fingers were cold as ice.

"I'm sure Cindy is equally curious about us," Thorne

said, squeezing her hand reassuringly. "Why don't we ask what she'd like to know about us?"

"I...know everything I need to," she murmured with a feeble smile. The instant the words were out, Cindy wanted to grab them back, realizing she'd said the wrong thing. She'd made it sound as if all she cared about was Thorne's money. Nothing could be less true. She would've fallen in love with Thorne had he sold newspapers on a street corner. Now, in addition to being ill at ease, she was acutely embarrassed.

Dinner didn't help. They sat at a long table with a crystal chandelier she suspected was worth more than her uncle's limousine. Thorne was across from her, making her feel even more alone. His parents were at either end of the long table.

A large goblet of ice stood in front of Cindy, and her mouth was so uncomfortably dry that she picked it up, disappointed to find so little water inside. Thorne's mother gave her a pitying glance and instantly Cindy knew she'd committed some terrible faux pas. Her mortification reached its peak when the maid brought a shrimp cocktail, placing the appetizer inside the glass of ice. She dared not look at Thorne, certain he'd find the entire incident amusing.

"What does your father do?" Gwendolyn asked between bites of succulent shrimp.

Briefly Cindy closed her eyes to gather her composure. She'd already disgraced Thorne with her lack of finesse once and she was afraid she'd do it again. "I'm sorry, but I don't know. He deserted my mother and me shortly after I was born."

"Oh, my dear! How terrible for your mother."

"She's gone as well, isn't she?" Thorne asked. His loving gaze caressed her, his brow furrowed with concern.

"She died when I was five."

"Who raised you?" It was the elder Thorne who questioned her now. From the looks they were giving her, one would've thought she'd been beaten daily and survived on dry bread crumbs tossed under the table.

"My aunt and uncle were kind enough to raise me." Thorne's parents exchanged sympathetic glances. "Believe me," Cindy hurried to add, "there's no need to feel sorry for me. They loved me as they would their own daughter. We're a close-knit family with lots of cousins and other relatives." Her aunt and uncle, however, wouldn't dream of interrogating Thorne the way his parents were questioning her.... Then again, maybe they would. Cindy felt slightly better musing about how her uncle Sal would react to meeting Thorne. The first hint of amusement touched the edges of her mouth. She raised her eyes to meet Thorne's and they shared a brief smile.

Dinner couldn't be over soon enough for Cindy. She ate a sufficient amount to ensure that no one would comment. The prime rib rested like a lead weight in the pit of her stomach. Dessert, a frothy concoction of lime and whipped cream, was a cool respite, and she managed to consume a larger portion of that.

"While the women have their coffee, let me show you my new nine iron." The elder Prince addressed his son.

Thorne turned to Cindy. She nodded, assuring him that she'd be fine alone with his mother. She was confident that Gwendolyn Prince had arranged this time so they could speak frankly, and Cindy was prepared to do exactly that.

The men left the table.

Cindy took a sip of coffee and braced herself. She saw

that Gwendolyn's hand trembled slightly and she was reassured to realize that the older woman was just as nervous.

Neither spoke for a long moment.

"Mrs. Prince—"

"Cindy—"

They both began at the same instant and laughed, flustered and uneasy.

"You first, dear," Gwendolyn said.

Cindy straightened the linen napkin on her lap. "I wanted to apologize for drinking out of the wrong glass—" She paused, drew in a deep, steadying breath, deciding to do away with small talk and get to the point. "I believe I know what you want to say, and I couldn't agree with you more. You're absolutely right about me. It's perfectly obvious that Thorne and I aren't suited."

If the older woman's hand had trembled before, now it positively shook. "Why, Cindy, what makes you suggest such a thing?"

"You mean other than my drinking from the shrimp glass?"

The first indication that Thorne's mother was capable of a smile showed on her well-preserved face. "My dear girl, shall I tell you about the time I drank too much wine and told Thorndike's mother that she was a cantankerous old biddy?"

Cindy raised the napkin to her mouth to disguise her laugh. "You actually said that?"

"And he proposed the next day. He told me he needed a wife who could stand up to his mother. I'd been crazy about him for years, you see, and I didn't think he knew I was alive. We'd started dating off and on—mostly off—and our relationship seemed to be moving sideways. That

Sunday dinner with his family was the turning point in our courtship."

"And you've enjoyed a happy marriage." Cindy made it a statement.

"For over forty years now."

Silence followed.

"I want you to know that very little of what Thorndike and I say will influence our son. He's always been his own man, and he hasn't brought you here for our approval."

Cindy nodded, agreeing that Thorne wouldn't be intimidated by his family's reservations regarding her. "You don't need to say any more. I understand."

"But I'm afraid that you don't," Gwendolyn said hurriedly. "It's just that Thorne and Sheila seemed to be such an item that both Thorndike and I assumed...well, we naturally thought that he and Sheila...oh, dear, I do seem to be making a mess of this."

"It would only seem natural that they'd get married," Cindy said, understanding completely.

"And then out of the blue, Thorne mentioned meeting you." Gwendolyn looked away and reached for her coffee.

Cindy dropped her gaze. The Christmas Ball and her little charade had clearly upset the family's expectations.

"Thorne thinks very highly of you," Gwendolyn added.

"You and your husband must be special people to have raised a son as wonderful as Thorne." Cindy meant that sincerely. "He's touched my life in ways I'll always value."

"I believe you mean that."

"I do, but I realized early on that I'm not the woman for him. He needs a different type." Although she would've given anything to be wrong, she knew she wasn't.

Gwendolyn's cup clanked against the saucer when she set it down. "I don't suppose you've told Thorne that?"

"Not yet."

"He won't give up on you so easily."

Cindy agreed, remembering the detective he'd hired. "He can be as stubborn as an ornery mule."

Gwendolyn laughed outright. "He's quite a bit like his father."

"I'm doing a poor job of expressing myself," Cindy said, not hiding her pain. "I want to reassure you that I won't upset you or your family further by complicating Thorne's life."

"Oh, dear." Gwendolyn looked startled. "Now that I've met you, I was rather hoping you would."

The words were a soothing balm to Cindy. "Thank you."

"Oh, my." Gwendolyn touched her face with her fingertips. "I wonder if I'm making an idiot of myself again. Thorndike swears I should never drink wine."

"He married you because of it," Cindy reminded the older woman, and they exchanged a smile.

"Thorne would never forgive me if I offended you."

"You haven't."

The men joined them a minute later and Thorne's searching gaze sought out Cindy's. She told him with a smile that everything had gone well between her and his mother and she saw him relax visibly. He'd been worried for nothing. She hadn't been raised in a large family without learning how to hold her own.

Thorne gave his parents a vague excuse and they left shortly afterward. Instead of heading toward the freeway, Thorne drove into a church parking lot and turned off the engine.

"My father was impressed with you."

"I can't imagine why," Cindy told him truthfully.

He ignored that. "What did my mother have to say?"

"What I expected."

"Which was?" he probed.

Cindy shook her head. "We came to an understanding."

"Good or bad?"

"Good. I like her, Thorne. She's straightforward and honest."

He rubbed his hand along the back of her neck. "So are you, my love," he said softly and directed her mouth to his, kissing her hungrily.

"So, Cindy Territo, it wasn't such a hard thing to reveal your name, was it?" He brushed his mouth over hers.

"No." Nothing was difficult when she was in his arms. Since the Christmas Ball, she'd allowed his touch to confuse the issue. She'd be so certain of what she had to do, and then he'd kiss her and she'd fall at his feet. It wasn't fair that he had such an overwhelming effect on her. She wasn't weak-willed, nor was her character lacking. She hadn't once suspected that love would do this to a person.

Her aunt was knitting in front of the television set when Cindy let herself into the apartment. Cindy glanced at her, said nothing and moved into the kitchen. Theresa put down the yarn and needles and followed her niece.

"So how was the Statue of Liberty?"

"We didn't go there." Her voice was strained with emotion.

"Oh." Her aunt opened the oven door and basted the turkey roasting inside. "So where'd you go?"

"Thorne took me to meet his family."

Surprised, Theresa let the oven door close with a bang. "His family? You must mean a great deal to him. So how did the introductions go?"

Cindy took a pitcher of orange juice from the refrigerator

and poured herself a glass, but not because she was thirsty. She was merely looking for something, anything, to occupy her hands. "I met his mother and father and…nothing."

"'Nothing'? What do you mean?"

Theresa knew her too well for Cindy to try to fool her. She set the glass of juice on the kitchen table and slumped into a chair, burying her face in her hands.

Theresa patted her shoulder gently. "Love hurts, doesn't it, honey?"

"I've been fooling myself…. It's just not going to work. I made such an idiot of myself—and everyone was so nice. Thorne pretended not to notice, and his mother told me she'd done silly things in her life, too, and his father just looked at me like I was this amusing alien from outer space. I could have died."

"I'm sure that whatever you did wasn't as bad as you think."

"It was worse!" she cried.

"Right now you think it is," Theresa said calmly. "Give it a year or so and you'll look back and laugh at yourself."

Cindy couldn't visualize laughing about anything at the moment. She was hurting too much. She raised her head, sniffling.

"I've decided I'm not going to see him again," Cindy said with iron determination, promising herself as well as informing her aunt. "It isn't going to work, and confusing the issues with love won't change a thing."

"Did you tell Thorne that?"

Miserably, Cindy shook her head. "I didn't want to invite an argument." She refused to spend their last minutes together debating her decision. Thorne had taken her to meet his family to show how easily she'd fit in, and the opposite had proven true. She'd enjoyed his parents.

She couldn't imagine not liking the two people most influential in Thorne's upbringing. They were decent folks, but Cindy had known the minute she'd walked inside their home that the chasm that divided their lifestyles was too wide to ever bridge.

She glanced around the Territo family kitchen at the pine table with its plain wooden chairs that had once belonged to her grandmother. There were no plush Persian carpets or Oriental rugs beneath it, only worn hardwood floors. Their furniture was simple, as were their lives. Comparing the two families would be like trying to…to mix spaghetti sauce and rough red wine with lobster and champagne.

Before they parted, Thorne had asked to meet her again. Distraught and too weak to argue with him, Cindy had agreed. Now she was sorry.

"The man's in love with you," Theresa said.

"But encouraging him will only hurt him more."

Theresa sadly shook her head. "Are you saying you don't love him?"

"Yes!" Cindy shouted, then winced at the searing look her aunt gave her. "I love him," she admitted finally, "but that doesn't make everything right. Some things in life were meant to be. Others won't ever work out."

Her aunt's expression was troubled. "You're old enough to know what you want. I'm not going to stand here and argue with you. Besides, anything I say is unlikely to change your mind. But I want you to know that you're a marvelous girl and a man like Thorndike Prince wouldn't fall in love with you if you weren't."

Cindy shrugged helplessly. For now he might have convinced himself that he loved her, but later, after he knew her better, he'd regret his love. Because of their unusual circumstances, he looked upon her as a challenge.

She'd made her decision, and although it was the most difficult thing she'd ever done, she was determined to stick by it.

"Yes?" Thorne flipped the intercom switch, his eyes still on the report he was studying. Interruptions were part of his day and he'd grown accustomed to doing several things at once.

Ms. Hillard cleared her throat. "Your mother is here."

Thorne groaned inwardly. He might be able to have Ms. Hillard fend off unexpected visits from Sheila, but his mother wouldn't be put off by her excuses. He sighed. "Go ahead and send her in."

"Thorne." His mother sauntered into the office, her expression resolutely cheerful.

He stood and kissed her on the cheek, already guessing that she was concerned about something. "To what do I owe this pleasure?" She unbuttoned her coat and he saw that she wore her diamond necklace. Absently Thorne wondered how Cindy would look in diamonds. No, he decided, with her blond hair, he'd buy her emeralds. He'd give her emeralds—earrings and a necklace—as an engagement present when they set their wedding date. He'd have her pearl comb repaired, too. He was anxious to give her all the things she deserved. She'd given him so much in so little time that it would take a lifetime to repay her.

"I was in town and thought I'd let you take me to lunch."

His mother had obviously taught Sheila that trick. "What about Dad?"

"He's tied up in a meeting."

"Ah." Understanding came.

"Besides, I wanted to talk to you."

Thorne bristled, automatically suspicious of her intentions. His mother wanted to discuss Cindy. He sighed, sensing an argument.

"What's the name of that nice little restaurant you like so well?" his mother asked, rearranging the small items on his desk, irritating him further.

"The Corner Bistro."

"Right. Oh. I made reservations at the Russian Tea Room."

Thorne managed to nod. It didn't matter where or what they ate as long as the air was cleared when they finished.

Half an hour later, Thorne studied his mother as they sat in a plush booth in the Russian Tea Room. Methodically she removed her white gloves one finger at a time. He knew her well enough to realize she was stalling.

"You wanted to say something, Mother?" He had no desire to delay the confrontation. If she disapproved of Cindy, he'd prefer to have it out in the open and dealt with quickly. Not that anything she said would alter his feelings toward the woman he loved. He'd prefer it if his family approved, but he wouldn't let them stand in his way.

"Sheila phoned me this morning and I'm afraid I may have done something you'd rather I hadn't." She sent him an apologetic glance and reached for the menu.

Thorne's fingers tightened around his water glass. "Perhaps you should start at the beginning."

"The beginning… Well, yes, I suppose I should." She set the menu aside. "I think you already know that I've had my reservations about Cindy."

"Listen, Mother, I need to tell you that your feelings about Cindy mean very little to me. I love her and, God willing, I plan to marry her and—"

"Please, allow me to finish." She silenced him with a

look she hadn't used since his youth. Her words were sharp. "As it happens, I find your Cindy a delight."

"You do?"

"Don't be a ninny! She's marvelous. Now stop acting so surprised." She shook her head lightly. "I thought at first that she might be too shy and retiring for you, which put me in a terrible position, since I doubted you'd care one way or another what I thought of her. But as it happens, I like her. The girl's got pluck."

"Pluck?"

"Yes. I'm pleased that you have the good sense to want to marry her."

Thorne was so astonished he nearly slid out of the booth and onto the floor. "I have every intention of making her my wife as soon as possible. She may put up a fight, but I'm not taking no for an answer."

His mother made a production of straightening the silverware, aligning each piece just so. "Well, dear, there may be a small problem."

"Yes?"

"Sheila seems quite broken up by the news that I'm giving Cindy my wholehearted approval. Mentioning that you'd brought her by to meet your father and me might not have been my smartest move. I had no idea Sheila would react so negatively. I'm afraid the girl may try to create problems for you."

"Let her." Thorne dealt with sensitive situations every day. He could handle Sheila. He'd calm her and end their relationship on a friendly note. "Don't worry, Mother, Sheila's been well aware of my feelings for Cindy for quite some time."

"She seemed to think you'd change your mind."

Thorne's mouth thinned with impatience. "She knows better."

"I'm worried about her, Thorne. I want you to talk to her."

Thorne ran his fingers along the fork tines. "Okay. I'm not sure it'll help. I regret any emotional trauma I may have caused her, but I'm not going to do anything other than talk to her."

"Do it soon."

Thorne agreed, elated with his family's acceptance of Cindy. He recalled the look on her face when he'd left her. She'd clung to him and kissed him with such fervor it had been difficult to leave. He thought about Cindy as his wife and the years that stretched before him—a lifetime of happiness and love. Even though he'd considered marrying Sheila at one point, he'd never thought about their future the way he did with Cindy, plotting the events of their lives.

"I'm seeing her tomorrow."

"Sheila?" his mother inquired.

He shook his head. "No, Cindy."

"But you will talk to Sheila? I'm afraid she might do… something silly."

"I'll speak to her," Thorne promised, determined to put an end to his relationship with the other woman.

Thorne stared at the wall clock in the lobby of the American Museum of Natural History. Cindy was half an hour late. It wasn't like her not to be punctual and he was mildly surprised. He had every minute of their evening planned. Dinner. Drinks. Dancing. Then they'd take a walk in Central Park and he'd bring out the engagement ring. Tonight was it.

All day he'd rehearsed what he was going to say. First, he'd tell her how knowing her had changed his life. It wasn't only singing in the shower and noticing the birds, either. Before she'd walked into his life, he'd fallen into a rut. His work had become meaningless, merely occupying his time. He'd lost his direction.

But her laughter and her smile had lifted him to the heavens, given him hope. He'd tell her that he'd never thought he'd experience the kind of love he felt for her. It had caught him unawares.

Naturally she'd be surprised by the suddenness of this proposal. She might even insist on an extended engagement. Of course, he hoped they could set the date immediately and begin to make the necessary arrangements for their wedding—a church wedding. He didn't want any rushed affair; when he made his vows to Cindy he wanted them spoken before God, not some fly-by-night justice of the peace. He intended their vows to last a lifetime.

Growing impatient, Thorne pulled the newspaper from his briefcase. Maybe if he read, the snail's pace minutes would go by faster. He scanned the business news and reached for the front page when the society section slipped to the floor.

Thorne retrieved it and was astonished to find Sheila's face smiling at him benignly. Interested, he turned the page right side up and read the headlines.

SHEILA MATHEWSON ANNOUNCES PLANS TO MARRY THORNDIKE PRINCE.

Thorne roared to his feet. The paper in his hand was crumpled into a wadded mass. So *this* was what his mother had come to prepare him for.... And worse, this was the reason Cindy hadn't shown up.

Ten

The minute Cindy walked into the apartment, Aunt Theresa and Uncle Sal abruptly cut off their conversation. Cindy studied their flushed faces; it wasn't difficult to ascertain that they'd been in the midst of a rousing argument. When Cindy arrived, they both seemed to find things to do. Her aunt opened the refrigerator and brought out a head of lettuce and her uncle reached for a deck of cards, shuffling them again and again, his gaze on his hands.

"I'll be in my room," Cindy said, granting them privacy. She was sorry they were fighting, and although it was uncommon, she knew from experience that it was best to let them resolve their differences without interference from her.

Sitting on the edge of her bed, Cindy eyed the clock. Thorne would be heading for the museum by now, anticipating their meeting. Only she wouldn't be there. She'd allowed him to think she'd agreed to this date, but she hadn't confirmed anything.

Coward! her mind accused her. But she had no choice, Cindy argued back. Every time she was with Thorne, her objections melted like snow under a springtime sun. She was so confused, she didn't know what she wanted anymore. Oh, she loved Thorne. But he was so easy to love. It would be far more difficult *not* to care for him.

Shaking her head vigorously, Cindy decided she couldn't leave Thorne waiting. That was silly and childish. It simply wasn't in her to let him waste his time worrying. She'd go to him and do her utmost to explain. All she'd ask him for was some time apart. A chance to test their feelings. Everything had happened so quickly that it would be wrong to act impulsively now. True love could wait, she'd tell him. A month was what she planned to suggest. Just a month. That didn't seem so long. Thorne would have to promise not to see her until Valentine's Day. If he truly cared for her, he'd agree to that.

Once she'd made her decision—the third one in as many days—she acted purposefully. She had her scarf wrapped around her neck by the time she entered the kitchen. She paused to button her coat.

Her uncle took one look at her and asked, "Where are you going?"

Sal so rarely questioned her about anything that his brusque inquiry took her by surprise. "I'm... The museum."

"You're not meeting that Prince fellow, are you?"

Her aunt pinched her lips together tightly and slammed the kitchen drawer closed, obviously annoyed by Sal's interrogation.

Cindy's gaze flew from Theresa back to her uncle. "I, uh, yes, I planned to meet Thorne there."

"No."

"No? I don't understand."

"I don't want you to have anything to do with that rich, spoiled kid."

"But, Uncle Sal—"

"The discussion is closed." Sal's hand pounded the tabletop, upsetting the saltshaker.

Cindy gasped and took a step backward. "I'm twenty-five years old! It's a little late to be telling me I can't meet someone."

"You are never to see that man again. Is that understood?"

"Cindy is more than old enough to make up her own mind," Theresa inserted calmly, her back to her husband.

"You keep out of this."

"So the big man thinks he can speak with the authority of a supreme court judge," Theresa taunted, her face growing redder by the second. "Well, I say Cindy can meet her Prince anytime she wishes."

"And I say she can't!" Sal yelled.

"Uncle Sal, Aunt Theresa, please…"

"He's not good enough for you," Sal said, more calmly this time. "Not nearly good enough for our Cindy."

"Oh, Uncle Sal—"

"Cindy…"

The compassion in her aunt's eyes was so strong that Cindy forgot what she wanted to say.

The room went still. Her uncle stared at the floor and Theresa's eyes glistened with tears.

"Something happened." Cindy knew it without a doubt. "It's Thorne, isn't it?"

Her aunt nodded, her troubled gaze avoiding Cindy's.

"Is he hurt?" She felt alarm bordering on panic. "Oh, you must tell me if he's injured. I couldn't bear it if he—"

"The man's a no-good bum," Sal interrupted. "You're best rid of him."

It was all so confusing. Everyone seemed to be speaking in riddles. She glanced from her uncle back to her aunt, pleading with them both to explain and to put an end to this nightmare of fear.

"I think we'd better tell her," Theresa said softly.

"No!" Sal insisted.

"Tell me what?"

"It's in the paper," Theresa said gently.

"I said she doesn't need to know," Sal shouted, taking the evening paper and stuffing it in the garbage.

"Uncle Sal!" Cindy pleaded. "What is it?"

Theresa crossed the room and reached for Cindy's hand. The last time Cindy could remember seeing her aunt look at her in exactly that way had been when she was a child, and Theresa had come to tell the five-year-old that her mother had gone to live in heaven.

"What is it?" Cindy asked, her voice low and weak. "He's not dead. Oh, no. Don't tell me he's dead."

"No, love," her aunt said softly.

Some of the terrible tension left Cindy's frozen limbs.

Theresa closed her eyes briefly and glanced over her shoulder to her husband. "She'll find out sooner or later. It's better she hear it from us."

For a moment it seemed as if Sal was going to argue. His chest swelled, then quickly deflated. He looked so unlike his robust, outgoing self that Cindy couldn't imagine what was troubling him.

"Sal read the announcement in the paper and brought it to me."

"The announcement?" Cindy asked. "What announcement?"

"Thorne's marrying—"

"—some high-society dame," Sal broke in. He shook his head regretfully as though he would've done anything to have spared Cindy this.

"But I don't understand," Cindy murmured.

"It was in the society pages."

"Sheila?"

Her aunt nodded.

Cindy sank into a kitchen chair, her legs unable to support her. "I'm sure there's some mistake. I... He took me to meet his family."

"He was using you." Sal came to stand behind her. He patted her shoulders awkwardly, trying to comfort her. "He was probably using his family to give you the impression that he was serious so he could get you into bed."

"No!" Cindy cried. "No, it was never like that. Thorne didn't even suggest...not once."

"Then thank God. Because it's where he was leading. He's a smart devil, I'll say that for him."

Theresa claimed the chair next to Cindy and took her numb fingers, rubbing them. "I refused to believe it myself until Sal showed me the article. But there it was, bold as can be. It's true, Cindy."

Cindy nodded, accepting what her family was telling her. No tears burned for release. No hysterical sob rose up within her. She felt nothing. No pain. No sense of betrayal. No anger. Nothing.

"Are you going to be all right?" Theresa asked.

"I'll be fine. Don't worry. It was inevitable, you know. I think I knew it from the beginning. Something deep inside me always realized he could never be mine."

"But...oh, Cindy, I can hardly believe it myself."

Cindy stood and hugged her aunt close. "You fell for the

magic," she whispered. "So did I for a while. But I'm not really Cinderella and Thorne isn't really a prince. It had to end sometime."

"I hurt so much for you!" Theresa whispered.

"Don't. I'm not nearly as upset as you think," Cindy told her. "I'm going to study for a while." Cindy was fighting off the terrible numbness, knowing she had to do something. Anything. Otherwise she'd go crazy.

Sal slipped an arm around his wife and Theresa pressed her head to his shoulder. "Okay," Sal told his niece softly. "You hit those books and you'll feel better."

Cindy walked back to her room and closed the door. It seemed so dingy inside. Dingy and small. She didn't feel like studying, but she forced herself to sit on the bed and open her textbook. The words blurred, swimming in and out of focus, and Cindy was shocked to realize she was crying.

"I want a retraction and I want it printed in today's paper," Thorne stormed at the society-page editor. The poor woman was red with indignation, but Thorne was beyond caring.

"I've already explained that we won't be able to do that until tomorrow's paper," the woman said for the sixth time.

"But that could be too late."

"I apologize for any inconvenience this may have caused you, Mr. Prince, but we received Ms. Mathewson's announcement through the normal channels. I can assure you this kind of thing is most unusual."

"And you printed the wedding announcement without checking with the alleged groom?"

The woman sat at her desk, holding a pencil at each end with a grip so hard it threatened to snap. "Let me assure you, Mr. Prince, that in all my years in the newspaper business, this is the first bogus wedding announcement that's ever crossed my desk. In the past there's never been any need to verify the event with the, uh, alleged groom—or bride for that matter."

"Then maybe you should start."

"Maybe," she returned stiffly. "Now, if you'll excuse me, I've got work to do."

"You haven't heard the end of this," Thorne said heatedly.

"I don't doubt it," the editor responded.

Thorne did an abrupt about-face and left the newspaper office, unconcerned with the amount of attention his argument had caused.

On the street, he caught the first taxi he could flag down and headed back to the office. As it was, he was working on a tight schedule. He'd already attended an important meeting early that morning—one he'd tried to postpone and couldn't. The minute he was free, he'd had Ms. Hillard contact the PI, Mike Williams, and he'd paced restlessly until he'd learned that Mike was out of town on a case and not expected back for another week.

The detective could well be his only chance of finding Cindy. Mike had gotten close once, but after Cindy had shown up outside his office building, Thorne had done as she requested and asked Mike to halt his investigation. After all, he'd gotten what he'd wanted—Cindy was back. Now he wished he'd pursued it further. He had no more chance of finding her now than when she'd left him the night of the Christmas Ball.

A feeling of desperation overpowered him. When Cindy hadn't appeared at the museum, Thorne had spent the evening calling every Territo in the phone book—all fifty-seven—to no avail. By the time he'd finished, he was convinced she'd given him a phony name. Either that, or she had an unlisted number. From there he had no more leads.

Thorne dreaded returning to his office. No doubt there'd be enough phone and e-mail messages to occupy his afternoon—and he was supposed to be working on a merger! Thank goodness it was almost completed. Still, this was not the week to be worrying about Cindy. He had neither the time nor the patience to be running around New York looking for her.

Ms. Hillard stood up when Thorne entered his office.

"Yes?" he barked, and was instantly contrite.

"Mr. Jenning would like to talk to you when you have a moment." Her eyes didn't meet his and Thorne felt a twinge of guilt. He'd been abrupt with her just now, but it was tame in comparison to his treatment of Sheila. She'd been to see him first thing that morning and he'd hardly been able to look at her as the anger boiled within him. The woman had plotted to ruin his life. It was her fault that he couldn't locate Cindy. He'd said things to Sheila that he'd never said to anyone. He regretted that now.

Perhaps he might have found it in his heart to forgive her, but she'd revealed no contrition. It almost seemed as if she was proud of what she'd done. He hadn't been the only one to lose his composure; Sheila had called Cindy the most disgusting names. Even now, hours later, Thorne burned with outrage.

In the end, he'd ruthlessly pointed at the door and asked her to leave. Apparently she'd realized her mistake. She began sobbing, ignoring his edict. He'd told her firmly that he planned to marry Cindy and nothing she could do would change his plans. Then, not knowing what else to do, Thorne had called in his secretary.

"Ms. Hillard," he'd said, his eyes silently pleading with the older woman. "It seems Ms. Mathewson needs to powder her nose. Perhaps you could show her the way to the ladies' room."

"Of course."

Mentally Thorne made a note to give his secretary a raise. The older woman had handled the delicate situation with finesse. Tenderly she'd placed her arm around the weeping Sheila's shoulders, and with nothing more than a few whispered words she'd directed her away from Thorne's desk and out of his office.

Sighing, Thorne sank down in his chair and looked over his messages. Paul Jenning had asked to see him, probably about his upcoming retirement and his not-so-secret proposal that Thorne succeed him. But even though this was what Thorne had always wanted, he couldn't feel excited about it. If only he knew how to contact Cindy...

"Have you been in *his* office yet?"

Cindy didn't need to guess whose office Vanessa was referring to. Her coworker hadn't stopped talking about Thorne from the moment Cindy had arrived for work. "Not yet."

"Are you going in there?"

"Vanessa, it's my job—nothing more and nothing less."

The other woman pushed her cleaning cart down the hallway, casting Cindy a worried glance now and then. "How can you be so calm? Aren't you tempted to booby-trap his desk or something? As far as I'm concerned, Prince is the lowest form of life. He's lower than low. Lower than scum."

Cindy pressed her lips together and said nothing.

"You're taking this much too calmly."

"What do you want me to do?" Cindy asked, losing patience.

"I don't know," Vanessa returned. "Cry, at least. Weep uncontrollably for a day or two and purge him from your system."

"It would take more than a good bout of crying to do that," Cindy mused. "What else?"

Vanessa looked confused. "I'd think you'd want to hate him."

Cindy wasn't allowed that luxury, either. "No, I can't hate him." Not when she loved him. Not when she wished for his happiness with every breath. Not when everything within her was grateful for the short time they'd shared. "No," she repeated softly. "I could never hate him."

They paused outside Thorne's office. "You want me to clean it for you?"

"No." Cindy didn't need to think twice about it. From this night forward, Thorne's office would be the only contact she had with him. It was far too much—and yet, not nearly enough.

"You're sure?"

"Positive."

The outer office, which Ms. Hillard occupied, was neat, as always, but Cindy brushed her feather duster over the desk and around the computer keyboard. Next, she plugged in the vacuum cleaner. With a flip of the switch it roared to life, but she hadn't done more than a couple of swipes when it was suddenly switched off. Surprised, Cindy whirled around to discover Thorne holding the plug in his hand.

"Can't this wait?" he snapped, tossing the plug onto the carpet. "In case you hadn't noticed, I'm working in here."

Cindy was too stunned to react. It was obvious he hadn't

even looked at her. She was, after all, only the cleaning woman.

She turned, prepared to leave without another word, but in her rush, she bumped against the side of the desk and knocked over a stack of papers. They fluttered down to the carpet like autumn leaves caught in a gust of wind.

"Of all the inept…"

Instantly, Cindy crouched down to pick them up, her shaking fingers working as quickly as she could make them cooperate.

"Get out before you do any more damage or I'll have you fired."

Cindy reared up, her eyes spitting fire. "How *dare* you speak to me or anyone else in that demeaning tone?" she shouted. She had the satisfaction of watching Thorne's jaw sag open. "You think that because you're Mr. Almighty Vice President you can treat other people like they're your servants? Well, I've got news for you, Thorndike Prince. You can't have me fired because—I quit!" With that she removed the feather duster from her pocket, shoved it in his hand and stormed out of his office.

Eleven

Thorne moved quickly, throwing the feather duster aside and hurrying out of his office. So this was Cindy's terrible secret. He'd never been more relieved about anything in his life. A flash of pinstriped coveralls and red bandana caught his attention in the office across from his own and he rushed in.

"Cindy, you crazy idiot." He took her by the shoulders, whirled her around and pressed her close to hug the anger out of her.

She struggled, her arms flailing ineffectively, but Thorne wasn't about to set her free. Her cries were muffled against his broad chest.

"Honey, don't fight me. I'm sorry—"

She gasped, braced her palms against him and pushed with all her might until she broke free. If Thorne had been surprised to find Cindy cleaning his office, it was an even greater shock to discover that the woman he'd been holding wasn't Cindy.

"I'm not your 'honey,'" Vanessa howled.

"You're not Cindy."

"Any idiot could see that." Disgruntled, she rearranged her bandana and squared her shoulders. "Do you always behave like an ape-man?"

"Where's Cindy?"

"And you're not exactly the love of *my* life, either," Vanessa continued sarcastically.

Thorne rushed from the office and down the hall, stopping to search every room. Cindy was gone. Vanished. This was how it happened every time. Just when he thought he'd found her, she disappeared, sending him into agony until she stumbled into his life again. No more. They were going to settle this once and for all!

He rushed back to the other young woman, leaned both hands against the office doorway and shouted, "Where'd she go?"

"I don't know if I should tell you." She idly dusted the top of Rutherford Hayden's desk, obviously enjoying her moment of glory.

"You—what's your name?"

"Vanessa, if it's any of your business."

Thorne clenched his fists, growing more impatient. He wasn't going to let this impertinent Vanessa person keep him from the woman he loved. "Either you tell me where she is or you're out of here."

"I wasn't all that keen to keep this job anyway," Vanessa said, faking a yawn. She sauntered to the other side of the office. "Do you love her?"

"Yes!"

"If that's the case, then why was your engagement to another woman announced in the paper?"

"Sheila lied. Now, are you going to tell me where Cindy went?"

"So, you aren't going to marry this other woman?"

"That's what I just got through telling you. I want to marry Cindy."

Vanessa raised her index finger to her lips, as if giving the matter consideration. "I suppose I *should* tell you, then."

"Could you do it fast?"

"I was the one who brought Cindy your picture and told her you might be her prince."

"We'll name our first daughter after you." Thorne said the words from between gritted teeth.

"Fair enough," Vanessa said with a sigh. "Take the elevator all the way to the basement, go left, then at the end of the corridor go left again, and it's the first room on your right. Have you got that?"

"Got it." Thorne took off running. "Left, left, right. Left, left, right," he mumbled over and over while he waited for the elevator. The ride to the basement had never seemed slower, especially when he realized that he had to change elevators on the main floor. When he couldn't locate the service elevator, the security guard, Bob Knight, came to his aid.

Just before the heavy door glided shut, Thorne yelled, "We'll name one of our children after you, too!"

Cindy was too furious to think straight. She removed her coveralls and flung them carelessly into the laundry bin. "Can't you see I'm working in here," she muttered, sarcastically mimicking Thorne's words. The red bandana followed the coveralls, falling short of the bin, but Cindy couldn't have cared less.

"Cindy."

At the sound of Thorne calling her name, Cindy turned, closed the door and slid the lock into place.

Thorne tried the door, discovered it was locked, then pounded on it with both fists. "Cindy, I know you're in there!"

She refused to answer him.

"Cindy, at least hear me out."

"You don't need to say a word to me, Mr. Almighty Thorndike Prince." Dramatically she brought the back of her wrist to her forehead. "I suggest you leave before you do any more damage and I'm forced to have you fired." She taunted him with his own threat.

"Cindy, please, I'm sorry. I had no idea that was you."

She reached for her jeans, sliding them over her hips and zipping them up, her hands shaking in her hurry to dress. "I think you're...despicable. Vanessa was right. You are the lowest of the low."

"She'll change her mind. I just promised to name our first daughter after her."

"Oh, stop trying to be clever!"

"Cindy," he tried again, his voice low and coaxing, "hear me out. I've had a rotten day. I was convinced I'd never find you again and one thing after another has gone wrong. You're right, I shouldn't have shouted at you, but please understand. I didn't know you were the cleaning lady."

She rammed her arms into the long sleeves of her sweatshirt and jerked it over her head. "It shouldn't have mattered who I was...as you kept telling me."

"And I meant it. If you'd let me explain..."

"You don't need to explain a thing to me... I'm only the cleaning woman."

"I love you, cleaning woman."

Telling her that was cheating, since he knew the effect it

would have on her. Cindy threw open the door and faced him, arms akimbo and eyes flashing. "I suppose you love Sheila, too."

"No, I—"

"Don't give me that. Did you think I'm so socially inept I wouldn't find out about your wedding announcement? I do happen to read the paper now and again."

"Sheila had that published without my knowledge. I have no intention of marrying her. How could I when I'm in love with you?"

That took some of the wind from her sails, as her aunt might have said, and her temper went with it. She closed her eyes and bowed her head. "Don't tell me you love me, Thorne. I don't think I'll be able to leave you if you do."

Thorne reached for her, astonished anew at how right it felt to hold her. He held her tight and sighed in relief. He had his Cindy, his princess, his love, and he wasn't going to lose her again.

"That night was all a game," she whispered. "I never dreamed...never hoped you'd come to care for me."

"The magic never stopped and it never will. You're mine, Cindy Territo. And I'm yours."

"But, Thorne, surely you understand now why I couldn't let you know."

"Do you think it matters that you're a janitor? I love you. I want you to share my life."

Cindy tensed. "Thorne, I'm scared."

"There's no reason to be." His hand smoothed the curls at the back of her head.

"Are you crazy?" Cindy asked with a sobbing laugh. "Look at us."

Thorne blinked.

"You're standing there in your thousand-dollar suit and I'm wearing bargain-basement blue jeans."

"So?"

"So! We're like oil and water. We don't mix."

Thorne smiled at that. "It just takes a little shaking up. You can't doubt that we were meant to be together, Cindy, my very own princess."

"But, Thorne—"

He kissed her then, cutting off any further objection. His mouth settled firmly over hers; the kiss was both undeniably gentle and magically sweet. When he held her like this, it was easy to believe that everything would always be wonderful between them.

"I want to meet your family."

"Thorne, no." Cindy broke out of his arms, hugging her waist.

He looked puzzled. "Why not?"

"Because—"

"I'll need to meet them sometime."

Her uncle Sal's contorted, angry face flashed before Cindy. She knew he disapproved of Thorne. If Cindy were to bring Thorne to the apartment, Sal would punch first and ask questions later. Any of her uncles would behave the same way. Her family was highly protective of all their loved ones, and there'd have to be a whole lot of explaining before Cindy brought Thorne into their midst.

"Meet them?" Cindy repeated. "Why?"

"Cindy." He held her squarely by the shoulders. "I plan to marry you. If you'll have me, of course."

She stared at him, overwhelmed by happiness—and then immediately swamped by doubts.

"You will be my wife, won't you?"

He asked her with such tenderness that Cindy's eyes brimmed with tears. She nodded wildly. "Yes..."

Thorne relaxed.

"No," she said quickly, then covered her face with both hands. "Oh, good grief, I don't know!"

"Do you love me?"

Her response was another vigorous nod.

"Then it's settled." He removed her hands from her face and kissed her eyes and her nose. Then his lips descended slowly toward her mouth, pausing at her earlobe, working their way across the delicate line of her jaw....

"But, Thorne, nothing's settled. Not really. We... I need time."

"Okay, I'll give you time."

The organ music vibrated through the church. Cindy stood at the back of St. Anthony's and her heart went still as the first bridesmaid, holding a large bouquet of pink rosebuds, stepped forward. The second and the third followed. Cindy watched their progress, and her heart throbbed with happiness. This was her wedding day and within the hour she would experience the birth of her dreams. She would become Thorne's wife. Somehow they'd crossed every hurdle. She'd claimed she needed time. He'd given it to her. She'd been so sure her family would object, but with gentle patience Thorne had won over every member. Now it was June and almost six months had passed since the night of the Christmas Ball. Thorne had convinced her the magic of that night would last throughout their lives, and finally Cindy could believe him. There wasn't anything in this world their love couldn't overcome. They'd proved it.

Thorne stood at the altar, waiting for her. His eyes were

filled with such tenderness that Cindy had to resist the urge to race into his arms.

His smile lent her assurance. He didn't look the least bit nervous, while Cindy felt as if a swarm of bees was about to invade her stomach. From the first, he'd been the confident one. Always so sure of what was right for them. Never doubting. Oh, how she loved him.

The signal came for four-year-old Carla to join the procession, and dressed in her long lavender gown, the little girl took one measured step after another.

Cindy stood at the back of the church and looked out over the seated guests. To her left were the people who'd loved and nurtured her most of her life. Aunt Theresa sat in the front row, a lace handkerchief in her hand, and Cindy saw her dab away an escaped tear. Cousins abounded. Aunts, uncles, lifelong friends, Vanessa, Bob Knight and others who'd come to share this glorious day. She lifted a hand to the pearl comb Thorne had returned to her. The combs secured her delicate veil. Cindy thought of her mother and how happy she would've been today.

To her right was Thorne's family. Wealthy, cultured, sophisticated. St. Anthony's parking lot had never hosted so many Cadillacs and Mercedes, nor had this humble sanctuary witnessed so many designer dresses and expensive suits. But they'd come, filling the large church to capacity, wanting to meet the woman who was about to marry Thorne Prince.

The organ music reached a crescendo when Cindy stepped onto the trail of white linen that ran the length of the aisle. The train of the satin and lace dress that had been worn by both her mother and her aunt flowed behind her. Cindy walked at a slow and stately pace, each resounding note of the organ drawing her closer to Thorne, her prince, her love.

The congregation stood and Cindy felt a surge of excitement as the faces of those she loved turned to watch her progress.

Thirty minutes later Cindy moved back down the same aisle as Thorne's wife. Family and friends spilled out of the church, crowding the steps. Cindy was repeatedly hugged and Thorne shook hand after hand.

The limousine arrived, and with his guiding hand at her elbow, Thorne led her down the steps and held open the car door.

Almost immediately, he climbed in after her.

"Hello, Mrs. Prince," he whispered, his voice awed. "Have I told you today how much I love you?" he asked.

"You just did that with a church full of witnesses," she reminded him softly. "I do love you, Thorne. There were so many times I didn't believe this day could ever happen, and now that it has, I know how right it is."

He gathered her in his arms and kissed her to the boisterous approval of their guests, who were still watching from the sidewalk.

"Did you see the banner?" Thorne asked, pointing to the church.

"No."

"I think Vanessa had something to do with that."

Cindy laughed. There, above the doors, a banner was hung, the words bold and bright for all the world to read:

CINDY AND HER PRINCE LIVED HAPPILY EVER AFTER.

* * * * *

SOME KIND OF WONDERFUL

One

"Once upon a time in a land far away," Judy Lovin began in a still, reverent voice. The intent faces of the four-year-olds gathered at her feet stared up at her with wide-eyed curiosity. Hardly a whisper could be heard as Judy continued relating the fairy tale that had stirred her heart from the moment she'd first heard it as a youngster no older than these. It was the story of *Beauty and the Beast*.

Today, however, her thoughts weren't on the fairy tale, which she could recite from memory. As much as she was trying to focus her attention on her job, Judy couldn't. She'd argued with her father earlier that morning and the angry exchange troubled her. She rarely disagreed with her father, a man she deeply loved and respected. Charles Lovin was an outspoken, opinionated man who headed one of the world's most successful shipping companies. At the office he was regarded as demanding but fair. At home, with his family, Charles Lovin was a kind and generous father to both Judy and her older brother, David.

Charles's Wedgwood teacup had clattered sharply when he'd placed it in the saucer that morning. "All those years of the best schooling, and you prefer to work as a preschool teacher in a day-care center." He'd said it as though she were toiling among lepers on a South Pacific island instead of the peaceful upper east side of Manhattan.

"I love what I do."

"You could have any job you wanted!" he'd snapped.

His unprovoked outburst surprised Judy and she'd answered quietly. "I have exactly the job I want."

He slapped the table, startling her. Such behavior was uncommon—indeed, unheard of—in the Lovin household. Even her brother couldn't disguise his shock.

"What good are my wealth and position to you there?" he roared. "Beauty, please…"

He used his affectionate name for her. She'd loved the fairy tale so much as a child that her father had given her the name of the princess. Today, however, she felt more like a servant than royalty. She couldn't recall a time when her father had looked at her in such a dictatorial manner. Swallowing a sip of tea, she took her time answering, hoping to divert the confrontation.

She was a gentle soul, like her mother, who had died unexpectedly when Judy was in her early teens. Father and daughter had grown close in the years that followed and even during her most rebellious teen period, Judy had hardly ever argued with him. And certainly not over something like this. When she'd graduated from the finest university in the country at the top of her class, she'd gone to work as a volunteer at a local day-care center in a poor section of town. She'd come to love her time with these preschoolers. Charles hadn't objected then, or when she'd been asked to join the staff full-time, although her pay was only a fraction of what she could make in any other job. But after all these months, it seemed unfair that her father should suddenly object.

"Father," she said, forcing herself to remain calm. "Why are you concerned about the day-care center *now?*"

He'd looked tired and drawn and so unlike himself that she'd immediately been worried.

"I'd assumed," he shouted, his expression furious, "that given time, you'd come to your senses!"

Judy attempted to disguise a smile.

"I don't find this subject the least bit amusing, young lady."

"Yes, Father."

"You have a degree from one of the finest universities in this country. I expect you to use the brain the good Lord gave you and make something of yourself."

"Yes, Father."

"Try living off what you make taking care of other women's children and see how far that gets you in this world."

She touched her mouth with her linen napkin and motioned with her head to Bently, who promptly removed her plate. The English butler had been with the family since long before Judy was born. He sent her a sympathetic look. "Do we need the money, Father?" she asked.

In retrospect, she realized she probably shouldn't have spoken in such a flippant tone. But to hear her father, it sounded as if they were about to become destitute.

Charles Lovin completely lost his temper at that, hitting the table so hard that his spoon shot into the air and hit the crystal chandelier with a loud clang, shocking them both.

"I demand that you resign today." And with that, he tossed his napkin on his plate and stormed from the room.

Judy sat for a long moment as the shock settled over her.

Gradually the numbness subsided and she pushed back her genuine Queen Anne chair. All the furniture in the Lovin home had been in the family for generations. Many considered this a priceless antique; Judy considered it a dining-room chair.

Bently appeared then, a crisp linen towel folded over his forearm. He did love ceremony. "I'm sure he didn't mean that, miss." He spoke out of the corner of his mouth, barely moving his lips. It had always amused Judy that Bently could talk like that, and she assumed he'd acquired this talent from years of directing help during dinner parties and other formal gatherings.

"Thank you, Bently," she said, grinning. "I'm sure you're right."

He winked then and Judy returned the gesture. By the time she arrived at the day-care center, she'd put the thought of resigning out of her mind. Tonight when she got home, her father would be his kind, loving self again. He would apologize for his outrageous tantrum and she would willingly forgive him.

"Miss Judy, Miss Judy!" Tammi, a lively little girl, jumped to her feet and threw her arms around her teacher's neck. "That's a beautiful story."

Judy returned the wholehearted hug. "I love it, too."

"Did Beauty and the Beast love each other forever and ever?"

"Oh, yes."

"Did they have lots of little beasts?"

"I'm sure they did, but remember, the Beast wasn't a beast any longer."

"Beauty's love turned him into a handsome prince," Jennifer exclaimed, exceedingly proud of herself.

Bobby, a blond preschooler with pale blue eyes, folded

his arms across his chest and looked grim. "Do you know any stories about policemen? That's what I want to be when I grow up."

Judy affectionately ruffled the little boy's hair. "I'll see if I can find a story just for you tomorrow."

The boy gave her a wide smile and nodded his head. "Good thing. I'm tired of mushy stories."

"Now," Judy said, setting the book aside. "It's time to do some finger painting."

A chorus of cheers rose from the small group and they scurried to the tables and chairs. Judy stood up and reached over her head to the tall cupboards for the paper and paints.

"You know what I love most about the Beast?" Jennifer said, lagging behind.

"What's that?" Judy withdrew an apron from the top shelf and tied it around her waist. Her brown hair fell in soft curves, brushing her shoulders, and she pushed it back.

"I love the way Beauty brought summer into the Beast's forest."

"It was her kindness and gentleness that accomplished that," Judy reminded the little girl.

"And her love," Jennifer added, sighing.

"And her love," Judy repeated.

"I have the report you requested."

John McFarland glanced up from the accounting sheets he was studying. "Put it here." He pointed to the corner of his beech desk and waited until his business manager, Avery Anderson, had left the room before reaching for the folder.

McFarland opened it, stared at the picture of the lovely brown-eyed woman that rested on top and arched his brows appreciatively. Judy Lovin. He'd seen her picture in the *New*

York Times several months ago, but the photo hadn't done her fragile beauty justice. As he recalled, the article had described her efforts in a day-care center. He studied her photograph. Although she was lovely, he knew women who were far more beautiful. However, few of them revealed such trusting innocence and subtle grace. The women he dealt with all had a seductive beauty, but lacked heart. Seeing Judy's photograph, McFarland was struck anew at the contrast.

He continued to stare at the picture. Her dark brown eyes smiled back at him and McFarland wondered if she had half the backbone her father possessed. The thought of the man caused his mouth to tighten with an odd mixture of admiration and displeasure. He had liked Charles Lovin when he'd first met him; he'd been openly challenged by him several years later. Few men had the courage to tangle with McFarland, but the older man was stubborn, tenacious, ill-tempered...and, unfortunately, a fool. A pity, McFarland mused, that anyone would allow pride to stand in the way of common sense. The U.S. shipping business had been swiftly losing ground for decades. Others had seen it and diversified or sold out. If McFarland hadn't bought them outright, he'd taken control by other channels. Charles Lovin, and only Lovin, had steadfastly refused to relinquish his business—to his own detriment, McFarland mused. Apparently, leaving a dying company to his beloved son, David, was more important than giving him nothing.

Lovin was the last holdout. The others had crumpled easily enough, giving in when McFarland had applied pressure in varying degrees. Miraculously, Lovin had managed to hang on to his company. Word was that he'd been cashing in stocks, bonds and anything else he could liquidate. Next, he supposed, it would be priceless family heirlooms.

It was a shame, but he felt little sympathy. McFarland was determined to own Lovin Shipping Lines and one stubborn old man wouldn't stand in his way. It was a pity, though; Lovin had guts and despite everything, McFarland admired the man's tenacity.

Leafing through the report, he noted that Lovin had managed to get a sizable loan from a New York bank. Satisfied, McFarland nodded and his lips twisted with wry humor. He was a major stockholder of that financial institution and several other Manhattan banks, as well. He pushed the buzzer on his desk and Avery appeared, standing stiffly in front of him.

"You called, sir?"

"Sit down, Avery." McFarland gestured to an imposing leather wing chair. Avery had been with McFarland four years and John had come to respect the other man's keen mind.

"Did you read the report?"

"Yes."

McFarland nodded and absently flipped through the pages.

"David Lovin is well thought of in New York," Avery added. "He's serious and hardworking. Wealth doesn't appear to have spoiled the Lovin children."

"David?" McFarland repeated, surprised that he'd been so preoccupied that he'd missed something.

"The young man who will inherit the Lovin fortune."

"Yes, of course." McFarland had examined the Lovin girl's photograph and been so taken with her that he hadn't gone on to read the report on her older brother. He did so now and was impressed with the young man's credentials.

"Many people believe that if Lovin Shipping Lines can hold on for another year..."

"Yes, yes." McFarland knew all that. Congress was said to be considering new laws that would aid the faltering shipping business. McFarland was counting on the same legislation himself.

"Father and son are doing everything possible to manage until Washington makes a move."

"It's a shame," McFarland murmured almost inaudibly.

"What's a shame?" Avery leaned forward.

"To call in his loan."

"You're going to do it?"

McFarland studied his employee, astonished that the other man would openly reveal his disapproval. John knew that to all the world, he seemed to be a man without conscience, without scruples, without compassion. He *was* all those things—and none of them. John McFarland was an entity unto himself. People didn't know him because he refused to let anyone get close. He had his faults, he'd be the first to admit that, but he'd never cheated anyone.

He stood abruptly, placed his hands behind his back and paced the area in front of his desk. David Lovin was a fortunate man to have a heritage so richly blessed; McFarland knew nothing of his own family. Orphaned at an early age, he'd been given up for adoption. No family had ever wanted him and he'd been raised in a series of foster homes—some better than others.

McFarland had clawed his way to the top an inch at a time. He'd gotten a scholarship to college, started his first company at twenty-one and been a millionaire by twenty-five. At thirty-six, he was one of the wealthiest men in the world. Surprisingly, money meant little to him. He enjoyed the riches he'd accumulated, the island, his home, his Learjet; money brought him whatever he desired. But wealth and position were only the by-products of success. Unlike those whose

fortunes had created—or were created by—family businesses, McFarland's empire would die with him. The thought
was a sobering one. Money had given him everything he'd
ever wanted except what he yearned for most—love, acceptance, self-worth. A paradox, he realized somewhat sadly.
Over the years, he'd grown hard. Bitter. Everything in him
demanded that he topple Lovin as he had a hundred other
businesses. Without sentiment or regret. The only thing stopping him was that damnable pride he'd recognized in Charles
Lovin's eyes. The man was a fighter and he hated to take
him down without giving the old boy a chance.

"Sir, do you wish to think this matter through?"

McFarland had nearly forgotten Avery's presence. He
nodded abruptly and the other man quietly left the room.

Opening the doors that led to the veranda, McFarland
stepped outside, leaned on the wrought-iron railing and
looked out on the clear blue waves crashing against the shore
far below. He'd purchased this Caribbean island three years
earlier and named it St. Steven's. It granted him privacy
and security. Several families still inhabited the far side of
the island, and McFarland allowed them to continue living
there. They tended to avoid him, and on the rare occasions
he happened to meet any of them, they slipped quickly away.

A brisk wind blew off the water, carrying with it the
scent of seaweed, and he tasted salt on his tongue. Farther
down the beach, he saw a lazy trail of foam that had left
its mark on the sand, meandering without purpose into the
distance. Sometimes that was the way McFarland viewed
his life; he was without inner purpose and yet on the surface, his activities were dominated by it. Another paradox,
he mused, not unhappily, not really caring.

Unexpectedly, he made a decision and returned to his
desk, again ringing for his assistant.

Avery was punctual as usual. "Sir?"

McFarland sat in his chair and rocked back, fingering his chin. "I've decided."

Avery nodded, reaching for his paper and pen.

McFarland hesitated. "I wonder how much that business means to the old man."

"By all accounts—everything."

McFarland grinned. "Then we shall see."

"Sir?"

"Contact Lovin as soon as possible and give him an ultimatum. Either I'll call in the loan—immediately—or he sends me his daughter." He picked up the file. "I believe her name is Judy.... Yes, here it is. Judy."

Avery's pad dropped to the carpet. Flustered, he bent to retrieve the paper, and in the process lost his pen, which rolled under McFarland's desk. Hastily, he rescued them both and, with nervous, jerky movements, reclaimed his place. "Sir, I think I misunderstood you."

"Your hearing is fine."

"But...sir?"

"Naturally there will be a number of guarantees on my part. We can discuss those at a later date."

"Sir, such a...why, it's unheard of—I mean, no man in his right mind—"

"I agree it's a bit unorthodox."

"A...bit? But surely...sir?" Avery stuttered.

Watching, McFarland found him highly amusing. The man had turned three shades of red, each deeper than the one before. A full minute passed and he'd opened his mouth twice, closed it an equal number of times and opened it again. Yet he said nothing.

"What about the young lady? She may have a few objections," Avery finally managed.

"I'm confident that she will."

"But…"

"We'll keep her busy with whatever it is women like to do. I suppose she could redecorate the downstairs. When I tire of her, I'll set her free. Don't look so concerned, Avery. I've yet to allow my baser instincts to control me."

"Sir, I didn't mean to imply…it's just that…"

"I understand." McFarland was growing bored with this. "Let me know when he gives you his decision."

"Right away, sir." But he looked as if he would've preferred a trip to the dentist.

Judy returned home from work that afternoon, weary in both body and spirit. She smiled at Bently, who took her coat and purse.

"Is my father home?" Judy asked, eager to settle this matter between them. If he felt as strongly as he had that morning about her job at the day care, then she'd do as he requested.

"Mr. Lovin is still at the office, Miss Judy."

Judy checked her watch, surprised that her father was this late. He was almost always home an hour or so before her. "I'll wait for him in the study," Judy said. Something was worrying him; Judy was positive. Whatever the problem was, Judy yearned to assure him that she'd help in any way possible. If it meant leaving the day-care center then she would, but she was happy working with the children. Surely he wanted her happiness. Being a success shouldn't be judged by how much money one happened to make. Contentment was the most important factor, and she was sure that someone as wise and considerate as her father would agree.

"In the study, miss? Very good. Shall I bring you tea?"

"That would be lovely. Thank you."

He bowed slightly and turned away.

Judy entered the library, which was connected to her father's study by huge sliding doors. She chose to wait among the leather-bound volumes and settled into the soft armchair, slipped off her pumps and rested her feet on the ottoman, crossing them at the ankles. The portrait of her mother, hanging over the marble fireplace, smiled down on her. Judy would sometimes sneak into the room and talk with her mother. On occasion, she could've sworn Georgia's eyes had moved. That was silly, of course, and Judy had long ago accepted that her mother was gone and the portrait was exactly that—a likeness of a lovely woman and nothing more.

Judy stared up at her now. "I can't imagine what got into Father this morning."

The soft, loving eyes appeared to caress Judy and plead with her to be patient.

"I've never known him to be in such an unreasonable and foul mood."

Her mother's look asked her to be more understanding and Judy quickly glanced away. "All right, all right," she grumbled. "I'll be more patient."

Bently came into the study, carrying a silver tray. "Shall I pour?"

"I'll do it," she answered with a smile. She reached for the pot. "Bently?"

"Yes, miss?" He turned back to her.

"Whatever happened to the Riordan sculpture that was on Father's desk?" The small bronze statue was a prized piece that her father had always loved.

"I…don't really know, miss."

"Did Father move it to his office?"

"That must be it."

"He'd never sell it." Judy was convinced of that. The Alice Riordan original had been a Christmas gift from her mother a few months before she died.

"I'm sure he didn't," the butler concurred and then excused himself.

Now that she considered it, she realized there were other things missing from the house—a vase here and there, a painting that had disappeared. Judy hadn't given the matter much thought, but now she found it odd. Either her father had moved them to another location for safekeeping or they'd simply vanished into thin air. Even to entertain the notion that the staff would steal them was unthinkable. Bently, Cook and Anne had been with the Lovins for years.

Judy poured her tea and added a squeeze of fresh lemon. Bently had been thoughtful enough to bring two extra cups so that when her father and David arrived, they could have tea, as well.

She must have drifted off to sleep because the next thing Judy heard was the sound of gruff male voices. The door between the two rooms had been closed, but she could hear the raised impatient voices of her father and brother as clearly as if they were in the library with her.

Judy sat upright and rubbed the stiffness from the back of her neck. She was about to interrupt her father and brother and cajole them into a cup of tea, but something held her back. Perhaps it was the emotion she recognized in their voices—the anger, the outrage, the frustration. Judy paid little attention to the business; that was her brother and father's domain. But it was apparent that something was dreadfully wrong.

"You can't mean you actually sold the Riordan?" David's astonished voice echoed off the paneled walls.

"Do you think I wanted to?" Charles Lovin said, and the

agony in his voice nearly caused her heart to stop. "I was desperate for the money."

"But, Father—"

"You can't say anything to me that I haven't told myself a thousand times."

"What else?" David sounded worried and grim.

"Everything I could."

The announcement was followed by a shocked gasp, but Judy didn't know if it had come from her throat or her brother's.

"Everything?" David repeated, his voice choked.

"As much as possible without losing this house...and it still wasn't enough."

"What about Bently and the others?"

"They'll have to be let go."

"But, Father—"

"There's no other way," he cried. "As it is, we're still millions short."

Judy didn't know what was happening, but this had to be a nightmare. Reality could never be this cruel. Her father was selling everything they owned? In addition to this estate, they owned homes all over the world. There were securities, bonds, properties, investments.... Their family wealth went back for generations.

A fist slammed against the desk. "Why would McFarland call in the loan?"

"Who knows why that beast would do anything? He's ruined better men than me."

"For what reason?"

Her father paused. "Perhaps he enjoys it. God knows, I've been enough of a challenge for him. From what I've been able to learn about the man, he has no conscience. He's a nobody," he said bitterly. The next words were smothered, as though her father had buried his face in his hands. "...something I didn't tell you...something you should know... McFarland wants our Beauty."

"What?" David shouted.

Judy bolted upright, her back rigid. It was apparent that they weren't aware she was in the other room.

"I heard from his business manager today. Avery Anderson spoke for McFarland and stated that either we come up with the amount of the loan plus the accumulated interest or send Judy to St. Steven's."

"St. Steven's?"

"That's the name of his private island."

"What does he want with...her?"

"Only God knows." The suffering in her father's voice ripped at Judy's heart. "He swears he won't abuse her in any way, and that she'll have free run of the island, but..."

"Oh, Dad." David must have slumped into a chair. "So you had to decide between a business that's been in our family for four generations and your daughter?"

"Those were exactly my choices."

"What...did you tell him?"

"You don't want to hear what I said to that man."

"No," David whispered, "I don't suppose I do."

"We have no option," Charles Lovin said through gritted teeth. "McFarland wins. I won't have Judy subjected to that beast." Despair weighed down his words.

Numb, her whole body trembling, Judy leaned back in the chair. Lovingly she ran her hand over the soft brown leather. This chair, like so much of what they owned, had been part of a heritage that had been in their family for generations. Soon it would all be lost to them.

And only she could prevent it from happening.

Two

Judy's hand tightened around the suitcase handle as she stood on the deserted dock. The powerboat that had brought her to St. Steven's roared away behind her. She refused to look back, afraid that if she did, her courage would abandon her.

The island was a tropical paradise—blue skies, soft breezes, pristine beaches and crystal clear water. Huge palm trees bordered the beach, swaying gently. The scent of magnolias and orchids wafted invitingly toward her.

A tall man Judy guessed to be in his late forties approached her. He wore a crisp black suit that revealed the width of his muscular shoulders. His steps made deep indentations in the wet sand.

She'd only brought one suitcase, packing light with the prayer that her stay would be a brief one. The single piece of luggage now felt ten times heavier than when she'd left New York that morning.

Her father had driven her to the airport, where McFarland's private jet was waiting to take her to a secluded airstrip. From there, she was told, it would be a short boat trip to the island. Tears had glistened in her father's faded blue eyes. He'd hardly spoken and when the moment came for Judy to leave, he'd hugged her so tightly she hadn't been able to breathe.

"Goodbye, Judy." His whispered words had been strangled by emotion. "If he hurts you…"

"He won't," she assured him. "I'll be fine—and back home so soon you won't even know I've been gone."

A pinched look had come over his face and he'd whispered, "I'll know. Every minute you're away, I'll know."

Leaving her family hadn't been easy for Judy, especially when she felt as though she was being ripped from their arms.

After innocently eavesdropping on her father and David's conversation, Judy had openly confronted them. She would go to McFarland and they could do nothing to stop her. Her stubborn determination had stunned them both. But she'd refused to hear their arguments and had simply gone about packing. Within twenty-four hours she was on her way to St. Steven's.

She was here now, outwardly calm and mentally prepared to do whatever she must.

"Ms. Lovin?" the man asked politely, meeting her at the end of the pier.

Judy nodded, momentarily unable to find her voice.

"We've been expecting you." He reached for her suitcase, taking it from her hand. "Come with me, please."

Judy followed the stranger. He led her into the nearby trees to a cart that reminded her of something she'd seen on the golf course. Only this one was far more powerful and surged ahead at the turn of a key.

When they came upon the house, Judy's breath was trapped in her lungs. It was the most magnificent place she'd ever seen. Built on the edge of a cliff, it was nestled in foliage and adorned with pillars and balconies. Tropical vines climbed the exterior walls, twisting upward.

"This way," the man said, standing on the walkway that led into the grand house.

Judy climbed out of the cart and followed him through the massive doors. In the marble entryway she was met by a short, thin man. She identified him immediately as McFarland's assistant, the man she'd heard her father mention. He looked like an Avery, she thought—efficient, intelligent...bookish.

"Ms. Lovin," he greeted her with an embarrassed smile. "I trust your journey was a pleasant one."

"Most pleasant." She returned his smile, although her knees felt like tapioca pudding. "You must be Mr. Anderson."

If he was surprised that she knew his name, he didn't reveal it. "Your rooms are ready if you'd like to freshen up before dinner."

"Please."

He rang a bell and a maid appeared as though by magic. The woman's gaze didn't meet Judy's as she silently escorted her up the stairs. The maid held open a pair of double doors, and Judy walked into a parlorlike room complete with fireplace, television, bookshelves and two sofas. Off the parlor was a bedroom so lovely Judy stared in amazement at the elegant pastel colors. The view of the ocean from the balcony was magnificent. She stood at the railing, the wind whipping her hair about her face, and saw a swimming pool and a tennis court. To her far right, she located another building that she assumed must be the stables. Her heart gladdened. She'd been riding almost from the time she could walk and loved horses. Her cage was indeed a gilded one.

"Dinner will be in fifteen minutes," the maid informed her.

"Thank you," Judy responded. She squared her shoulders and her heart pounded faster. Soon she'd be meeting the infamous McFarland—the man her father called the Beast.

But Judy was wrong. When she descended the stairs, armed with questions to which she was determined to find answers, she learned to her dismay that she'd be dining alone.

Mr. Anderson lived in a small house on the island and had departed for the day. McFarland had sent his regrets, but business prevailed. His brief note indicated that he was looking forward to meeting her in the morning.

The dining-room table was set for eight with a service of the finest bone china. The butler seated Judy at one end. The servants brought in course after course, their footsteps echoing in the silent room. Each course was delectable, but Judy ate little. Afterward, she returned to her room.

Her sleep was fitful as questions interrupted her dreams. She wondered if McFarland was playing some kind of psychological game meant to intimidate her. If he was, then she'd fallen an unwilling victim to it. She didn't know much about John McFarland. He was rarely if ever seen in public and she'd been unable to locate any photos of him on any Internet site. Her father insisted he was arrogant, impudent, insolent, unorthodox and perhaps the worst insult—beastly.

What a strange place this was, she thought tiredly, staring up at the darkened ceiling. The house was built in a paradise of sun and sea and yet a chill pervaded her bones.

By six, she couldn't bear to stay in bed any longer.

Throwing back the covers, she rose and decided to head for the stables. She yearned to ride, to exorcise the fears that plagued her.

The house was like a tomb—silent, dark, somber—as Judy crept down the stairs. The front door opened easily and she slipped outside. The sun was rising, cloaking the island in golden threads of light.

At a noise behind her she twisted around. A stranger on horseback was approaching her slowly. Even from a distance, Judy noticed that he sat tall and straight in the saddle. He wore a cowboy hat pulled low over his eyes.

She hesitated. No doubt he was a security guard and from the way he regarded her, he was either looking for trouble or expecting it.

"Good morning," she called out tentatively.

He touched the brim of his hat in greeting. "Is there a problem?" His voice was deep and resonant.

"A…problem? No, of course not."

His finely shaped mouth curved with amusement as he studied her from head to foot.

Not knowing what else to do, Judy returned his look, staring into those compelling blue eyes. She thought for a moment that he was silently laughing at her and she clenched her fists. Hot color climbed up her neck, invading her cheeks. "It's a beautiful morning."

"Were you thinking of going for a walk?" He shifted his weight in the saddle and at the sound of creaking leather, Judy realized that he was dismounting. He took a step toward her.

Before she could stop herself, Judy stepped back in retreat. "No… I was going to the stables. McFarland said I could go anyplace I wanted on the island and… I thought

I'd have someone choose a horse for me. Of course, I could saddle it myself."

Bold blue eyes looked straight into hers. "I frighten you?"

"No...that's ridiculous." She felt like a stuttering fool. He didn't frighten her as much as he enthralled her. He radiated a dark energy with his brooding eyes and tall, lean build.

He grinned at her response and the movement crinkled the lines around his eyes and creased his bronze cheeks. "Relax, I'm not going to pounce on you."

She stiffened. "I didn't think you would." Surely the help respected McFarland's guests—if she could call herself that.

"I'll walk you to the stables." He reached for the reins and the huge black horse followed obediently behind.

"Have you been on the island long?" she managed shakily, and attempted to smile.

"Three years."

She nodded, clasping her hands tightly in front of her. This was the first person she'd had the opportunity to speak with and she wanted to find out as much as she could about McFarland before actually meeting him. In her mind she'd conjured up several pictures, none of them pleasant. She knew he had to be an unhappy, lonely man. Old, decrepit, cantankerous. "What's he like?"

"Who?"

"McFarland."

A muscle worked in his lean jaw and when he looked at her again, his eyes were dark and enigmatic. "Some say he's a man without a heart."

Judy grinned and lowered her own eyes to the ground. "My father calls him the Beast."

"The Beast." He seemed to find that amusing. "Some

claim there's no compassion in him. Others say he has no conscience."

She glanced at the man's lathered, dusty horse and then at him. Pride showed in the tilt of his strong chin and the set of his shoulders. Thoughtfully, she shook her head. "No," she said slowly, "I don't agree with that."

"You don't?"

"No," she repeated confidently. "He appreciates beauty too much. And if he didn't have a conscience he would've—" She realized she was saying much more than she should to one of McFarland's employees. McFarland could have ruined her father ten times over, but hadn't. He might not have a heart of gold, but he wasn't without conscience. Nor was he cruel.

"What do *you* think he's like? I take it you haven't met the man."

"I'm not sure how I feel about him. As you say, we haven't met, but from what I've seen, I'd guess there's precious little joy in his life."

The man laughed outright. "Look around you," he said. "He's said to be one of the richest men in the world. How could any man have so much and not be happy?"

"Joy comes from within," she explained. "There's too much bitterness in him. He obviously hasn't experienced true contentment."

"And who are you? A psychiatrist?"

It was Judy's turn to laugh; she'd grown more at ease with this dark stranger. "No. I formed my opinions before I came to the island."

"Wait until you meet him, then. You may be pleasantly surprised."

"Perhaps." But Judy doubted it.

They arrived at the stables and were met by a burly older man, who ambled out.

"Good morning, Sam."

"Morning," the other man grumbled, eyeing Judy curiously.

"Saddle Princess for Ms. Lovin and see to it that Midnight gets extra oats. He deserves it after the ride I gave him this morning."

Judy turned abruptly. "How did you know my name?"

He ignored her, but his eyes softened slightly at her questioning look. "Tomorrow morning, saddle both horses at five-thirty. Ms. Lovin and I will be riding together."

"Consider it done, Mr. McFarland."

Embarrassment washed over Judy. She dared not look at him.

"I'll see you at lunch, Ms. Lovin."

It was all she could do to nod.

The morning passed with surprising speed. Judy hadn't ridden in months and her body was unaccustomed to the rigors of the saddle. She hadn't gone far, preferring to investigate the island another day. A hot breakfast awaited her after she'd showered and she ate eagerly. When she'd finished, she had written her father a long letter. She'd been told that no direct contact—like phone calls or e-mail messages—would be allowed; letters were permitted, however, and would be mailed for her. Once she'd completed and addressed the letter, she lay back on the velvet sofa and closed her eyes, listening to music. The balcony doors were open and the fresh sea air swirled around her.

Someone knocked politely at her door. A maid had been sent to inform Judy that lunch would be served in ten minutes.

Experiencing dread and excitement at once, Judy stood, repaired the damage to her hair and makeup and slowly descended the stairs. She paused at the bottom, gathered her resolve and forced a smile, wondering how long it would last. She didn't expect to maintain the cheerful facade, but it was important to give McFarland the impression that she'd been unruffled by their earlier encounter. Her palms were already damp in anticipation of the second meeting with the man who ruled an empire from this island.

He stood when she entered the dining room.

"I trust your morning was satisfactory," he said.

Boldly, Judy met his probing gaze. "Why am I here?" She hadn't meant to immediately hurl questions at him, but his discerning look had unnerved her.

"I believe it's to eat lunch. Please sit down, Ms. Lovin. I, for one, am hungry, and our meal will be served as soon as you're comfortable."

The butler held out a mahogany chair at the end of the table, where she'd eaten the night before. With rebellion boiling in her blood, Judy sat on the brocade cushion.

A bowl of consommé was set in front of her. When Judy lifted her spoon, she discovered that her hand was trembling and she tightened her grip.

"How long do you plan to keep me here?" she asked. Six place settings separated them; the distance could've been far greater for all the notice McFarland gave her.

"You'll be free to go shortly," he announced between courses, having waited a full five minutes before responding.

"I can leave?" she said in astonishment. "When?"

"Soon." He gauged her expression grimly. "Are you so miserable?"

"No," she admitted, smoothing the linen napkin across her lap. "The island is lovely."

"Good." His eyes grew gentle.

"Whose decision was it for you to come?" he asked unexpectedly.

"Mine."

He nodded and seemed to approve. "I imagine that your father and brother were opposed to your willingness to sacrifice yourself." He said this with more than a hint of sarcasm.

"Adamantly. I probably never would've been told of your...ultimatum, but I accidentally overheard them discussing it."

"You were wise to come."

"How's that?"

"I wouldn't have hesitated to call in the loan."

"I don't doubt that for a second," she said, disliking him. Her fingers gripped the napkin in her lap, but that was the only outward sign of anger that she allowed herself.

His grin lacked humor. "If you'd refused, you would've been burdened with a terrible guilt. In time, your peace and happiness would have been affected."

The butler took away her untouched salad and served the main course. Judy stared down at the thin slices of roast beef, smothered in gravy and mushrooms, and knew she wouldn't be able to eat.

"Have you always been this dictatorial?" Judy demanded.

"Always." He carefully sliced his meat.

She thought of the class of four-year-olds she'd left behind. "You must have been a difficult child." His teen years didn't bear contemplating.

Slowly, deliberately, McFarland lowered his knife and fork to the table. His eyes were sad. "I was never a child."

Princess was saddled and ready for her early the following morning. Judy patted the horse's nose and produced a carrot from the hip pocket of her jeans.

"At great personal danger, I sneaked into the kitchen and got you this," she whispered, running her hand down the mare's brown face. "Now, don't you dare tell Sam, or he'll be mad at me." Judy had quickly realized that Sam ruled the stables like his own castle and she could well be stepping on the older man's toes.

"Do you have something for me, as well?" The deep male voice spoke from behind her.

Judy whirled around to see McFarland. "No," she said, shaking her head. "I hope you don't mind..." She eyed the rapidly disappearing carrot.

He was dressed in black this morning, his expression brooding. Once again his hat brim shadowed his face. His mood seemed as dark and dangerous as his clothes. "You needn't worry about stealing vegetables."

Without another word, he mounted his horse with supple ease. He hesitated long enough to reach for the reins and sent Judy a look that said she was welcome to join him or go her own way.

Quickly, Judy placed her foot in the stirrup and swung onto Princess's back, grabbed the reins and cantered after him.

McFarland rode at an unrelenting gallop, leading her into the jungle. The footpath was narrow and steep. Birds cawed angrily and flew out of their way, their wings beating against the underbrush. Leaves and branches slapped at Judy's face; mud spattered her boots and jeans. Still he didn't lessen his furious pace. It took all of Judy's skill just to keep up with him. She barely managed. By the time he slowed, she was winded and her muscles ached. He directed Midnight onto the beach and Judy followed gratefully, allowing Princess to trot along the sandy shoreline.

Judy stared at him. Panting, she was too breathless to speak coherently. "Good—grief, McFarland—do you always tear—through the jungle like that?"

"No." He didn't look at her. "I wanted to see how well you ride."

"And?"

"Admirably well." He grinned, and his eyes sparkled with humor. Judy found herself involuntarily returning his smile.

"Next time," she said between gasps, "*I* choose the route." Dark mud dotted her clothes and face. Her hair fell in wet tendrils around her cheeks and she felt as though they'd galloped through a swamp.

He, on the other hand, had hardly splattered his shiny boots.

"Tell me about Judy Lovin," he demanded unexpectedly as they trotted side by side.

"On one condition. I want you to answer something for me."

"One question?"

"Only one," she promised, raising her right hand as though swearing an oath.

"All right."

"What do you want to know?"

"Details."

She nodded curtly. "I weighed just under seven pounds when I was born—"

"Perhaps current information would be more appropriate," he cut in.

Judy threw back her head and laughed. "Fine. I'm twenty-six—"

"That old?"

She glowered at him. "How am I supposed to tell you anything if you keep interrupting?"

"Go on."

"Thank you," she muttered sarcastically. "Let me see—I suppose you want the vitals. I'm five-five, which is short, I know, and I weigh about… No." She shook her head. "I don't think that's information a woman should share with a man."

He chuckled and Judy drew back on the reins, surprised at the deep rich sound. She suspected he didn't often give in to the urge.

He sent her an odd, half-accusing look. "Is something wrong?"

"No," she responded, feeling self-conscious. He really should laugh more often, she thought. He looked young and carefree and less—she couldn't find the word—*driven,* she decided.

"What about men?"

"Men?"

"As in beaux, boyfriends, dates, male companionship—that kind of thing."

"I date frequently." Although that was a slight misrepresentation of the truth…

"Anyone special?"

"No—unless you consider Bobby. He's four and could steal my heart with a pout." She stopped Princess, swung her leg over the horse's back and slowly lowered her feet to the ground.

McFarland dismounted, as well.

"My turn."

He shrugged. "Fire away."

"May I call you by your name?" She found it ridiculous that a man would be called simply McFarland.

"My name? You mean my first name?"

"Yes."

He hesitated long enough for her to become uneasy. Then he nodded.

"Thank you." She dropped her gaze to her mud-coated boots. "John," she whispered.

"Well?" he prompted. "Do you think it suits me?"

"It does," she told him.

"I'm glad to hear it," he said, and she wasn't sure whether he was mocking her. Then she decided it didn't matter if he was.

"You really aren't a beast, are you?" she murmured.

He frowned at that and brushed a wet strand of hair from her cheek. His fingers trailed across her face, causing her stomach to lurch at the unexpected contact.

"But you, my dear, are a Beauty."

Judy went cold. "How did you know my father called me that?"

"I know everything about you. Right down to that wimp you thought you were in love with a couple of years back. What was his name again? Richard. Yes, Richard. I'm also aware that you've rarely dated since—disillusionment, I suppose."

Judy felt the blood drain from her face.

"I know you fancy yourself a savior to that group of four-year-olds. How noble of you to squander yourself on their behalf, but I doubt they appreciate it." His blue eyes were as cold as glacial ice.

Judy thought she might be sick.

He waited, his expression filled with grim amusement. "What, no comment?"

"None." She threw the reins over Princess's head. "Thank you for the ride, John. It was quite exhilarating." Her chin held at a proud angle, she mounted and silently rode away, her back rigid.

McFarland watched her go and slammed his boot viciously against the sand. He didn't know what had made him speak to her like that. He'd known from the moment he'd seen her picture that she was like no other woman he'd ever encountered. Another woman would have thrown angry words at him for the unprovoked attack. Judy hadn't. She'd revealed courage and grace, a rare combination. McFarland didn't think he'd seen the two qualities exemplified so beautifully in any one woman. Most were interested in his wealth and power.

He didn't like the feelings Judy Lovin aroused in him. Studying her picture was one thing, but being close to her, feeling the energy she exuded, watching her overcome her natural reserve, had all greatly affected him.

Judy was good—too good for him. As other people said, he chewed up little girls like her and spit them out. He didn't want to see that happen to Judy.

What an odd position to be in, he mused darkly. He had to protect her from himself.

Three

Princess's hind feet kicked up sand as Judy trotted her along the beach. Her thoughts were in turmoil. What a strange, complex man John McFarland was. His eyes had been gentle and kind, almost laughing, when he'd asked her to tell him about herself, and yet he'd obviously known everything there was to know. Her cheeks burned with humiliation that he'd discovered what a fool she'd made of herself over Richard. She'd been so trusting, so guileless with her affection and her heart—so agonizingly stupid to have fallen in love with a married man. The pain of Richard's deception no longer hurt Judy, but her own flagrant stupidity continued to embarrass her.

Judy was so caught up in her memories that she didn't notice the children at first. Their laughter drifted on the cool morning air and she drew in her reins. As always, the mare responded instantly to Judy's signal.

"Princess, look," she said excitedly. "Children." They were playing a game of hide-and-seek, darting in and out of the jungle and rushing to the water's edge. Judy counted seven children between the ages of eight and twelve, from what she could guess.

They didn't seem to notice her, which was just as well since she didn't want to disturb their game. The smallest, a boy, had apparently been chosen as "it" and the others scattered, smothering their laughter as they ran across the sand.

Judy swung out of the saddle.

Her action must have drawn their attention because the laughter stopped abruptly. She turned around to find all the youngsters running to hide. Only the one small boy remained.

Judy smiled. "Good morning," she said cautiously, trying not to frighten him.

He was silent, his deep brown eyes serious and intense.

Digging in the pocket of her jodhpurs, Judy pulled out two sugar cubes. The first she fed to Princess. The second she held out to the boy.

He eyed it for a long time before stepping forward and grabbing it from her hand. Quickly, he jumped away from her. Holding it in his own palm, he carefully approached the horse. When Princess lowered her sleek head and ate the cube from his hand, he looked up and grinned broadly at Judy.

"She's very gentle," Judy said softly. "Would you like to sit in the saddle?"

He nodded enthusiastically and Judy helped him mount.

Astride Princess, the boy placed both hands on the saddle and sat up straight, as though he were a king surveying his kingdom. Gradually, the other children came out from their hiding places among the trees.

"Good morning," Judy greeted each one. "My name is Judy."

"Peter."

"Jimmy."

"Philippe."

"Elizabeth."

"Margaret."

They all rushed toward her, eager to be her friend and perhaps get the chance to sit on her beautiful horse.

Judy threw up her hands and laughed. "One at a time, or I'll never be able to remember." She laid her hand on the slim shoulder of one of the younger girls. "I'm pleased to make your acquaintance." She was rewarded with a toothless smile.

From a ridge high above the beach, McFarland looked down on the scene below, a silent witness to Judy's considerable charm. She was a natural with children, and although he shouldn't be surprised at the way they gravitated toward her, he was. More often than he could count, he'd come upon the island children playing in the surf or along the beach. Usually he saw little more than a fleeting glimpse of one or two running away as though they were afraid of him.

Until he'd watched Judy enchant these children, McFarland hadn't given a second thought to the few families who made this island their home. He allowed them to remain on St. Steven's, not for any humanitarian reason, but simply because his feeling toward them was one of indifference. They could stay or leave as they wished.

Unfortunately, he couldn't say the same about Judy Lovin. The sound of her laughter swirled around him. As he watched her now with these children, an unwilling smile touched his mouth. He, too, was a victim of the enchantment she'd brought to his island.

And he didn't like it, not one damn bit.

Pulling back sharply on Midnight's reins, McFarland

turned the horse and rode toward the other side of the island as if the fires of hell were licking at their heels.

By the time Judy returned to the house, McFarland had
already eaten breakfast and sequestered himself in his office. Judy wasn't disappointed. She'd purposely stayed away
in an effort to avoid clashing with him a second time that
morning. The man puzzled her and she didn't know how
to react to him.

Feeling increasingly unsettled as morning turned to mid-
day, she ordered a light lunch and ate in her room. In the
afternoon, she swam in the Olympic-size pool, forcing herself to swim lap after lap as she worked out her confusion
and frustration. She had no clue as to why McFarland had
sent for her other than to torment her family, and she hated
to think he'd purposely do that. If she'd understood him
better, she might be able to discern his motives.

Breathless from the workout, Judy climbed out of the
pool and reached for her towel, burying her face in its plush
thickness. As she drew it over her arms and legs, goose
bumps prickled her skin and she realized she was being
watched. A chill shivered up her spine and she paused to
glance around. She could see no one, but the feeling persisted and she hurriedly gathered her things.

In her own rooms, Judy paced, uncertain and unsettled.
Eventually she sat down at the large desk and wrote another
long, chatty letter to her father and brother. The hallway
was silent when she came out of her room. She hesitated
only a moment before making her way downstairs and into
the wing of the house from where she suspected McFarland ruled his empire.

"Ms. Lovin?"

Avery Anderson's voice stopped her short when she

turned a corner and happened upon a large foyer. "Hello," she said with feigned brightness. "I apologize if I'm intruding."

Avery stood, his hands on the top of his desk as he leaned forward. "It's no intrusion," he said, obviously ill at ease at her unexpected appearance.

Judy hated to fluster him. "I have some letters I'd like to mail."

"Of course."

Judy raised questioning eyes to his. "They're to my family?" She made the statement a question, asking if there'd be any objection. "Do you have regular mail delivery to and from the island?"

"All correspondence is handled by courier."

"Then there's no problem with writing my father?"

"None whatsoever."

Judy hated to be suspicious, but Avery didn't sound all that confident, and it would be easy for him to deceive her.

"I'll see to it personally if that will reassure you, Ms. Lovin." McFarland's voice behind her was brisk and businesslike.

Judy blushed painfully as she faced him. "I'd appreciate th-that," she said, stammering slightly. The virility of his smile made her catch her breath. That morning, when they were out riding, he'd been sneering at her and now she could feel her pulse react to a simple lift of his mouth.

"Thank you, John," she said softly.

"John?" Avery Anderson echoed, perplexed, but his voice sounded as though it had come from another room—another world.

"Would you care to see my office?" McFarland asked, but the sparkle in his eyes made Judy wonder if he was taunting her.

"I don't want to interrupt your day." Already she was retreating from him, taking small, even steps as she backed away from Avery Anderson's desk. "Perhaps another time."

"As you wish." His eyes grew perceptibly gentler at her bemused look. "We'll talk tonight, during dinner."

The words were as much a command as an invitation. It was understood that she'd show up in the dining room when called.

Judy nodded. "At dinner."

By the time she closed the doors to her suite, her heart was thumping wildly. She attempted to tell herself she feared John McFarland, but that wasn't entirely true—the man was an enigma. But instead of gauging her responses by his mood, Judy decided she could only be herself.

She dressed for dinner in a black skirt and a blouse that had been favorites of her father's. Charles had said the pink and maroon stripes enhanced the brown of her eyes, reminding him of her mother.

At the top of the stairs, Judy placed her hand on the railing, then paused. She was excited about this dinner, yet apprehensive. Her stomach rebelled at the thought of food, but she yearned to know this man—"the Beast." Exactly why he'd brought her to St. Steven's had yet to be explained. She had a right to know; she *needed* to know. Surely that wasn't too much to ask.

He was standing by the fireplace, sipping wine, when she entered the dining room. Once again she was struck by his virility. He, too, had dressed formally, in a pinstriped suit that revealed broad, muscular shoulders and narrow hips.

"Good evening, Judy."

She smiled and noted that he'd used her given name for the first time. Some of the tension drained out of her.

"John."

"Would you care for a glass of wine before dinner?"

"Please." The inside of her mouth felt as though it was stuffed with cotton. The wine would help…or it might drown whatever wit she still possessed. As he approached her with a goblet, Judy was unsure whether she should take it. His blue eyes burned into her, and, without further thought, Judy accepted the wine.

"Why do you hate my father?" she asked, the words slipping from her mouth as she met his gaze.

"On the contrary, I hold him in high regard."

Judy's eyes widened with disbelief.

"Charles Lovin has more grit than twenty men half his age."

"You mean because he's managed to hold you off against impossible odds?"

"Not so impossible," McFarland countered, before taking a sip of wine. "I did allow him a means of escape."

Judy considered his statement, momentarily baffled by his reasoning. "You wanted me on the island," she said.

"Yes, you."

It wasn't as though he desired her company. In the two days since her arrival, he'd barely spoken to her; indeed, he seemed to avoid doing so.

"But why? What possible good am I to you?"

"None at all. I require no one." A hardness descended over his features, and his eyes narrowed, his expression shutting her out. His face showed his arrogance—and his pride. Judy frowned, aching to soothe the hurt, erase it from his life. She longed to understand what made him the way he was. Somehow, somewhere, a cruel and heartless person had mortally wounded John McFarland's spirit. From the torment in his eyes, she knew the scars hadn't healed.

"Am I to be your slave?" she asked, without anger, her voice even.

"No."

"Y-your pet?"

"Don't be ridiculous!" he shouted. "You're free to do as you wish."

"Can I leave?"

He gave a curt laugh and took another sip of his wine. "You're here to amuse me."

"For how long?"

He shrugged. "Until you cease doing so."

Muted footsteps drew Judy's attention to the manservant who stood just inside the dining room. He nodded once in McFarland's direction.

"I believe our dinner is ready. Chicken Béarnaise." He moved to her end of the table and held out her chair. Judy was grateful for the opportunity to sit down; her legs felt wobbly. No man had ever affected her the way John did. But he claimed he needed no one, and by all outward appearances he was right.

Once she was seated, John took the chair at the opposite end of the table.

Judy spread out the linen napkin on her lap. "I came across some children today," she said after several tense minutes.

"There are a number of families who live on the island."

"The kids were friendly. At first I wasn't sure they spoke English, but then I realized that they speak it so fast it sounds like a foreign language."

John smiled at that. "I haven't had the opportunity to talk to them myself, but I'll remember that when I do."

"They asked about you."

"The children?"

"Yes, they call you the Dark Prince."

A brief smile flickered across his face. "They usually avoid me."

"I know."

Humor flashed in his eyes as he studied her. Once again, she'd surprised him. He'd expected her to be outraged, spitting angry tirades at him, ruining his meal. Instead, she sat at his table with the subtle grace of royalty when he knew she must be dying inside at his callousness.

"If they call me the Dark Prince, did they give *you* a name?"

Judy shifted her gaze. "I asked them to call me Judy."

"But they didn't."

"No." Color invaded her face, and she obviously had difficulty swallowing.

"Tell me what they decided to call you."

"I—I'd prefer not to."

"Finding out would be a simple matter," he said in low, unthreatening tones.

Judy found little amusement in her predicament. "They called me 'the Dark Prince's woman.' I tried to explain that I was only a friend, but it didn't seem to do any good. This probably embarrasses you, but I couldn't seem to change their minds."

McFarland felt the laughter leave his face. He'd meant to tease her, but she was concerned that these people, these strangers who occupied his land, had offended him by suggesting she was his woman. He felt as though someone had given him a swift kick in the behind. He raised his eyes, studying her to be sure she wasn't taunting him, and knew in his heart that it wasn't in her to insult man or beast. And he was both.

Their meal arrived, but McFarland had little appetite.

"Do you like the island?" he asked, wanting to hear her speak again. The sound of her voice was soothing to him.

"It's lovely."

"If there's anything you wish, you need only ask."

"There's nothing." Judy saw that his tone, his look, everything about him, had changed. His mocking arrogance had vanished; no longer did he look as though he meant to admonish her for some imagined wrong, or punish her for being her father's daughter. She found it impossible to eat.

"Do you dislike the solitude?"

She searched his face, wondering why he cared. "It's not Manhattan, but that's fine. To be honest, I needed a vacation and this is as close to paradise as I'm likely to find."

"You've had a nap."

She nodded.

"You're to have complete run of the house and island."

"Thank you, John," she said humbly, "you've been very kind."

Kind? He'd been kind to force her into staying here? Kind to have blackmailed her into leaving everything familiar in her life? He stared at her, not understanding how she could even suggest such a thing. Abruptly, he pushed aside his plate and stood. "If you'll excuse me, I have some business matters that require my attention."

"Of course."

He stormed out of the room as if she'd offended him. For a full minute, Judy sat frozen, uncertain of what had happened between them. He had seemed to want her company, then despised it.

She, too, had no desire to finish her meal, and feeling at odds with herself, she stood. It was still early, and she had no intention of returning to her rooms. John had said she could freely explore the house and she'd barely seen half of it.

Judy never made it beyond the center hall. The doors were what had attracted her most. The huge mahogany panels stretched from the ceiling to the polished floor, reminding her of ancient castles. Unable to resist, she turned both handles, pushed open the massive doors and entered the dimly lit room.

She paused just inside, and sighed with pure pleasure. It was a library, elegantly decorated with comfortable leather chairs, two desks and a variety of tables and lamps. Every wall was filled with books. Judy couldn't have been more pleased if she'd inadvertently stumbled upon a treasure. A flip of the switch bathed the room in light and she hurried forward to investigate.

An hour later, when the clock chimed, Judy was astonished to realize how long she'd been there. Reverently, she folded back the pages of a first edition of Charles Dickens's *A Christmas Carol*. Each book she saw produced a feeling of awe and respect. Mingled with the classics were volumes of modern literature; one entire wall was dedicated to nonfiction.

With such a wide variety to choose from, Judy finally selected a science fiction novel. She sat in a high-backed leather chair and read for an hour before slipping off her shoes and tucking her feet beneath her. Suddenly thirsty, she went to the meticulous kitchen and made herself a cup of tea. Carrying it into the library, Judy returned to her chair.

McFarland found her there after midnight, sleeping contentedly in the chair, her legs curled under her. Her head was nestled against the upholstery, with one arm carelessly draped over her face. The other dangled limply at her side so that the tips of her fingers almost touched the Persian carpet. Transfixed, he stood there for a moment studying her, unable to look away.

A tender feeling weakened him, and he sat in the chair opposite hers. For a long time, he was content to do nothing but watch her sleep. He wondered at the wealth of emotion she aroused in him. He knew it wasn't love—not even close. He felt protective toward her and yearned to take away the troubles that plagued this young woman's life. Surprisingly, he wanted her to be happy.

She looked as innocent as a child, but was very much a woman. She was gentle and kind, honorable without being lofty. Generous without being a pushover. He'd never known a woman like her, and was shocked to find himself consumed with fear. He could hurt Judy Lovin, hurt her beyond anything she'd known in her life, hurt her more than Richard, who'd stolen her trust and wounded her heart with his greed.

McFarland knew she'd fall in love with him at the slightest encouragement. His conjecture wasn't based on ego, but on the knowledge that Judy, by nature, was giving and loving. If he were to ask, she would deny him nothing. His own power frightened him, but that wasn't what stopped him. He wasn't any knight in shining armor. No, the simple truth was that the thought of Judy's control over him was more terrifying than any pleasure he'd get from obtaining her love.

He considered waking her and it seemed only natural to lean over and kiss her. Her lips would be soft under his. He pictured her raising her arms and hugging his neck. She would smile at him and they'd stare at each other. She'd blush in that way she had that made her all the more beautiful, and she'd lower her thick lashes as she struggled to hide her feelings from him.

Forcefully, McFarland's fingers clenched the arm of the leather chair. He'd have a maid wake Judy and see her to her room.

She was just a woman, he reminded himself, and no doubt there were a million others like her. Who needed Judy Lovin? Not him.

"Midnight," Judy called, standing on the bottom rung of the corral fence. "If you want it, you'll have to come to me." She held out the carrot to the prancing black horse, who snorted and pawed the ground.

"It's yours for the taking," she said soothingly. Winning the trust of the sleek, black horse had become paramount in the four days that had passed since the night she'd fallen asleep in the library. John had been avoiding her; Judy was convinced of that. The only times they were together were at dinner, and he was always preoccupied with business, avoiding conversation and generally ignoring her.

Judy wasn't offended as much as bewildered. At any moment, she half expected to receive word that he no longer required her presence on St. Steven's, or some other stiffly worded decree. She'd be happy to leave, although she'd miss the children, who had fast become her friends. She'd been on the island a week now and surely that was enough time to serve whatever purpose he had in mind.

But she *would* miss the children. She met them daily now on the beach. They brought her small, homemade gifts— a flowerpot and a hat both woven from palm leaves, cleverly done. A huge conch shell and a hundred smaller ones had been given to her with great ceremony. In return she told them stories, laughed at their antics and played their

games. She met their mothers and visited their homes.
She would miss them, but she wouldn't forget them.

"Midnight," she coaxed again. "I know you want this
carrot." If John wouldn't allow her to be his friend, then
she'd work on the horse. Judy had noticed several similarities between the two; both were angry, arrogant, proud.

The horse remained in the farthest corner of the corral,
as determined to ignore her as John seemed to be.

"I suppose all the women tell you how good-looking you
are?" she said with a laugh. "But I'm not going to say that.
You're much too conceited already."

Midnight bowed his powerful head and snorted.

"I thought that would get you." Jumping down from the
fence, Judy approached the gate. "You're really going to
make me come to you, aren't you?"

The stallion pranced around the yard, his tail arched.

"You devil," Judy said with a loud sigh. "All this time together and you're more stubborn now than when I started."

The horse continued to ignore her.

"What if I told you I had a handful of sugar cubes in my
pocket?" She patted her hip. "Sweet, sweet sugar cubes that
will melt in your mouth." As she spoke, she released the
clasp to the gate and let herself into the corral.

Midnight paused and stared at her, throwing his head
back and forth. "You'll have to come closer, though," she
said softly.

His hoof dug at the hard dirt.

"Honestly, horse, you're more stubborn than your master."

She took three steps toward the huge black stallion, who
paused to study her. He jerked his neck, tossing his thick mane.

With one hand on her hip, Judy shook her head. "You
don't fool me one bit."

Someone walked up behind her, but Judy paid no attention, suspecting it was Sam. He was bound to be angry with her. He'd told her repeatedly not to go inside the corral, but since Midnight refused to come to her, she'd decided she had no choice.

"Don't move." John's steel-edged words cut through her. "If you value your life, don't move."

Four

Judy went still, her heart pounding wildly. She wanted to turn and assure John that Midnight wouldn't hurt her. She longed to tell him she'd been working for days, gaining the stallion's trust. All her life she'd had a way with animals and children. Her father claimed she could make a wounded bear her friend. Midnight had a fiery nature; it was what made him such a magnificent horse. He'd been a challenge, but she believed he'd never purposely injure her. But Judy said none of these things. She couldn't. John's voice had been so cold, so cutting, that she dared not defy him.

The clicking sound behind her told Judy that Midnight's master had entered the corral. He walked past her and his clipped, even stride revealed his fierce anger. He didn't even glance at her and as she noticed the hard look in his eyes, she was glad.

Midnight pranced around the corral, his satiny black head held high, his tail arched, his hooves kicking up loose dirt.

McFarland gave one shrill whistle, to which the stallion responded without delay. Midnight cocked his head and galloped past Judy to his master's side, coming to an abrupt halt. He lowered his head. With one smooth movement, McFarland gripped the horse's mane and swung onto his back. Midnight protested violently and reared, kicking his powerful front legs.

Judy sucked in her breath, afraid that McFarland wouldn't have time to gain control of the animal. She was wrong; when the horse planted his feet on the ground, John was in charge.

"Get out."

The words were sharp and he didn't so much as look at her, but then he didn't need to. She could feel his contempt and his anger. Judy did as he said.

McFarland circled the paddock a few times before swinging off the stallion's back and joining her at the corral gate.

"You stupid idiot," he hissed. He grabbed her by the shoulders and gave her one vicious jerk. "You could've been killed!"

When he released her, Judy stumbled backward. Her eyes were wide with fear. In all her life no one had ever spoken to her in such a menacing tone. No one had dared raise a hand to her. Now she faced the wounded bear, and was forced to admit that Charles Lovin had been right— John McFarland was a beast no woman could tame.

"Who let you inside the corral?"

Her throat had thickened, making speech impossible. Even if she'd been able to answer him, she wouldn't have. Sam had no idea she'd ever been near Midnight.

"Sam!" McFarland barked the stableman's name.

The older man rushed out of the barn, limping. His face was red and a sheen of perspiration had broken out on his forehead.

McFarland attacked him with a barrage of swear words. He ended by ordering the man to pack his bags.

Sam went pale.

"No," Judy cried.

McFarland turned on her, his eyes as cutting as his words. He stood no more than a foot from her, bearing down on her as he shouted, using language that made her gasp. Her eyes widened as she searched his face, attempting to hide her fear. Her chin trembled with the effort to maintain her composure as she squarely met his cold gaze, unwilling to let him know how much he intimidated her.

McFarland couldn't make himself stop shouting at her. The boiling anger erupted like fire from a volcano. By chance, he'd happened to look out his window and he'd seen Judy as she opened the corral gate. The fear had nearly paralyzed him. All he could think of was getting to her, warning her. A picture of Midnight's powerful legs striking out at her had almost driven him insane. He hadn't been angry then, but now he burned with it.

McFarland could see the shock running through Judy's veins as the pulse at the base of her throat pounded frantically. Still, the words came and he hated himself for subjecting her to his uncontrollable tantrum.

"Anyone who pulls an asinine trick like this doesn't deserve to be around good horses," he shouted. "You're a hazard to everyone here. I don't want you near my stables again. Is that understood?"

Her head jerked back as though he'd slapped her.

"Yes." She nodded weakly, signaling that she'd abide by his edict.

She left him then, with such dignity that it took all his strength not to run after her and beg her forgiveness.

The air was electrified and McFarland rammed his hand

through his hair. Sam stood there, accusing him, silently reprimanding him with every breath. The older man had once been a friend; now his censure scorched McFarland.

"I'll be out of here by morning," Sam muttered, and with a look of disgust, he turned away.

The remainder of the day was a waste. McFarland couldn't stop thinking of what he'd said to Judy, and he experienced more than a twinge of conscience. That woman had eyes that could tear apart a man's soul. When he'd ordered her to stay away from the horses, she'd returned his look with confused pain, as though that was the last thing she'd expected. He had wanted to pull her into his arms, hold her against his chest and feel the assurance of her heart beating close to his. Instead, he'd lashed out at her, unmercifully striking at her pride when all he'd really wanted to do was protect her.

His vehement feelings shocked him most. He tried to tell himself that Judy deserved every word he'd said. She must have been crazy to get into a pen with an animal as unpredictable as Midnight. He'd warned her about him; so had Sam. Anyone with a brain would have known better. There were times when even he couldn't handle that stallion.

Damn! McFarland slammed his fist against the desk. He couldn't afford to feel like this toward a woman. Any woman, but particularly Judy Lovin.

As she came down the stairs for dinner that evening, Judy's stomach tightened and fluttered with nerves. Her face continued to burn with humiliation. She would've preferred to have dinner sent to her room and completely avoid John, but she had to face the beast for Sam's sake.

"Good evening, John," she said quietly as she entered the dining room.

He stood with his back to her, staring out the window. He turned abruptly, unable to disguise his surprise. From all appearances, he hadn't expected to see her.

"Judy."

They stood staring at each other before taking their places at the elegant table.

Not a word was exchanged during the entire meal. In all her memory, Judy couldn't recall a more awkward dinner. Neither had much appetite; eating was a pretense. Only after their plates had been removed and their coffee poured did she dare appeal to the man across the table from her.

"Although I'd rather not talk about what happened this afternoon, I feel we need to discuss Sam."

John took a sip of his coffee. His eyes narrowed slightly, and he seemed affronted that she'd approach him on a matter he was sure to consider none of her business.

She clutched her napkin and forced herself to continue. "If you make Sam leave the island you might as well cut off both his legs. St. Steven's is his home. The horses are his family. What happened wasn't his fault. He'd told me repeatedly to stay away from Midnight. If he'd known I'd gone into that corral he would've had my hide. I snuck in there when Sam wasn't looking. He doesn't deserve to lose his job because of me."

John lowered his cup to the saucer without speaking.

"Despite everything people say about you, John McFarland, I trust you to be fair."

He arched his brows at that comment. This woman had played havoc with his afternoon, caused him to alienate a man he'd considered a friend, and now she seemed to believe that by pleading softly she could wrap him around her little finger.

"Sam leaves in the morning, as scheduled."

Without ceremony, she rose from her chair. Her eyes steadily held his. "I see now that I misread you," she told him. "My judgment is usually better, but that isn't important now." She turned to leave the room. After only a few steps, she paused and looked back. "My father once told me something, but I didn't fully appreciate his wisdom until this moment. He's right. No man is so weak as one who cannot admit he's wrong."

By the time she reached her rooms, Judy discovered she was shaking. She sat on the edge of her bed and closed her eyes. The disillusionment was almost more than she could bear. She'd been mistaken about John McFarland. He was a wild, untamable beast—the most dangerous kind...one without a heart.

Several hours passed, and although John had forbidden her to go near the stables again, Judy couldn't stay away. She had to talk to Sam, tell him how deeply sorry she was.

She changed from her dress into shorts and a T-shirt. As usual the house was silent as she slipped down the stairs and out the front door.

Even the night seemed sullen and disenchanted. The still, heavy air was oppressive. The area around the house was well lit, but the stable was far enough away to be enveloped in heavy shadows. The moon shone dimly and provided little light.

As Judy walked along the path that led to the stables, she felt a chill invade her limbs. She longed for home and the comfort of familiarity. Folding her arms around her middle, she sighed. She tried not to wonder how long John intended to keep her on the island. Surely he'd send her away soon. After the incident with Midnight, he must be eager to get rid of her. She was a thorn in his side—a festering one.

Not for the first time did she feel like an unwelcome stranger to the island. Although she'd done everything possible to make the best of the situation, she was still John's prisoner. In the days since her arrival, she'd struggled to create some normalcy in her life. She'd begun to feel at ease. Now that had changed. Without access to Princess, she wouldn't be able to see the children as frequently and with Sam's dismissal, the other servants would avoid her, fearing they, too, could lose their positions. Loneliness would overwhelm her.

The door to the stable was open, revealing the silhouette of Sam's elongated shadow. His actions were quick and sure and Judy strained her ears, thinking she heard the soft trill of his whistle.

"Evening, Sam," she said, pausing just inside the open doorway.

"Ms. Lovin." His eyes brightened with delight, then quickly faded as he glanced around. "Ms. Lovin, you shouldn't be here—"

"I know," she said gently, interrupting him. "I came to tell you how sorry I am."

He shrugged his shoulders, seemingly unconcerned. "Don't you worry about that. It's all taken care of now."

The words took a moment to sink in. "You mean you aren't leaving?"

Sam rubbed the side of his jaw and cocked his head. "I've never known Mr. McFarland to change his mind. A man doesn't become as wealthy as that one without being decisive. I knew I'd done wrong to let you get close to that stallion—I figured I deserved what I got. Can't say I agree with the way he laid into you, though, you being a lady and all, but you took it well."

"You aren't leaving the island?" Judy repeated, still not convinced she could believe what she was hearing.

"No. Mr. McFarland came to me, said he'd overreacted. He asked me personally to stay on. I don't mind telling you I was surprised."

So was Judy. She felt warm and wonderful. The sensation was so strong that she closed her eyes for a moment. She hadn't misjudged John. He was everything she hoped.

"Mr. McFarland's here now," Sam continued, his voice low. "Midnight's still in the corral and he went out there. I don't suppose you saw him or you wouldn't be here." The man who ruled the stables removed his hat and wiped his forehead, then gave Judy a sheepish grin. "He didn't say anything to me about letting you in the stables again."

"I'll leave," she said, unable to restrain a smile. Sam was back in John's good graces, and she'd become a threat.

The older man paused and looked around before whispering, "You come see me anytime you want. Princess will miss you if you don't bring her a carrot every now and then."

Judy laughed and gently placed her hand on his forearm. "Thank you, Sam."

He grinned in response, and she was grateful that she could count him as her friend.

Judy left the barn, intent on escaping before John discovered her presence. Her world had righted itself and there was no reason to topple it again—at least not this soon.

She was halfway to the house when she changed her mind, realizing she wanted to thank John. Like his stallion, he was dangerous and unpredictable. He was different from any man she'd ever known, and it frightened her how much she wanted to be with him. How much she wanted to thank him for not firing Sam.

John's shadow moved in and out of the dim moonlight as she approached. As Sam had told her, he stood by the corral, one booted foot braced against the bottom rung, his arms resting on the top.

A minute or so later she joined him. "It's a lovely night, isn't it?" she said, tentatively leaning against the fence.

McFarland tensed, his face hard and unyielding. He avoided looking at her. "There's a storm brewing."

"No," she said with a soft smile. "The storm has passed."

He gave a low, self-mocking laugh. "I asked you to stay away from here."

"I won't come again if you wish."

What he wished would have shocked her all the way to those dainty feet of hers, just as it had shocked him. He liked his women spicy and hot; Judy Lovin was sweet and warm.

"I'd like to show you something," she said, breaking into his thoughts. "But I need your trust."

He didn't answer her one way or the other. All evening he'd been toying with the idea of sending her back to her family and he was at a loss to understand why that no longer appealed to him. The woman had become a nuisance. She forced him to look deep within himself; she invaded his dreams and haunted his days. He hadn't had a moment's peace since she'd stepped onto the island.

"John, will you trust me for one moment?"

He turned his head slightly.

Standing on the bottom rung of the corral, she gave a shrill whistle that was an imitation of the one John had used earlier that day to attract Midnight's attention.

The stallion snorted once, jerked his head and casually walked toward her.

"Here, boy," she said, patting his nose and rubbing her hands and face over his as he nuzzled her. "No, I don't have any sugar cubes with me now, but I will another day. I wanted to show your master that we're friends."

Midnight whinnied softly and seemed to object when she stepped down and moved away.

McFarland wouldn't have been any more shocked if she'd pulled out a gun and fired on him. She'd made Midnight look as tame as a child's pony. His throat tightened.

"I was never in any real danger," she explained in a low voice. "Midnight and I are friends. Most of his arrogance is show. It's expected of him and he likes to live up to his reputation."

"When?" McFarland growled.

"I've been working with him in the afternoons. We made our peace two days ago. He'd even let me ride him if I wanted to, but he's your horse and I wouldn't infringe on that."

Why not? She had infringed on everything else in his life! His peace of mind had been shot from the minute she'd turned those incredible eyes on him.

Without a word, he left her standing at the corral, not trusting himself to speak.

Hours later, unable to sleep, McFarland gazed around his still bedroom. He didn't know what to make of Judy Lovin; she could be either angel or demon. She tamed wild animals, was beloved by children and made his cynical heart pound with desires that were only a little short of pure lust.

The maid woke Judy early the next morning just as dawn dappled the countryside.

"Mr. McFarland is waiting for you, miss."

Judy sat up in bed and rubbed the sleep from her eyes. "Mr. McFarland?"

"He's at the stables, miss."

"He wants me to go riding with him?"

"I believe so."

With a surge of energy, Judy tossed back the covers

and climbed out of bed. "Could you please tell him I'll be there in ten minutes?"

"Right away."

Judy was breathless by the time she arrived at the stables. Princess was saddled and waiting for her; Midnight stood beside the mare. John appeared from inside the barn.

"Good morning," she said brightly. He was dressed in black again, his eyes a deep indigo-blue. "It's a glorious morning, isn't it?"

"Glorious," he echoed mockingly.

She decided to ignore his derision. The earth smelled fresh in the aftermath of the night's storm. The dewdrops beaded like sparkling emeralds on the lush green foliage.

"Are you ready?" McFarland asked as he mounted.

"Yes." She swung onto Princess's back.

As he had the first time she'd ridden with him, John rode furiously. Judy was able to keep pace with him, but when they reached the far side of the island, she was exhausted from the workout.

He slowed, and they trotted side by side on the flawless beach.

"You never cease to amaze me," he said, studying her. He'd ridden hard and long, half expecting her to fall behind, almost wishing she had.

"Me? I find *you* astonishing. Do you always ride like that?"

"No," he admitted sheepishly.

"You must've been born in the saddle."

"Hardly. I'd made my first million before I ever owned a horse."

"When was that?"

A slow, sensual smile formed as he glanced in her direction. "You're full of questions, aren't you?"

"Does it bother you?"

He stared at her. "No, I suppose not."

"I imagine you had a colorful youth."

He laughed outright at that. "I'd been arrested twice before I was thirteen."

"Arrested?" Her eyes widened. "But why?"

"I was a thief." He threw back his head and laughed. "Some say I still am."

Judy dismissed his joking. "I don't believe that. You're an honorable man. You wouldn't take anything that didn't belong to you, not without a good reason."

Her automatic defense of him produced a curious hurt in his chest. There *had* been a good reason—someone had tried to cheat him. In the same circumstances, he'd react the same way. He wasn't bad, but in all his life, only one man had ever believed in him. From grade school, he'd been branded a renegade, a hellion. He'd been all that and more. But he wouldn't be where he was today if he hadn't been willing to gamble. He'd had to be tough.

When he didn't respond, Judy sought his gaze. The look in his eyes made her ache inside. He wore the wounds of his past proudly, like medals of valor, but the scars went deep.

"What about you?" he taunted. "Haven't you ever done anything wrong? Other than falling in love with a married man?"

The pain in her eyes was so clear that McFarland felt ashamed of asking.

"Actually, I have," she said, recovering quickly. "But since you don't know, I'm not going to tell you."

She laughed, slapped the reins against Princess's neck and sped off, leaving a cloud of sand in her wake.

McFarland caught up with her easily.

She smiled at him, her brown eyes sparkling. Dismounting, she brushed the wind-tossed hair from her face and stared into the sun. "I love this island. I love the seclusion and the peace. No wonder you had to have it."

McFarland joined her on the beach. He knew he was going to kiss her, knew he'd regret it later, but he was beyond caring. He touched her shoulder and turned her so that she faced him, giving her ample opportunity to stop him if she wanted to.

She didn't. Her pulse surged as his mouth moved to cover hers.

His arms went around her, bringing her close. He groaned and dragged his mouth away. She tasted like paradise and he didn't know how he could avoid wanting more. "I wish I hadn't done that," he said with a moan.

"I'm glad you did," she whispered.

"Don't tell me that."

"Yes…"

She wasn't allowed to finish as he held her face and kissed her again, unable to get enough of her. She leaned against him, letting him absorb her weight. Their bodies were pressed close. His fingers became tangled in her hair as he kissed her. He felt a tremor work its way through her and heard the soft sounds of passion that slid from her throat.

Instantly, he sobered, breaking off the kiss.

Judy sagged against him and released a long breath, resting her forehead on his chest. "You kiss the same way you ride."

McFarland slowly rubbed his chin against her hair as a lazy smile touched his mouth. She made him tremble from the inside out. He'd been right the first time; he shouldn't have let this happen. He should've found the strength to resist. Now that he'd held her, now that he'd kissed her, there was no turning back.

"John?"

He wanted to blame her for what she did to him, punish her for dominating his thoughts and making him hunger for her touch, but he didn't. He couldn't. His rage was directed solely at himself.

"I shouldn't have said those things."

"I know," she whispered. She seemed to sense intuitively that he was talking about Midnight. "I understand."

"Why didn't you say something?"

"I couldn't—you were too angry. I'd frightened you."

He slipped his arm around her shoulder. He should be begging forgiveness, but all she seemed to do was offer excuses for him. "I want to make it up to you," he said.

"There's no need. It's forgotten."

"No," he said forcefully. "I won't pass it off as lightly as that. Anything you want is yours. Just name it."

She went still.

"Except leaving the island." There must be a thousand things she longed to own, he thought. Jewels, land, maybe stocks and bonds. He'd give them to her. He'd give her anything she asked for.

"John, please, there's no need. I—"

"Name it." His eyes hardened.

She bit her lower lip, realizing it would do little good to argue. He was making amends the only way he knew how—with money. "Anything?"

He nodded sharply.

"Then I want the school on the island rebuilt. It's rundown and badly in need of repairs and unsafe for the children."

Five

Paulo, a gleeful year-old baby, rested on Judy's hip. Other children followed her around the cluster of homes as though she were royalty. The small party walked to the outskirts of the schoolyard, where the workers were busily constructing the new schoolhouse.

"Mr. McFarland told me the school will be ready by the end of the month," Judy told the children. The building had gone up so quickly that it had astonished both Judy and the islanders. The day after she'd made her request, a construction crew had arrived, followed by several shiploads of building supplies. Judy shuddered to think of the expense, but John hadn't so much as blinked when she said she wanted a school. And when John McFarland ordered something, there were no delays.

Paulo's mother joined Judy and the other children. The baby gurgled excitedly, stretched out his arms and leaned toward his mother. Judy gave him a kiss and handed him over.

"Paulo likes you."

"As long as his mother isn't around," Judy responded with a laugh.

"The children are very happy," the shy young woman added, looking toward the school. "Thank you."

"Don't thank me. Mr. McFarland's having it built, not me."

"But you're his woman and you're the one who told him...."

Judy had long since given up explaining that she wasn't John's "woman," although the thought wasn't as objectionable as when she'd first come here. In the weeks since, her attitude toward John had altered dramatically. He was the beast her father claimed; Judy had seen that side of him on more than one occasion. But he possessed a gentleness, too, a kindness that touched her heart.

Now that she knew him better, she hoped to understand his idiosyncrasies. He'd told her so little of his life, but from what she'd gleaned, he'd been abandoned at a young age and raised in a series of foster homes. A high-school teacher had befriended him, encouraged his talents and helped him start his first business. Although the teacher had died before John had achieved his financial empire, the island had been named after him—Steven Fischer.

Since the kiss they'd shared that early morning, Judy's relationship with John had changed subtly. As before, he didn't seek out her company and the only time she could count on being with him was at dinner. She was allowed to take Princess whenever she wished, but the invitation to ride with John had come only twice. He treated her with the politeness due to a houseguest, but avoided any physical contact, which told her that he regretted having kissed her.

Judy didn't regret it. She thought about that morning

often, relived it again and again, fantasizing, wishing it hadn't ended so quickly.

She exchanged letters with her family regularly now. Her father and her brother worried about her, but Judy frequently assured them she was happy, and to her surprise, realized it was the truth. She missed her old life, her family and her home, but she kept them close in her heart and didn't dwell on the separation.

John had given no indication when she could return and she hadn't asked. For now she was content.

After spending the morning with the children, Judy went back to the house, wearing a wreath of flowers on her head. The children and Paulo's mother had woven it for her and she'd been touched by their generosity.

Since it was an hour until lunch, Judy decided to find a new book to read. The library doors were open and beckoned her inside. Judy walked into the room.

McFarland sat at the desk, writing.

"John," she said, surprised. "I'm sorry, I didn't mean to intrude."

He glanced up and the frown that creased his forehead relaxed at the sight of her. She wore a simple yellow sundress with a halo of flowers on her thick, dark hair. He couldn't pull his eyes away from her.

"You didn't disturb me," he told her.

"It's a fantastic morning," she said eagerly, seeking a topic of conversation.

In the weeks since her arrival, Judy had acquired a rich, golden tan. Her healthy glow mesmerized him. "Beauty" did little to describe this woman, whose charm and winsome elegance appealed to him so strongly. McFarland had never known anyone like her. Her goodness wasn't a sweet coating that disguised a greedy heart. Judy Lovin was pure and good; her simple presence humbled him.

The memory of their kiss played havoc with his senses. He hadn't touched her since, doing his utmost to be the congenial host. The sweetest torment he'd ever endured was having her so close and not making love to her. He feared what would happen if he kissed her again, and yet the dream of doing so constantly interrupted his sleep.

He'd planned to return Judy to her family before now, but couldn't bring himself to do so. He was at odds with himself, knowing it was foolish to keep her on the island with him. If she'd revealed some sign of being unhappy and asked to go home to New York, he would've allowed it, but Judy showed no desire to leave and he selfishly wanted to keep her with him, despite her family's constant pleading.

"I spent the morning with the children," Judy said, still only a few steps inside the room. "They're excited about the school."

John nodded, unconcerned. "Did they give you the flowers?"

She raised one hand to her head, having forgotten about the orchid wreath. "Yes, they're talented, aren't they?" Out of the corner of her eye, she saw an elaborate chess set. When he didn't respond to her first question, she asked another. "Do you play?"

McFarland's gaze followed her own. "On occasion."

"Are you busy now?"

He glanced at his watch, more for show than anything. He was always busy, but not too busy to torture himself with her. "Not terribly."

"Shall we play a game, then?" She longed for his company. "That is, if it wouldn't be an intrusion."

His eyes held hers; he couldn't refuse her. "All right," he agreed.

"Good," she said, smiling, and brought the chess set to the desk, then pulled up a chair to sit opposite him.

"Shall we make it interesting?" McFarland asked, leaning forward.

"Money?"

He grinned. "No."

"What then?"

"Let the winner decide."

"But…"

"How good are you?"

Judy dropped her gaze to the board. "Fair. If I lose, what would you want from me?"

What a question. The possibilities sent his blood pressure soaring. He wanted her heart and her soul. And he wanted to feel her body beneath his own. The image clawed at his mind and his senses. He forced himself to rein in his desire.

"John?"

"What would I want?" he repeated hurriedly. "I don't know. Something simple. What about you? What would you want?"

Her laughter echoed off the book-lined walls. "Something simple," she echoed.

His eyes softened as he studied her. Afraid that he'd be caught staring, McFarland tried to look away and discovered that he couldn't—her eyes held his.

"It's your move."

McFarland brought his attention to the board, unaware that she'd placed her pawn in play. "Right." He responded automatically, sliding his own man forward.

By sheer force of will, he was able to concentrate on the

game. Her technique was straightforward and uncomplicated and a few moves later, he determined that her strategy was weak. He should be able to put her in checkmate within ten or fifteen minutes, but he wasn't sure he wanted to. If he lost, albeit deliberately, he'd be obligated to give her "something simple." He thought about how she'd look in a diamond necklace and doubted that the jewels could compete with her smile. Emeralds would draw out the rich color of her deep brown eyes, but no necklace could do her eyes justice. A sapphire brooch perhaps. Or...

"John? It's your turn."

Slightly embarrassed to be caught dreaming, he slipped his bishop forward with the intent of capturing her knight, which was in a vulnerable position.

Judy hesitated. "That wasn't a good move, John. Would you like to do it over?"

He agreed with her; it wasn't a brilliant play, but adequate. "No, I released my hand from the bishop."

"You're sure?"

He studied the pieces again. He didn't think he was in imminent danger of losing his king or the match. If he did forfeit the game it would be on his terms. "Even if this was a bad move, which it isn't," he added hastily, "I wouldn't change it."

Her eyes fairly danced with excitement. "So be it, then." She lifted her rook, raised her eyes to his before setting it beside his undefended king, and announced, "Checkmate."

Tight-lipped, John analyzed her play and was astonished to discover she was right. So much for her being straightforward and uncomplicated! The woman had duped him with as much skill as a double agent. The first couple of plays had been executed to give him a sense of false security while she set him up for the kill.

"I won," she reminded him. "And according to our agreement, I'm entitled to something simple."

McFarland still hadn't taken his eyes off the chessboard. The little schemer. Now that he could see how she'd done it, he was impressed with her cunning and skill. All right. He'd lost in a fair game; he was ready for her to name her price.

"Okay," he said a bit stiffly. "What would you like? A diamond necklace?"

She looked horrified. "Oh, no! Nothing like that."

"What then? A car?"

For an instant she was too stunned to reply. "Good heavens, no. Your idea of something simple and mine seem to be entirely different."

"What do you want then?"

"Your time."

His expression grew puzzled. "My what?"

"Time," she repeated. "You work much too hard. I don't recall even one afternoon when you weren't cooped up in that stuffy office. You own a small piece of paradise. You should enjoy it more often."

"So what's that got to do with anything?"

"For my prize I want us to pack a lunch and take it to the beach. It'll be a relaxing afternoon for both of us."

He grinned at the idea that she would assume he had a few hours to do nothing but laze on the beach. Surely she wasn't so naive that she didn't know he ruled a financial empire. Offices around the globe were awaiting his decisions. "I don't have time for that nonsense," he finally said.

"That's a shame." Judy looped a dark strand of hair around her ear. "Unfortunately, you're the one who decided to place a wager on our chess match. You should never have made the suggestion if you weren't willing to follow through."

"I'll buy you something instead. I know just the thing."

Judy shook her head adamantly. "I would've sworn you were a man who kept his promises. The only thing I want is this afternoon."

He frowned. "I can't afford to waste time lollygagging around the beach."

"Yes, John."

"There are cost sheets, reports, financial statements— all of which need to be reviewed."

"Yes, John."

"There are decisions to be made." His voice rose in volume. "Offers to be considered."

Judy let neither his tone nor his words intimidate her. "I'll be at the door in half an hour and I'll leave with or without you. But I honestly believe that you're a man of honor."

She left the room and McFarland continued to sit at his desk, seething with frustration. She'd tricked him; she'd set him up, waited patiently and then waltzed in for the kill. His laugh was filled with bitterness. An innocent woman? He didn't think so.

Half an hour later, Judy stood in the foyer waiting for John. When he didn't come, she lingered for an additional five minutes. Deeply disappointed, she picked up the large wicker picnic basket and walked out of the house alone.

In his suite of offices, McFarland stood at the balcony door staring into space. It wasn't just that he didn't have time to spend lazing on the beach. If he truly wanted to, he could have joined her. The problem was Judy. Whenever he was with her, the need for her burned within him. A curious ache tore at his heart. Perhaps his upbringing— or lack of one—was the problem. At no other time in his life had he wanted to know a woman the way he did Judy. He yearned to hold her in his arms and hear tales from her childhood, and tell her about his. From the little she'd described, he recognized how close she'd been to her mother. She rarely spoke of her brother or father and McFarland didn't encourage it, afraid she missed them and would ask to be released.

For his own part, McFarland had told her more of his life than he'd ever revealed to anyone. Being with her made him weak in ways he couldn't explain. That kiss was a good example. He'd promised himself he wouldn't do it and then… A low groan of frustration welled up in his throat and he momentarily closed his eyes.

Pivoting, he walked over to the liquor cabinet, poured himself a stiff drink and downed it in two swallows. He wanted her. This soul-searching led to one thing and one thing only. He hungered to take Judy in his arms and kiss her until she felt a fraction of his desire. And when the moment came, she'd smile up at him with those incredible eyes and give him her very soul and ask nothing in return.

"Mr. McFarland?" Avery Anderson stepped into the office.

"Yes?" he snapped.

"I'm sorry to disturb you."

McFarland shook his head, dismissing the apology. "What is it?"

Avery shifted his feet. "It's Ms. Lovin."

"Yes. Is there a problem? Is she hurt?" He strove to keep his voice unemotional, although his heart was hammering anxiously against his ribs.

"No…no. Nothing like that."

"Then what?"

Avery ran a finger inside his stiff white collar. "She's been on the island nearly a month now."

"I'm aware of that."

"I was wondering how much longer her family will be kept waiting before she's returned."

"Have they been pestering you again?" Grim resolve tightened his features. Judy enjoyed the island; he could see no reason to rush her departure.

Avery gave one barely perceptible shake of his head and dropped his gaze. "No…"

"Then who's doing the asking?"

Avery squared his shoulders and slowly raised his eyes to his employer's. "I am, sir."

"You?"

"That's right, Mr. McFarland."

"How long Ms. Lovin stays or doesn't stay is none of your concern." His tone was cold.

"But, sir…"

"That'll be all, Avery."

He hesitated for a long moment before turning, white-lipped, and walking out of the room.

McFarland watched his assistant leave. Even his staff had been cast under her spell. Sam, who could be decidedly unpleasant, rushed to do her bidding. Princess had never been groomed more frequently or better. When asked about the extra attention he'd paid to the mare, Sam had actually blushed and claimed it was for Ms. Lovin.

The maids fought to serve her. The chef had somehow managed to learn her favorite dishes and cooked them to the exclusion of all else. Pleased by his efforts, Judy had personally gone to thank him and kissed the top of his shining bald head. The island children followed her the way they would a pied piper. Even Midnight had succumbed to her considerable charm. McFarland wiped a hand over his face. The entire island rushed to fulfill her every command. Why should *he* be exempt from yearning to please her?

"Avery!" he barked.

"Sir?" The other man hurried into the room.

"Cancel my afternoon commitments."

"Excuse me?" Incredulous disbelief widened the other man's eyes.

"I said wipe out any commitments I have for the remainder of the day."

Avery checked his watch. "Are you feeling ill, Mr. McFarland? Should I contact a doctor?"

"No. I'm going swimming."

Avery's eyes narrowed. "Swimming?"

"In the ocean," McFarland said, grinning.

"The one outside—the one here?"

"That's right." Purposefully, he closed the folder on his desktop lest he be tempted to stay. "Avery, when was the last afternoon you had free?"

"I'm not sure."

"Take this one off. That's an order."

An instantaneous smile lit up the fastidious man's face. "Right away, Mr. McFarland."

McFarland felt as young as springtime and as excited as a lover on Valentine's Day. He walked through the house to his quarters and changed clothes. With a beach towel slung around his neck, he strolled down the front lawn and searched the outskirts of the beach. He found Judy lying in the shade of a tall palm tree. She wore a demure swimsuit and had kicked off her sandals. A large blanket was spread out on the grass; the picnic basket was open. He glanced inside and saw enough food to hold off a siege.

Judy lay on her back with her eyes closed. She knew she appeared tranquil, but her thoughts were spinning. She shouldn't be on St. Steven's. She should be asking when John intended to release her so she could go home to her family. Instead she was lazing on the beach feeling sorry for herself because she'd misjudged John McFarland. Her pride was hurt that he'd refused such a simple request. She liked being with John; the highlight of her day was spending time with him. She savored those minutes, and was keenly disappointed whenever he left her. The kiss they'd shared had changed everything; nothing could be the same anymore. They'd come to trust each other enough to be friends, but now they feared each other. The kiss hadn't satisfied their curiosity. Instead, it had left them yearning for more.

A soft protest sounded from her throat. She was falling in love with John. She didn't want to love him, nor did he want her love. He would hurt her and send her away when he tired of her. It would embarrass him—and her—if he ever guessed how she felt.

"You knew I'd come, didn't you?" McFarland said, standing over her.

Judy's eyes shot open, blinked at the bright sunlight and closed again. Shielding her eyes with one hand, she leaned on one elbow and looked at him again. "John." She sat upright.

He didn't seem pleased to be there, but she was too happy to care.

"Sit down." She patted the blanket beside her. "And no, I didn't know you were coming, but I'm so glad you did."

He joined her, looping an arm around his bent knee. He stared into the rolling blue surf as he spoke. "I left Mc-Donnell Douglas on the line so I could fulfill this wager."

"They'll call you tomorrow."

"You hope."

"I know," she said, hiding a smile. "Now don't be angry with me. You're the one who suggested we make things interesting."

"Why can't you be like every other woman and ask for diamonds?"

"Because some things are worth more than jewels."

"What's the problem? Do you have so many that more don't interest you?" His face was hard and unyielding, but his anger was directed more at himself than at Judy.

"My mother left me three or four lovely pieces." She slowly trailed her finger in the sand. "But I seldom wear jewelry." He wouldn't understand and she couldn't explain that being with him was worth more to her than rubies and pearls.

A strained silence followed. "I shouldn't have snapped at you," he eventually said.

She turned to face him and was caught once again by his tortured gaze. Her breath stalled in her lungs. Not knowing what drove her, she brought her hand to his face, yearning to wipe away the pain. John's eyes closed as her fingers lightly brushed his cheek. He took her hand, then raised his eyes to hers, kissing the inside of her hand.

The sensation of his lips against her palm made Judy gasp.

"I shouldn't do this," he said and groaned, directing her face to his. He kissed her cheek, her temple, her eyes.

They broke apart momentarily, and when he reached for her again, Judy met him halfway. This time the kiss was much deeper, and when he lifted his head they were both dazed and more than a little shocked. The kiss was better, far better, than either had anticipated.

McFarland rose to his knees, pulling Judy with him. Her look of innocent desire stabbed at his conscience. He hadn't meant to kiss her; he feared hurting her more than he feared losing his wealth. But the soft, feminine feel of her was irresistible. And in the end, he kissed her again and again until his heart thundered and roared. He lost himself in her sweetness as years of loneliness melted away.

John's kisses made Judy feel light-headed. The finest wine couldn't produce a sensation as potent as this. She trembled in his arms and her gaze met his.

He dragged his eyes away from her.

"Let's swim," he said abruptly.

Judy nodded and he helped her to her feet.

The turquoise water wasn't far, and they stepped into the rolling surf together. The cool spray against her heated flesh took Judy's breath away.

John dove into an oncoming wave and Judy followed him. He broke the surface several feet from her, turned and waited for her to swim to him.

"Have you ever body surfed?" He shouted to be heard above the sound of the churning sea.

"No, but I'd like to."

"Good." He reached out and clasped her waist. "We'll take this wave together."

With no option, Judy closed her eyes and was thrust into the swelling wall of water. Her hold on John tightened as they were cast under the surface by a giant surge of unleashed power.

Judy threw back her head and laughed once the wave washed them onto the beach. "That was wonderful." She wrapped her arms around John's neck.

"You're slippery," McFarland said, using the excuse to draw her closer. He held her firmly against him, his fingers brushing the wet strands of hair from her face. Her pulse went wild at his touch.

His eyes darkened just before his mouth descended on hers. Judy gave herself to the kiss, responding with all the love in her heart. The water took them again, and when they emerged from the wave, Judy was breathless and weak.

McFarland's chest heaved. He'd thought he could escape his need for her in the water, but it hadn't worked out that way. "You feel even better like this...."

"Pardon?"

"Nothing," he grumbled. How was he ever going to let her go? "Judy?"

She wound her arms around his neck and smiled shyly. Maybe he'd admit that he loved her. No, she told herself. It was a fanciful dream. Earning John's love would take more than a few playful moments in the surf. He had to learn to trust.

"Listen," he said in a low voice, "I have to tell you something."

She raised her head, afraid that he was going to send her away.

"I'm leaving."

Her heart slammed against her ribs. "When?"

"In the morning."

"How long?"

"A few days," he said, and continued to brush the wet strands from her face, although they'd long since been smoothed into place. "Four, possibly five."

Perhaps he'd decided to send her away. Her eyes must have revealed her distress.

"Will you wait here for me, Beauty?"

She nodded, overcome with relief.

"Good," he whispered, and greedily sought her mouth once again.

Not until he kissed her did she realize he hadn't called her Judy.

Six

John left just after dawn the next morning. Judy was awake and at the sound of muted voices, reached for her robe and rushed down the winding stairs. By the time she arrived, John was already gone, but she could see his Jeep in the distance. She stood on the huge porch, leaning dejectedly against the marble column. She would've liked to have wished him well.

"Morning, Ms. Lovin."

Judy straightened and turned toward Avery Anderson.

"Good morning. I see John got off without a hitch."

"Mr. McFarland should only be away a few days."

"Four, possibly five." She quoted what John had told her, staring after the disappearing vehicle. "It won't be so bad."

"He's instructed me to see to your every wish."

She smiled. If she were to have a craving for pastrami from her favorite New York deli, Judy didn't doubt that speedy arrangements would be made.

"He doesn't go away often," Avery went on to explain as

he straightened his bow tie. "He wouldn't now if it wasn't necessary."

Judy nodded. John hadn't wanted to leave her. She'd seen the regret in his eyes.

"Some say he's a recluse," Avery commented thoughtfully, studying Judy.

"No," she countered. "Not in the true sense of the word, but he does care about his privacy."

"He does," the older man agreed.

They turned to go back inside, walking through the wide doors and parting at the foot of the stairs.

Four or five days wouldn't seem long, Judy told herself as she dressed. The time would fly. She glanced at her watch; already fifteen minutes had passed.

Slumping onto the edge of the bed, Judy released a long, slow breath. She loved John and was only beginning to understand the consequences of blithely handing him her heart. Caring for him excited her, and it made her afraid. John wouldn't be an easy man to love; he knew so little about it. Judy had been surrounded by love. Her feelings for John gave him the power to hurt her and she wasn't convinced that telling him how she felt would be in her best interests—or his.

The first day passed without incident. The second was equally dull. Mealtimes were the worst. She sat at the end of the table and experienced such an overwhelming sense of loneliness that she scolded herself for being so dramatic. Nothing seemed right without John. Not riding Princess around the island; not visiting the children; not writing letters to her family; not swimming.

She was lonely and bored, at odds with herself. One man had toppled her world and a few days without him taxed the balance of her existence.

The night of the third day, Judy tossed and turned in her bed, unable to sleep. She missed John dreadfully and was angry with herself for feeling at such a loss without him.

At midnight, she threw aside the blankets and silently crept down the stairs for a glass of milk, hoping that would help her sleep. John's office was on the opposite side of the house from the kitchen, and Judy carried her milk to the opulently paneled suite, turning on the lights. She slipped into his desk chair, tucking her bare feet beneath her. Briefly she closed her eyes and smiled, inhaling his scent. She could practically feel his presence, and that eased the ache of loneliness and despair.

Weary to the bone, McFarland entered the house and paused in the foyer, resisting the urge to climb the stairs and wake Judy. The thought of holding her sleepy head against his chest was almost more than he could resist.

The business meetings hadn't gone well and in part he blamed himself. Negotiations had come to an impasse and, in his impatience to return to the island, he'd asked that the meeting be adjourned while both parties considered the lengthy proposals. He would've stayed in Dallas if he'd felt it would do any good, but he figured it was probably better to return to St. Steven's rather than buckle under to United Petroleum's unreasonable demands.

He paused, rubbed a hand over his face and smiled. He didn't need to wake Judy to feel her presence in his home. He had only to shut his eyes to see her bouncing down the stairs with a vitality that rivaled life itself. Her laughter was like sparkling water; her smile could blot out the sun.

His heart constricted with emotion. He would surprise her first thing in the morning. Until then he'd have to be content.

With that in mind, he headed toward his rooms, until a light in his office attracted his attention. It wasn't like Avery to work this late unless there was a major problem. Frowning, McFarland decided to check.

One step into his office and he stopped cold. Judy was curled up in the chair behind his desk, sound asleep. She was the picture of innocence with her head to one side, the thick coffee-colored hair falling over her cheek. She wore a plain nightgown beneath an equally unfeminine robe. Neither did much to reveal the womanly curves beneath. However, McFarland had never experienced a stronger stab of desire. It cut through him, sharp and intense, and trapped the breath in his lungs.

Had it been any other woman, he would've kissed her awake, then carried her into his room and satisfied his yearning. He couldn't do that with Judy; her innocence prevented him.

He hesitated, debating how he should wake her. His impulse, despite everything, was to bend over and kiss her, but he knew that would never satisfy him and the potency of his desire would only shock her. Shaking her or calling her name might frighten her.

Of her own accord, Judy stirred and stretched her arms above her head, arching her back and yawning loudly. She hadn't meant to fall asleep. When she opened her eyes, she discovered John standing on the other side of the desk. She blinked. At first she was convinced he wasn't real but the embodiment of her deepest desires. When she realized he was actually there, she leaped from the chair, nearly tripping on the hem of her nightgown.

"John." She brought her hand to her chest. "I'm so sorry… I don't know what came over me to come into your office. It must've startled you to find me here. I... I apologize."

"My home is yours. No apology is necessary," he said softly as his gaze fell on the empty glass.

"I couldn't sleep." She shook back her hair, still flustered and more than a little embarrassed. "When did you get in?"

He felt a smile twitch at the corners of his mouth. She looked like a guilty child with her hand in the cookie jar. "A few minutes ago."

She clasped her hands and smiled brightly. "Welcome home."

"It's good to be here."

Judy tightened her hands to restrain the urge to run into his arms, hold on to him and beg him never to leave her again. Her heart continued to pound, but she didn't know if it was from being caught in his office or just the sight of him.

"Did anything happen while I was away?" he asked, reaching for his mail and idly flipping through it.

"Nothing important." She stood across from him, drinking in his presence as though he might disappear at any moment. "Are you hungry? I'd be happy to fix you something." She prayed he was famished, so she'd have an excuse to stay with him longer.

"Don't go to any trouble."

"I won't. Will a sandwich do?" She smiled, inordinately pleased to be able to do this one small thing for him.

"A sandwich would be fine."

He followed her into the kitchen and pulled a stool up to the stainless-steel table while Judy opened the refrigerator to take out the necessary ingredients.

"How was the trip?" she asked, liberally slathering two

slices of bread with mayonnaise before placing turkey and tomato on them.

McFarland had never discussed business matters with anyone outside his office. The temptation to do it now was strong, but he didn't. "Everything went as expected," he said matter-of-factly, which was only half true.

Judy cut the sandwich in half, set it on a plate and handed it to him. She poured them each a glass of milk, then sat on a stool across from him.

Elbows braced on the table, she cupped her face in her hands and studied him while he ate. Her brow creased with concern. "You look exhausted."

"I am. I didn't make it to bed last night."

"The meetings didn't go well, did they?"

Her intuition surprised him; he hadn't thought he was that easy to read. "I didn't expect them to."

"What happened?"

McFarland shrugged. "I made an offer, they rejected it and came back with a counteroffer."

"And you rejected that?"

He paused, the glass halfway to his mouth. "Not exactly. Not yet, anyway," he elaborated.

"But you will?"

Again he shrugged, and his eyes met hers. "I'm not sure."

Judy continued to study John. He was physically exhausted, but his mental stress weighed far more heavily on him. As a young girl, she'd often watched her mother soothe away her father's tension. Georgia Lovin hadn't made suggestions; she'd had no expertise in business, but she possessed the ability to get her husband to relax and talk out the problem. More often than not, he found the solution. Judy prayed she could do the same for John.

"You want this deal, don't you?" she asked him softly.

McFarland nodded. "I've been working on it for over a year. The offer I made United Petroleum is a fair one—it was more than fair. But I'm at a disadvantage."

"Why?"

He set the glass down hard. "Because they know I want this."

"I see."

"Now that you mention it, I may have appeared too anxious to settle." He couldn't deny his eagerness. He'd wanted to get those papers signed so he could get back to the island and Judy, his mission accomplished. He'd thought he'd been more subtle, but perhaps not. "Let me explain," he said, taking a napkin and scribbling down a series of figures.

He spoke nonstop for fifteen minutes. Much of what he said was beyond Judy's comprehension, although she pretended to understand every bit of it. She nodded at the appropriate times, occasionally asking a question, and smiled when he finished.

"You're right," he said with a wide grin. "Why didn't I think of that?"

Judy understood only some of what he was talking about, but it didn't seem to matter. The weariness was gone from his eyes. He stood and paced the kitchen.

"That's it," he said, pausing in front of her. "Has anyone ever told you what a marvel you are?" His hands cradled her face and he kissed her soundly.

Judy's breath lodged in her chest. "What was that for?"

"To thank you." He checked his watch. "It's late, but I think I'll call my attorney and talk this latest strategy over with him."

"John," she protested. "It's one o'clock in the morning!"

"For the money I pay that man it shouldn't make any difference what time I call him."

Before she could protest further, John was at the kitchen door. He opened it, paused and turned back. "Will you ride with me in the morning?"

She smiled and nodded eagerly, grateful that he'd asked.

In his office, McFarland emptied his briefcase and set the file for United Petroleum on his desk. It struck him then, sharply. He didn't know how, but Judy had gotten him to reveal the minute details of this buyout. He'd told her everything without any hesitation. He wasn't worried about what she'd do with the information; there *was* nothing she could do.

But he was shocked by the way she'd so completely gained his confidence—to the point that he cheerfully gave out industry secrets without a second thought. This woman had him tied in knots a sailor couldn't untangle, and every one of them was choking off his independence. Because she was making herself essential.

He paused as he analyzed the situation. McFarland didn't like the idea of a woman, any woman, controlling his life. Not one bit. Something had to be done to put an end to it.

At dawn Judy rushed to meet John at the stables. She'd slept well after leaving him. When the maid had come to wake her, she'd resisted climbing out of the warm bed, preferring to hold on to the memory of John's arms around her. It took her a moment to realize she'd been dreaming.

Midnight and Princess were saddled and waiting.

"Morning," she called to Sam and smiled at John, who immediately swung onto Midnight's back.

The burly trainer waved. Judy stroked Princess's smooth neck before mounting. She noticed that John's look remained stoic.

"How'd you sleep?" she asked when they'd gone a few

hundred feet. He was quiet, withdrawn and taciturn— nothing like the warm, gentle man he'd been when they'd parted.

"I didn't get to bed," he answered crisply.

"Oh, John, again? You must be ready to fall out of the saddle."

"No. After you left last night, I started to analyze the proposal and decided there were still things I wanted to change before I talked to Butterman."

Judy assumed Butterman was his attorney. "What did he have to say?"

John's expression was thoughtful. "Not much. But he seemed to think the new strategy would work. Unless United Petroleum wants to play games, I should hear back sometime this afternoon." He tipped back the brim of his hat and glanced at his watch. "The fact is, I should probably cut our ride short and get back to the office in case they contact me this morning."

Judy was aghast. "You don't intend to work, do you? Good heavens, you've been away on an exhausting business trip."

"So?"

"You haven't slept in who knows how long!"

McFarland's mouth thinned. "What's that got to do with anything?"

"Everything," she cried, losing her own temper. She didn't know what was wrong with him, but she had a hunch that a few hours' rest would cure it.

"Just what am I supposed to do?"

"Sleep."

"I'm expecting a phone call."

"Avery will wake you."

"What are you? My nurse?"

Judy's gloved hands tightened around the reins at the harsh edge to his voice. "Someone needs to look after you."

"And you're volunteering for the job?" McFarland didn't want to shout at her, but he couldn't seem to make himself stop. She was right. He hadn't seen a bed in over forty-eight hours, but he sure didn't want a woman dictating his actions.

Judy clamped her mouth shut, refusing to rise to the bait.

They rode together for half an hour without saying a word. McFarland derived little pleasure from the outing. He regretted having snapped at Judy, especially when he would much rather have taken her in his arms and kissed her. He searched for a way to apologize without losing his pride, and found none.

When they'd returned to the stable, Judy lowered herself from Princess's back and turned toward John. "As I recall, only a few hours ago you considered me wise and insightful. I don't know what happened since then, but I really do wish you'd rest."

"Why?"

She clenched her fists. "You're killing yourself working day and night for no reason."

"I call a hundred million dollars a damn good reason."

"Is it worth your health?" she cried, tears glistening in her eyes. "Is it worth becoming so unreasonable no one can even talk to you? Is it worth saying things you don't mean?"

"You seem to be doing exactly that."

"No. I mean everything I say." She paused. "I care about you."

"Is that supposed to excite me?" he asked. "You care about everything—horses, children…bugs. It would be hard to find something you *didn't* care about. Listen, Miss Bleeding Heart, I can do without your meddling. Got that?"

"No," she said with pride, her face pale and grim.

"You've been nothing but a nuisance since you came to the island. There isn't a man or woman here who doesn't bend to your every wish. Well, I refuse to be one of them. You'll do what I tell you. It won't be the other way around. Is that clear?"

If possible, her face went even paler, and her eyes widened with unmistakable pain. She opened her mouth to say something, then closed it again. But she refused to look away.

"I won't bother you again, John McFarland," she whispered with quiet dignity and turned away from him. How quickly everything had changed. She'd missed John desperately. She'd longed to savor this morning's outing with him and instead had been subjected to an outburst she didn't understand.

In her rooms, she sat and stared at the wall as the tears began to flow down her cheeks. She was in love with a beast. The possibility of ever gaining his heart struck her as ludicrous. In his own words, she was a nuisance and, with that, Judy realized that he'd probably never be capable of loving her.

At lunchtime, she sent a message that she wouldn't be joining him and requested that all her meals be sent to her room. If John found her company so taxing, there was no need to punish him with it. She was determined to avoid him until he saw fit to summon her.

A day passed.

A night.

Another day.

Another long, sleepless night.

A third day came and went, and still John didn't ask for her. She thought about him, yearned for him. She loved him and he considered her an annoyance. All these weeks when she'd treasured every moment with him, he'd seen her as a bother, a pest.

Still, he didn't summon her. To escape her rooms, Judy walked along the beach in the early morning. For the first time in weeks she entertained thoughts of leaving, but ultimately rejected them. They'd struck a bargain, and although it became increasingly difficult, she would stay on the island until he sent her away.

Countless times Judy wondered why he kept her there. She yearned to be with her family.

McFarland was not amused by Judy's stubbornness. Perhaps he'd been a bit unreasonable, but her reaction was even more so. For four days, she'd refused to have anything to do with him. That had been her choice, but enough was enough. The entire house was in an uproar.

Earlier McFarland had discovered the chef arguing with Avery. French insults gushed like water out of a spigot while the four-star chef gestured freely with his hands. The entire time, the man glanced accusingly in McFarland's direction.

"What was that all about?" he'd asked his assistant later.

"He—ah—is concerned," Avery commented, looking embarrassed.

"Concerned? Is there a problem with the kitchen staff?"

"No." Avery busied himself shifting papers around his desk.

"Then what is it?"

"He's concerned about Ms. Lovin."

McFarland's grin faded and his eyes grew cold. "Judy? What's wrong?"

"He claims she isn't eating properly and that she sends back her meals untouched. He's tempted her with his most famous recipes and nothing seems to work. He's afraid she's making herself ill."

A muscle jerked convulsively in McFarland's clenched jaw.

"I realize this isn't any of my business, Mr. McFarland, but..."

"You're right. It isn't."

Avery squared his shoulders, his own jaw tightening. "I've been with you for several years now, but these last three days have been the most difficult. You've been impatient and unreasonably demanding, and I can see no excuse for it. You have my notice, Mr. McFarland."

McFarland was stunned. Perhaps he *had* been a bit more demanding in the past few days, but that wasn't any reason for Avery to resign. "As you wish," he answered with some reluctance.

The afternoon went smoothly after that, but when they'd finished, Avery presented him with a brief but precise letter of resignation.

McFarland read it over twice, convinced there must've been some mistake. There wasn't; Avery was leaving him.

In an effort to think through this unexpected turn of events, McFarland got two cold beers and decided to visit Sam. To his additional shock, he discovered that the stableman regarded him with a black scowl.

"Don't tell me she's got you on her side, as well?" McFarland barked, angry because he should've known better. She'd had Sam twisted around her little finger from the minute she'd tamed Midnight. "Doesn't even one of you recognize the hand that feeds you? I don't believe it. Not you, too?"

In response, Sam chuckled, ambled to the back of the barn and brought out two rickety chairs.

"Women aren't worth the trouble they cause," McFarland said, pulling the tab from the aluminum top and guzzling a long swallow.

Sam joined him in the toast. "Can't say I blame you. You'd do well to be rid of her."

McFarland wiped his mouth with the back of his hand. "What do you mean?"

"You don't plan to keep her on the island? Not with the way she's been acting."

McFarland planned exactly that. He had no intention of letting her leave. She was there of her own free will—at any rate, she'd chosen to come. This disagreement between them was a spat, nothing more. She'd infringed on his private life and he wouldn't stand for it. Given time, she'd acknowledge that and she'd apologize and the situation would return to the way it used to be.

"She's a busybody, that one," Sam added. "Why, look at the way she stuck her nose in your affairs, dictating how you should run your business. No man should be expected to put up with that kind of intrusion."

McFarland nodded slowly, a little taken aback by Sam's vehemence.

"Look at the way she's always needling you, making one demand after another. I hear she constantly wants gifts."

McFarland shook his head. "She's never asked for a thing. Not for herself, anyway."

Sam took a swallow of beer. "If I were you, I'd put her in a rowboat and cast her out of my life. Let her fend for herself. As you said, she's a nuisance. She isn't worth the trouble."

McFarland mumbled something unintelligible. "Who said she was a nuisance?"

"You did! I heard you tell her so myself. You should've

seen the look in her eyes." Sam's laugh was loud and boisterous. "She's full of pride and spirit, that one. You'd better break it if you intend to keep her around."

"What else did I say to her?"

"Oh, lots of things."

"What things?"

McFarland felt sick as Sam told him. He'd been so exhausted that he didn't remember half of it. Now, every word,
every syllable, was like a vicious punch to his abdomen.

McFarland crushed the aluminum can with his hands
and stood.

"Where are you going?"

He didn't answer.

"You're going to get rid of her, aren't you?" Sam asked,
and noting the expression on McFarland's face, he chuckled, pleased with himself.

A little reverse psychology wouldn't go amiss, Sam
figured. It worked with stubborn horses. Why not their
owners?

Seven

Once again McFarland was in the uncomfortable position of having to seek Judy's forgiveness. His behavior gnawed at his conscience and wouldn't let him sleep. He rolled over and stared at the darkened ceiling. His heart constricted and his first serious doubts concerning what he was doing with Judy began to surface. He'd seen her picture in some newspaper and his interest had been awakened. He didn't quite understand what craziness had driven him to bring her to his island. In the weeks since her arrival, his life had been drastically affected. She'd been open, happy, guileless and unbelievably gentle when she had every excuse to hate him. He'd berated her, lashed out at her and still she turned those beautiful eyes on him and managed to smile.

By everything that was right, he should send her back to her family. His heart pounded slowly, painfully, at the thought of never hearing the sound of her laughter again, or having those eyes smile into his, or seeing her ride across his land with her hair in disarray. A heaviness weighed on his chest.

He couldn't do it—sending her away was unthinkable. The tenderness in her eyes and her smile filled him with an exhilaration he couldn't analyze. He wasn't even sure he wanted to. She made him feel things he'd never experienced, emotions he'd fought against most of his life. All he knew was that he needed her on St. Steven's for now. He'd deal with tomorrow later.

Judy punched her pillow and battled another wave of depression. She was wide awake. With nothing better to do, she climbed out of bed, dressed and crept out of the house, heading for the stables.

She felt incredibly weary.

The sky remained dark, but the promise of dawn lay just over the horizon. She could hear Sam stirring in the back of the barn as she saddled Princess and rode toward the beach.

Sam's features were twisted in a scowl as he searched McFarland's face in the half light of early dawn.

"She's gone," he announced harshly.

"Who?" McFarland stood beside Midnight, already saddled and waiting for him.

"Princess."

McFarland's eyes widened. No one would dare steal the mare. Only Judy rode her. "Has anyone checked the house to see—"

"The maid says there's no one in her room. Her bed barely looks slept in."

McFarland's own features hardened with determination, and in a single motion, he swung his weight onto Midnight's back. "What direction does she usually take?"

Sam gestured widely with both hands. "North. Sometimes east."

"I'll head west."

Sam's nod was curt, his eyes boring into McFarland's. "You bring her back. She belongs here."

McFarland raced out of the yard. He wouldn't come back until he found her. He'd punish whoever had helped her in this underhanded scheme. What good was security if she could carry out her own escape? He'd fire the lot of them, but first he had to find Judy.

McFarland would've ridden from one side of the island to the other, torn down the entire jungle to stop her. To his utter astonishment, all it took was a wild fifteen-minute ride. He came upon her with such ease that his heart began to slam against his chest. He paused, his frantic heartbeat stilling as he raised his eyes in gratitude.

She was walking on the beach with Princess following behind. The reins were draped over her shoulders as she ambled along. Although McFarland was high on the ridge above, he could see how distressed Judy was. Her head hung low, her shoulders were hunched and she moved slowly, despondently. He didn't need to see her tear-streaked face to know she'd been crying. That realization had the oddest effect on him. Guilt overwhelmed him and his chest constricted with a pain that was razor sharp. He couldn't take his eyes off her. Witnessing her sorrow brought such an intense desire to protect her that he could hardly breathe.

Since the night Sam had told him about the things he'd said to Judy, McFarland had sought a means of apologizing while salvaging his pride. He could give her a token gift, perhaps. Something that would convey his message without costing him emotionally. Watching her now, a sick feeling settled in the pit of his stomach and he admitted that he'd gladly fall to his knees and beg her forgiveness. He was a selfish bastard and Beauty—his Beauty—deserved so much better.

Judy wiped the tears from her cheeks, angry with herself for being so melancholy. From the first, she'd known it would be difficult to love John. She'd thought she had accepted that. In the long days since their ride together, she'd come to understand the cost that love demanded. But she had her pride, too—in some ways it was as great as John's—and she would die before she'd let him know that he held her heart in the palm of his hand.

A flash of ebony caught her attention and she turned and spotted John on the ridge above her. He pulled on the reins and she realized with a start that he was planning to meet her. It was one thing to know he'd found her, and another to let him see her tears.

Frantic to escape, she mounted Princess and slapped the reins hard. The mare shot across the beach, kicking up a flurry of sand. Judy decided her best chance of escape was the jungle and went in that direction. Risking a look behind her, she was astonished to see that John had already arrived at the beach.

"Hurry, Princess," she cried as the horse charged ahead.

Judy didn't see what darted across the beach, but Princess reared, her front legs kicking in terror. Unable to stop herself, Judy slipped sideways in the saddle. She made a desperate effort to regain her balance, but it was too difficult to stay on the bucking horse. A sense of unreality filled her. She hadn't been thrown by a horse since she was a child. She refused to believe it, but the ground that rushed up to meet her was certainly real. With a cry of panic she put out her arms to break the fall. Then the impact of her body against the beach brutally drove the air from her lungs.

McFarland saw Princess buck and watched helplessly as Judy teetered, frantically trying to regain her seat. He saw her fall and knew she'd landed hard. Swearwords scorched the morning mist and his heart thundered with alarm. The thoughts that flashed through his mind were completely illogical. He'd sell his business interests around the world if she was unhurt. If that didn't satisfy the powers that be, he offered his life, his soul—anything—as long as Judy wasn't hurt.

He pulled Midnight to an abrupt halt, vaulted from the stallion's back and ran across the sand, more frightened than he could remember ever being.

Falling to his knees at Judy's side, he gently rolled her over. The steady, even pulsing at the side of her neck made him go weak with relief. He yanked off his jacket and placed it under her head. Then, not knowing what else to do, he held her limp hand in his own, rubbing the inside of her wrist.

Judy's eyes fluttered open to see John leaning over her, looking sickly pale. "Princess?" she whispered and tried to sit up.

It took McFarland a moment to realize she was worried about the mare. He was astonished; Judy could have been maimed, or worse, killed, and she seemed to care nothing for her own well-being.

"Is she hurt?"

McFarland shook his head and responded in a husky voice. "She's fine. She's already on her way back to the stable. What about you? How do you feel?"

Her smile was little more than a slight trembling of her

lips. It was too soon to tell. She felt like she might throw up and the world spun crazily. "I'm all right," she said weakly.

"You're sure?" His eyes burned into hers.

"The only thing bruised is my pride." With some difficulty she stood, then stumbled and swayed toward him. Her ribs hurt badly, but she successfully hid the pain.

McFarland caught her, wrapping his arms around her, holding her against him, grateful for the excuse to bring her into his embrace. He brushed her disheveled hair away from her face, and Judy noted that he was shaking as much as she was.

"I'm fine, John. Something must have spooked Princess. I think it was a rabbit." She tilted her head back and saw the torment in his expression as he relived the moment of her fall.

Their eyes met. Neither moved; neither breathed. Slowly, he lowered his mouth to hers. Judy could find no way to describe the turbulent sensations that jolted her. It was as though she realized she could've been killed and forever denied the feel of John's arms around her. Judy wanted to cherish this moment forever and forget the pain.

They remained locked in each other's arms long after the kiss had ended. Timeless seconds passed, each more precious than the one before.

"You have to see a doctor," he said at last.

"John, I'll be fine."

"You're shaking."

She smiled, unable to tell him his kisses contributed to her trembling as much as the pain.

His low whistle brought Midnight to their side. "You'll ride with me."

"But…"

One look cut off any argument. McFarland climbed into Midnight's saddle first.

Judy stared at the stallion and felt her knees go weak. The last thing she wanted to do right now was get back on a horse. Although she strove to reassure John that she was unhurt, she felt as though someone had taken a baseball bat to her ribs. It hurt to breathe and she ached everywhere. Nothing seemed broken, but something wasn't right, either. "What if he won't let me?" she asked shakily.

John dismissed the idea with a curious smile. "You said yourself that Midnight is your friend."

She nodded, staring at the hand he offered her. She took it, and his strong fingers closed over hers as he prepared to lift her onto the stallion's back. However, the simple act of raising her arm caused her to gasp with pain.

Hurriedly, she drew it back to her side, closed her eyes and pressed her forehead against John's leg. The next thing she knew, she was on her knees in the sand, clutching her side.

"You idiot!" he shouted, dismounting. "Why didn't you say something?"

Tears welled in her eyes as she lifted her gaze to his. "Why do you always yell at me?" she asked in a hoarse whisper.

"Beauty, I'm sorry."

She held her arm protectively across her ribs. "Only my father calls me that."

"It's true, you know," he said, kneeling beside her, holding her with such tenderness that she couldn't identify the greater pain—loving John or the ache in her ribs.

"I'm not beautiful."

"Yes, you are. You're the most beautiful woman I know. Now don't argue with me anymore."

She gave him a weak smile.

The trip back to the house was torture and seemed to take hours. She pleaded with him to leave her there and send someone back for her. The injury wasn't so bad that she couldn't stand to be alone for half an hour. John adamantly refused and, in the end, she did ride Midnight, cradled in John's arms.

She rode facing him, her head against his chest, her arms around his middle. Their progress was slow and by the time they arrived she was hazy with pain and incredibly sleepy.

Sam and several others rushed out to greet them.

"Send for a doctor," John shouted urgently. That meant flying one in, which would take time, but there was no alternative.

With some effort, Judy lifted her head. "I thought you weren't going to yell anymore."

"I said that?" He pretended to be surprised.

She frowned and drew in a slow, painful breath. "Maybe you didn't."

He buried his fingers in her hair. "If it'll make the hurt go away," he whispered, "I promise never to raise my voice again."

The ache in her side immediately lessened.

He issued other orders, but in a subdued voice that moved her deeply, not because she found his shouting objectionable, but because he cared enough to try to please her. After the last four days of the bitter war that had raged between them, this sweet attention was bliss.

John helped her off Midnight and carried her into the house. She protested when he started up the stairs to her room, but it didn't stop him.

"I'm too heavy," she cried.

"Now look who's yelling."

"John, please, you're the one who'll need a doctor if you insist on hauling me up these stairs."

"I'll risk it."

"I wish you wouldn't." But it was useless to protest. Besides, he was already halfway up the stairs.

When he reached the hallway outside her suite, he nudged her door open, crossed the room and placed her carefully on the bed. Judy immediately recognized that lying down wasn't the thing to do and, kicking out her feet, she struggled to a sitting position.

"What's wrong?" McFarland saw the flash of pain in her eyes and felt it as strongly as if the agony were his own.

She shook her head and closed her eyes. "Nothing. Just go away, please. I'll be fine in a minute."

To her surprise he did leave her, but two maids were in her room within seconds. They were followed by the security guard who'd met her the day of her arrival.

Judy grinned. "So we meet again."

"I have some medical training," he explained. "Mr. McFarland asked that I check you over before the doctor gets here."

Judy nodded and slumped onto the end of her bed.

McFarland was pacing in the hallway outside her room when Wilson returned. "Well?" he asked anxiously.

"My guess is that she's cracked a couple of ribs."

"She's in considerable pain, isn't she?" Although Judy tried to hide it from him, McFarland could tell that she wanted to scream and once again he felt her agony.

"She's pretending it doesn't hurt, but I know better," Wilson said wryly.

"Give her something for the pain," McFarland demanded gruffly.

The other man looked uncertain. "I don't know if I should, Mr. McFarland. The doctor might want to—"

"It could be hours before he shows up. Give her something and do it now. That's an order."

Wilson nodded, swallowing any argument. "Right away."

He returned a few minutes later with two capsules, instructing Judy to take both. Within minutes she drifted into a troubled sleep. She lay tightly curled up, taking shallow breaths, trying to minimize the pain.

When she woke, she discovered John sitting at her bedside, staring at his hands, his face bleak.

"John?"

He straightened and turned toward her. "Yes, Beauty?"

"The island needs...something. A medical facility. What if one of the children gets hurt? Then...what? There's nowhere..." She felt so sluggish, so miserable. The pills hadn't taken the away pain; only her mind was numb.

"The doctor will be here soon," he assured her.

She nodded and moistened her lips with her tongue. "I'm thirsty."

"Here." He lifted her head and held a glass of cool water to her lips. She managed to take several sips. When she'd finished, he kissed her forehead.

"John?" Her voice was a slurred whisper. She struggled to keep her eyes open, but gave up the effort.

The catch in her voice stabbed at his heart. "Yes?"

"I'm sorry I've been such a nuisance."

The words burned him like a red-hot iron. "You were never a nuisance."

"But you said—"

He gripped her hand in his own and raised it to his lips,

kissing her knuckles. "I was wrong." McFarland couldn't remember ever admitting that to anyone.

He stayed at her bedside until the medical team arrived. Then he lingered outside her room until the physician had completed his examination, which seemed to take hours. McFarland paced the area in front of her room for so long that he grew dizzy.

His thoughts mingled with each other until they dashed through his mind in a muddled sequence. Judy running away from him, Judy falling, Judy in pain. It was all his fault.

When the physician finally did appear, McFarland found himself studying the other man, fearing what he might learn. "Will she be all right?" His eyes pleaded with the white-haired man for assurance.

"I believe so. We brought along a portable X-ray machine. She's cracked two ribs and has a slight concussion."

"Any internal damage?" That was McFarland's greatest fear.

"Not that we can detect."

He jerked his fingers through his hair. "Should she be hospitalized?"

The physician shook his head. "I don't see how that would do any good. What she needs now more than *anything* is rest. For the time being she isn't going to feel like getting out of bed. However, that's for the best. Let her sleep."

"How long?"

"A couple of days. After that, she should gradually increase her activity."

"What about the pain? I don't want her to suffer." He couldn't bear to see her face twisted in agony.

"I've left some medication with my nurse, Ms. Reinholt. Ms. Lovin is sleeping comfortably now."

McFarland let out his breath in a long, slow sigh. "Good. Thank you, doctor." He offered the physician his hand and had Wilson escort the medical team to the waiting helicopter. Except for the nurse, who'd be staying as long as necessary.

McFarland checked on Judy one last time before going to his office. He was stalled in the foyer by several of the staff members. They raised questioning eyes to him, their concern evident.

"How is Judy—Ms. Lovin—sir?" the chef asked as he bravely stepped forward.

Only hours earlier McFarland would've bitten off the man's head for daring to approach him on a subject that was none of his business. Now he patiently explained the extent of Judy's injuries and answered a legion of questions.

From there McFarland went to his offices. Avery stood when he entered the room.

Before his assistant could ask, he rattled off his now-rehearsed report. "Cracked ribs, bruises and a mild concussion. She'll be confined to her bed for a few days and good as new in a couple of months. Or so the doctor says."

Avery nodded. "How about you?"

"Me?"

"It doesn't appear to me that *you're* going to recover in a couple of months," he said boldly.

McFarland glared at his assistant before walking into his office and soundly closing the door. Avery was right; McFarland doubted he'd ever be the same. He'd been shaken to the very core of his existence. He buried his face in his hands and sat, unmoving, for what felt like hours.

Somehow he made it through the day, dictating memos,

making decisions, charting the course of numerous companies, but for all the emotion he put into it, he could've been playing Monopoly. Nothing seemed real; nothing seemed right.

The mere thought of food nauseated him. He couldn't eat, couldn't work. And when night came, he discovered that he couldn't sleep, either. He'd tried to stay away, to let her rest, and realized it was impossible.

The nurse in the stiff white uniform answered his knock at Judy's door.

"She's sleeping."

McFarland nodded, feeling foolish. "Go ahead and take a break. I'll stay with her."

The woman looked grateful and left soon afterward.

McFarland was thankful to spend the time alone with Judy. Her face was relaxed and revealed no signs of pain, which eased the guilt that had burdened him from the moment he'd watched Judy fall helplessly to the ground.

He couldn't tolerate the thought of her in pain. He wasn't squeamish, never had been, but Judy's accident had terrified him. He'd gone weak. With others, McFarland often battled feelings of rage; with Judy he could only blame himself. He felt sick with guilt.

"John." His name was a faint whisper.

"I'm here." Anxiously, he brought the chair closer to her bedside.

The clock on the nightstand said it was near midnight. Or was it noon? Judy didn't know anymore. Everything was so unclear. "Have you been here all this time?"

"No." He shook his head. "The nurse needed a break."

"The nurse?"

"Yes, the doctor felt you needed round-the-clock attention for a little while."

"That's ridiculous." She tried to laugh and sucked in a breath, her ribs protesting.

"Shh, you're supposed to keep quiet."

She ignored that and pushed herself up on one elbow. "Help me sit up, would you?"

"No."

"John, please, I need to talk to you."

"No, you don't."

"I'm on my deathbed, remember? Humor me."

He grudgingly helped her into a sitting position. Next he fluffed up her pillow and tucked the sheets securely around her waist.

A smile lit up her eyes and for the life of him, McFarland couldn't tear his gaze away. "There," he said, proudly, brushing his palms against each other as though he'd accomplished some impressive feat.

"What's that?" Judy pointed at a small crate on the floor next to the dresser.

"A gift."

"From whom?"

"Me."

Although it required some effort, she managed a smile. "Well, for heaven's sake, bring it to me."

He took it from the crate after breaking off the strips of wood. It was cradled in a thick blanket. "I meant to have it wrapped, but..."

"Oh, John, it doesn't matter. As it is, I don't really know why you'd want to buy me anything."

The room went quiet as McFarland reclaimed his chair. "Go ahead and open it."

The object was heavy and awkward in her lap. With infinite care, Judy unrolled the blanket, her excitement growing. As the bronze figure was gradually revealed, she raised her eyes to his. "John? Oh, John, could this be what I think it is?"

He arched both eyebrows playfully. "I don't know."

Tears filled her eyes and Judy bit her lip, too overcome to speak.

"Judy?"

She pressed her fingers to her mouth as she blinked back the tears. "It's the Riordan sculpture Mother gave Father. He was forced to sell it...recently."

"Yes."

"You knew?" Her hand lovingly traced the bronze, stroking it as though she hadn't believed she'd ever hold it in her hands again.

Reverently, she set the sculpture aside and lifted her arms to John. Tears shone in her eyes. "Come here," she whispered brokenly. "I want to thank you."

Eight

McFarland made excuses to visit Judy. Ten times a day he found reasons that demanded he go to her. He discovered it was necessary to confer with her nurse at least twice a day. He delivered Judy's lunch along with his own so they could share their meals. In the evening, he felt Ms. Reinholt, the nurse, should have some time off, so McFarland took it upon himself to stay with the patient. Seldom did he come empty-handed. Judy's injury was the perfect excuse to give her the things he felt she deserved.

Judy's eyes would light up with such happiness at his arrival that his excuses became flimsier with every day. The Riordan sculpture rested on the nightstand and more than once McFarland had caught Judy gazing at it longingly. He knew the piece reminded her of her life in New York, but she never mentioned leaving the island. Neither did he.

"John," Judy whispered the third day of her convalescence. "You have to send that woman home." She bobbed her head in the direction of the stiff-backed nurse who sat knitting in the opposite corner of the room.

"Why?" He lowered his voice conspiratorially, his eyes twinkling.

"I'm not joking, so quit laughing at me! Ms. Reinholt is driving me crazy. Every time I turn around she's flashing a light in my eyes or sticking a thermometer under my tongue. When I complained, she suggested there were other places she could stick the blasted thing."

Despite himself, McFarland burst into laughter.

Judy's eyes narrowed and she whispered, "I'm glad you consider this so amusing."

"I'm sorry," he said, but he didn't feel at all contrite.

In a huff, Judy crossed her arms over her chest and tried to be angry with him. She couldn't. He'd been so wonderful, so attentive, that it wasn't possible to find fault with him. It was as though he yearned to make up to her for his harshness since her arrival on the island.

"I'm tired of sitting in bed." She tried to appear stern, but the edges of her mouth quivered with suppressed laughter.

He grinned.

"You'd think I was the only woman who'd ever survived two cracked ribs, the way everyone's acting. Well, I've got news for you. I am not a medical marvel."

"I realize that."

"No, you don't," she said. "Otherwise you'd let me get up."

"You are allowed to get up."

"Sure, for five minutes every hour. Big deal." She thrust out her arm. "I'm losing my tan! I'll have you know I worked hard for this."

He chuckled, and Judy resisted the urge to poke her elbow into his ribs.

"You aren't taking me seriously, John!"

"All right, all right. I'll tell Ms. Reinholt you can get up more often."

"I want to sit in the sun," she pleaded.

"Perhaps tomorrow."

There was no point in arguing. "Promise?"

He nodded. His eyes held hers and were so warm and caressing that Judy wondered why she longed for sunshine when she had John.

"And…"

"Hmm?"

"No more gifts." Her room was filled to overflowing with everything he'd given her. There was hardly space for all the flowers—roses, orchids, daisies. In addition, he'd given her bottle upon bottle of expensive perfume, and box after box of jewelry until she swore she could open her own store. Her slightest wish had been fulfilled ten times over.

"I like giving you things."

Her hand reached for his. Intuitively Judy recognized that John was soothing his conscience. She frowned; it was important that he know she didn't blame him. "The accident wasn't your fault."

His fingers tightened on hers. "I caused you to fall…"

"John, no." Her free hand stroked his clenched jaw. "I was the one who ran from you. It was an accident." In her opinion, the pain of cracked ribs was a small price to pay for an end to the hostility between them.

Ms. Reinholt set her knitting aside and checked her watch. "It's time to take Ms. Lovin's temperature," she said crisply.

"See what I mean?" Judy muttered.

"I'd better get back to the office." John leaned over and

lightly brushed his lips over hers, then stood and left the room.

Obediently, Judy opened her mouth as the nurse approached. She lay back and closed her eyes, savoring the memory of those moments with John. Although he came often, he seldom stayed more than ten or fifteen minutes. Judy was so pleased to see him for any amount of time that she didn't complain.

John wasn't her only visitor. Avery Anderson arrived shortly after noon, pulled up a chair and talked for an hour. He was a fussy man, not much taller than she was and couldn't seem to finish a sentence without stuttering. She found him oddly charming, though, and toward the end of their conversation, he seemed to relax.

Ten minutes after Avery's visit, John reappeared, looking perplexed. He ran his fingers through his hair and studied her. "What did you say to Avery?"

"When?"

"Just now. He was here, wasn't he?"

Judy nodded. "I didn't say anything special. He came to see how I was doing. You don't mind, do you? I mean, if he should've been doing something else, I apologize."

John shook his head absently. "We'd finished for the day."

"What's wrong, then?"

"Nothing." John smiled then, a rich, rare smile. "He's decided to stay."

"Avery? I didn't know he was leaving."

"He isn't," John said. "At least, not anymore."

"I'm glad."

He stared at her. "You're sure you didn't say anything?"

"I said a lot of things."

His gaze returned to her. "Like what?"

"John, honestly. I don't know… I mentioned the weather and we talked about the stock market—he was far more knowledgeable about it than I'll ever be. We talked about you, but only a little. Now that you mention it, he did seem nervous at first."

"Avery's always nervous."

"Then there was nothing out of the ordinary."

McFarland sat on the edge of the bed and braced his hands on either side of her head. "It appears I'm in your debt again."

"Good, I like it that way."

He looked as though he wanted to kiss her. He even bent his head closer to hers, his gaze on her lips. Judy wished he would and tried to beckon him with her eyes, but he didn't and left soon afterward, leaving her frustrated and disappointed. He'd kissed her several times since the accident, light kisses that teased her with the memory of other more potent ones. He treated her like…like an indulgent older brother. But she was powerless to change his attitude until she could get out of bed.

Judy crossed her arms and sighed dejectedly. She couldn't blame John for not being tempted by her; she must look a sight in her plain nightgowns. What she wouldn't give for a skimpy piece of silk!

Feeling tired, Judy slept for the next hour and woke to distant hammering, or at least that was what it sounded like.

"What's that noise?" She sat upright, looking at the nurse.

"Is it bothering you? Mr. McFarland instructed me to let him know if the construction disturbed your rest."

"Construction?"

"Yes, Mr. McFarland is having a medical clinic built. I'll be staying on the island full-time following your recovery."

"He's building a clinic?"

"Yes, I've already seen several of the children for physical exams. Arrangements are being made to fly in a doctor twice a week from now on."

Judy was too astonished to make a sound. Grimacing at the pain, she tossed aside the sheets and climbed out of bed. She reached for her robe.

"Ms. Lovin, what are you doing?"

She tried to speak, but couldn't. Instead, she shook her head and walked out of the room.

"Just where do you think you're going?" Virginia Reinholt demanded, hands on her hips.

It was all Judy could do to point down the stairs.

"Ms. Lovin, I must insist that you return to your room immediately. Mr. McFarland will be displeased."

Judy ignored her and carefully moved down the stairs, taking one step at a time. It hurt to walk, but she discovered that pressing her arm against her sides lessened the pain.

The middle-aged nurse ran ahead of Judy and was waiting for her at the bottom of the stairs. "Please—go back to your room this instant."

"No," Judy said with as much resolve as she could muster.

"Then you leave me no option but to inform my employer." The nurse marched toward McFarland's suite of offices.

The flustered woman was standing in front of Avery's desk, visibly distressed, when Judy appeared. Avery wiped his forehead with his handkerchief, straightened his bow tie and nodded now and then.

Judy sidestepped them both, knocked politely on John's door and let herself into his office.

"Judy?" He rose to his feet. "What are you trying to do?

Kill yourself?" He noted her tears and lowered his voice sufficiently. "My Beauty, what is it?" He walked around his desk and pulled her into his arms.

Judy tried to tell him, but her voice refused to cooperate. Whimpering softly, she framed his face with her hands and spread kisses over his jaw and cheeks. Quick, random kisses. She found his eyes, his nose, his ear. She kissed him again and again, ignoring his faint protests.

"Judy," he said thickly, his hands on her upper arms.

He continued to speak, but Judy cut him off by placing her mouth over his, thanking him silently for his thoughtfulness.

The intensity of the kiss rocked them both and, feeling weak, he backed into a chair and sat with her nestled in his lap.

He drew her closer and teased her with feathery strokes of his tongue. Judy moaned, lost in the sensations.

McFarland had restrained himself from holding or touching her like this. Her innocence humbled him, and he was afraid he'd frighten her with the fierce passion she aroused in him.

Since the accident, he'd kissed her a handful of times, but each gentle kiss had only created more need than it satisfied. Now his desire for her mounted with such intensity that it sapped the strength from him. Emotions that had been hiding just below the surface gushed forth, nearly overpowering him with their intensity.

Groaning, McFarland tore his mouth away and nuzzled his face in her neck, holding her as close as he dared, afraid of causing her further pain. Her tenderness enveloped him, and with it a desire so overwhelming that he couldn't hold her much longer and remain sane.

"John," she pleaded, "don't stop."

He kissed her again because refusing her anything was beyond him. His mouth claimed hers, and when he'd finished, their breathing was labored.

He held her face and wiped the tears from her cheek with the side of his thumb, still aghast at the power she held over him. "What happened?"

She shook her head. "I heard pounding...or what I thought was...pounding."

McFarland nodded, encouraging her to continue.

"You're building a medical clinic?"

"Yes."

She drew her hands over his face, stroking, loving every inch of his features while she gathered her composure. "Thank you," she said in a small voice.

McFarland studied her, more perplexed than ever. He'd given her a host of gifts, but nothing had evoked this response. Not even the sculpture. A simple medical clinic had reduced her to tears.

A loud knock forced them apart.

"I apologize for this rude interruption, Mr. McFarland," the nurse said, standing just inside the door. "There was no stopping her—I did try."

"I flew the coop," Judy whispered and was rewarded with a quick smile from John.

"I really have to insist that she return to bed immediately."

"Oh, do I have to?" Judy asked with a ragged sigh.

McFarland stood, bringing Judy with him. "Yes, you do."

"Another day of this, and you might as well bury me in my nightgown." Playfully, she pressed the back of her hand to her forehead and rolled her eyes.

"Another kiss like that," McFarland said, low enough for only Judy to hear, "and you can bury me, too."

John scooped her into his arms, carrying her up the stairs. Virginia Reinholt led the way back to Judy's room, clucking as she went, listing Judy's myriad transgressions with every step.

McFarland followed Ms. Reinholt into the room and lowered Judy to the bed. She didn't release her arms from around his neck, but held him a moment longer while she whispered, "Just wait until you get sick!"

"Are you sure you're up to this?" McFarland asked for the fifth time in as many minutes. The thought of her on another horse made him wince.

"If you ask me that once more I think I'll scream," Judy told him with a scathing look that added credence to her threat. "It's been three weeks since the accident. I'm not recovering from brain surgery, you know!"

"But horseback riding…"

"If Ms. Reinholt approved, so should you. Besides, I want to ride again before I lose my nerve."

"Never mind yours," McFarland muttered. "Mine's completely shot."

Sam brought both Princess and Midnight to the front of the stables and held Princess while Judy slipped her foot into the stirrup and mounted the mare.

The movement caused a painful twinge, but nothing she couldn't readily disguise. "There," she said triumphantly.

"Right." McFarland swung himself onto Midnight and circled the yard. Judy hadn't fooled him; she was hurting and he was furious that she wouldn't put this off until she'd had time to heal completely.

"Are you coming or not?" She threw the question over her shoulder as she trotted ahead of him toward the beach.

"Judy, slow down!" he shouted, racing after her.

"No."

The wind carried her laughter and McFarland relaxed in his saddle, smiling as the sound washed over him. The last few weeks had drastically altered their relationship.

He'd never spent time like this with a woman. A shared look could have more meaning than an hour's conversation; a kiss in the moonlight could fill him with longing. She might have been innocent, but she aroused in him a sensual awareness far stronger than anything he'd ever known. When she laughed, he laughed; when she ached, he ached; when she was happy, he was happy.

He spent as much of his day with her as his business would allow. For the first time, he delegated his duties freely. He'd always known that Avery Anderson was a competent manager, but in the past three weeks, he'd learned to fully utilize and appreciate the man's talents.

If McFarland needed to read over papers regarding his business interests, he'd often do it in the evenings. Content simply to be at his side, Judy would sit across from him in the library reading, a book propped open in front of her, while he handled his affairs. Often he found his interest wavering. Watching her was by far the greater joy.

There'd been a time when he was reluctant to take an hour off; now he dedicated whole days to Judy. He couldn't imagine his life without her. Some inner part of himself must have known this would happen—that was the only possible explanation for the fact that he'd forced her to come to the island. For the very first time in his life he was utterly content. There were no more mountains to conquer, no more bridges to cross. There was nothing he desired more than what he possessed at that moment.

"I've missed riding," Judy said happily, breaking into his thoughts.

He'd ridden only five or six times himself, preferring to spend any free hours with her.

"John," she said, her voice softening, "I thought I asked you to stop buying me gifts."

"I vaguely recall something to that effect," he said glibly.

"If you think you've fooled me, you're wrong. I know exactly what's going on."

"I wouldn't dream of disregarding your wishes." He did his best to disguise a smile.

"I suppose you don't think I've noticed the way Sam's been walking around like a peacock. You've bought another horse."

Shaking his head, McFarland chuckled. "She's a beauty. You're going to love her."

"Oh, John, honestly. What am I going to do with you?"

Love me. Marry me. Have children with me. Fill my life with joy. The possibilities were endless.

"John, look," Judy cried. "The kids are playing in the surf."

McFarland paused, watched their antics and laughed.

"They haven't seen you in a couple of weeks," he said. "Go and talk to them. I'll wait for you here."

"Wait for me?" She turned questioning eyes to him.

"I'll frighten them away."

Judy frowned. She understood what he meant, but it was time the children got to know him the way she did, the way he really was. "But you're with me," she said, climbing down from Princess. "Come on." She held out her hand to him.

McFarland felt a twinge of nervousness as he joined her. He hadn't been around children much and if he admitted the truth, he felt as apprehensive as they did.

"Philippe. Elizabeth." Judy called their names and watched as they turned, then raced toward her.

"Judy!"

Arms went flying around her amid a chorus of happy cries.

Judy fell to her knees and joyously hugged each one.

"We heard you nearly died!"

"There's a nurse on the island now. Did you know that?"

"Paulo got a new tooth."

"It'd take more than a fall to do me in," she told them with a light laugh, dismissing their concern. She lifted her eyes to John's, daring him to contradict her. "Children, I have someone I want you to meet." She rose to her feet and slid her arm around John's waist. "This is Mr. McFarland. He owns the island."

All the children froze until Elizabeth and Margaret curtsied formally, their young faces serious as they confronted John McFarland. The boys bowed.

McFarland frowned, raised his brows at Judy and followed the boys' example, bending low. "I'm pleased to make your acquaintance."

"Did you build us the school?"

"The nurse stuck a needle in my arm, but I didn't cry."

"The doctor said I have to eat my vegetables."

The flurry of activity took him by surprise. Patiently, he was introduced to each child.

"Judy. Judy." Jimmy came running from the edge of the jungle, carrying a huge cage. "Did you see my bird?"

He was so obviously proud of his catch that Judy paid a great deal of attention to the large blue parrot. "Oh, he's lovely."

"I caught him myself," Jimmy went on to explain. "He

was trapped in the brush and I grabbed him and put him inside the cage."

The square box had been woven from palm leaves. "You did an excellent job."

"He sings, too. Every morning."

"I think you should set him free," Margaret said, slipping her hand into Judy's. "No one's happy in a cage."

"But he sings," Jimmy countered.

"He's such a pretty bird," Philippe said, sticking his fingers into the holes of the cage. The parrot's wings fluttered madly in an effort to escape.

"I give him food. He'll even let me hold him."

"But how do you know he's happy?" Margaret persisted.

"Because I just do!"

"But how do you know he'll be happy tomorrow?"

"Because he will!"

Judy felt the blood drain from her face. The chatter of the children abated. Even the ocean appeared to hold back the surf. Judy couldn't take her eyes off the parrot, and her throat clogged with emotion. She was like that bird. She'd been coerced into coming here. John had forced her to leave everything she loved behind. He'd given her gift after gift, admired her, held her in high regard, but it had changed nothing. She was still in a cage, a gilded one, but nevertheless a cage. She could flutter her wings, trying to escape, but she was trapped as effectively as the parrot.

"I...think I should get back to the house," she said, her voice shaky.

"It was too much for you." John took her by the elbow and led her over to Princess. "You've gone pale," he told her.

Judy felt as though someone had robbed her of her happiness. Seeing the bird brought her own situation into clear focus. She'd been playing a fool's game to believe she could ever be more than a plaything to John. He'd told her when she first arrived that she'd been brought to St. Steven's to amuse him. She'd fulfilled that expectation well, so content was she with her surroundings.

The ride back to the house seemed to require all her energy.

"I'm contacting the doctor," McFarland announced the minute they'd dismounted and the horses had been led away. "I knew it was too soon, but I went against my better judgment."

"No," Judy said, hardly able to look at him. "I'll go lie down for a moment. Then I'll be fine." That wasn't true, but she needed an excuse to get away from him and think.

A letter was waiting for her on the dresser in her room. She stared at the familiar handwriting and felt overwhelmingly homesick. Tears burned for release as she held the envelope and closed her eyes. Home. Her father. David. New York had never seemed so far from her, or so unattainable.

The content of the letter had a curious effect on her. Suddenly in control of herself again, she marched out of her room and down the stairs.

John was in his office dictating a memo to Avery when she approached him. He looked up, obviously surprised to see her standing here. "Judy," he said softly. "Are you feeling better?"

"I'm fine." She noticed how blithely he smiled, unaware of the change in her. "John, I need to talk to you."

He dismissed Avery with a shake of his head. Judy closed the door after his assistant and turned to face him, pressing her hands against the door. Her lack of emotion astonished even her.

"There was a letter from my family in my room when I returned."

"I'd heard one had been delivered."

She dropped her hands to her side. "My brother's getting married."

"Good." McFarland smiled. "It seems the shipping business has improved." With a little subtle help from him. The Lovins need never know, and it eased his conscience to repay them in some small measure for sending Judy to him.

"My father is thrilled with his choice and so am I. David has loved Marie for several years, but delayed the wedding because...well, you know why."

For having received such good news, Judy didn't appear very happy.

"John," she said, boldly meeting his gaze. "I've been here for nearly three months now."

"Yes."

"You asked me and I came without question. I've never asked to leave."

A sense of dread filled McFarland. "What are you saying?"

"I want to go home."

Nine

"I won't let you go," McFarland said.

Judy closed her eyes at the bittersweet pain. "I haven't amused you enough?" At his blank stare, she continued. "That was the reason you brought me to the island, or so you claimed."

"That has nothing to do with it."

"Then what does?"

McFarland's control was slipping and rather than argue, he reached for his pen and scribbled instructions across the top of a sheet. If he ignored her, maybe she would forget her request and drop the matter entirely.

"John," she said, "I'm not leaving this office until you answer me."

"I've already said everything I intend to. The subject is closed."

"The subject is standing in front of you demanding an answer!"

"You're my guest."

"But you won't allow me to leave."

A strained silence fell between them. Judy's breathing was fast and shallow. Her throat burned as she struggled to hold back her emotions.

"John, please."

"You are my guest."

"So I may leave?"

"No!" His rage was palpable. He didn't know why, after all these weeks, she'd ask him to release her. His heart felt like a stone in his chest.

The silence returned.

When Judy spoke again, her voice was soft yet tortured. "Then I'm your prisoner."

She turned and left him, feeling as though she was living out her worst nightmare. She dared not look back; tears threatened but she refused to let them fall.

McFarland watched her go, overcome by an unidentifiable, raw emotion. She called herself his prisoner, but there were chains that bound him just as strongly. She'd come to him and within weeks had altered the course of his life. He couldn't afford to lose Judy—she was his sunshine, his joy. She'd brought summer to the dark winter of his existence. How could he let her go?

Judy returned to her suite, weighed down by grief, sorrow, anger. She'd been happy with John and the island life. Everything had been good—until she'd seen the cage. Until she recognized the bars surrounding her. Perhaps she'd been blinded by her love for him and that was why she'd been able to tolerate this lack of choice, of independence. But now, like the bird wildly seeking escape, her wings were beating frantically, seeking freedom.

She took her brother's letter out of the envelope. For the third time, she read it. Every word was a form of torture.

Things she'd taken for granted returned to haunt her. Bently and the funny way he had of speaking out of the corner of his mouth; the dining-room chairs that were a family heritage; the drapes that hung over her bedroom windows.

Her beloved brother was getting married. Some of the weight lifted from her heart as she thought of David as a husband and someday a father. Marie would make him a good wife. His excitement and joy were evident in the letter. She could almost see him with his eyes sparkling and his arm around Marie's shoulder. How Judy wished she could be with him to share in this special moment.

At noon, although she had no appetite, Judy went downstairs, pausing just inside the dining room. John was waiting for her, standing at his end of the table, hands resting on the back of his chair.

"Are you feeling better?" he asked cordially.

"No." She dropped her gaze to the table. A small, beautifully wrapped gift lay beside her water glass. She raised questioning eyes to John. "What's this?"

"Go ahead and open it."

She wanted to tell him that she wouldn't accept any more gifts. He couldn't buy *her* as he'd bought everything else in his life. She wasn't for sale. The only thing she wanted from John McFarland was the freedom to return home, and he wouldn't give her that.

Dutifully, she sat down and peeled away the paper. Inside was a diamond bracelet of such elegance and beauty that she caught her breath. "It's beautiful."

John looked pleased. "I was saving it for just the right moment."

Judy gently closed the velvet box and set it aside. "Why now? Did you want to prove that my shackles are jewel-encrusted? You needn't have bothered, John. I've always known that."

His face convulsed and, as he stared at her, his eyes grew dark and hot.

Neither spoke another word during their meal, and when Judy walked out of the dining room, she pointedly left the bracelet behind.

A week passed, the longest, most difficult week of Judy's life. She didn't ask John to release her again, but her desire to leave the island hung between them at every meeting. Although she avoided him, he seemed to create excuses to be with her. He chatted easily, telling her little things, pretending nothing had changed. Judy wasn't that good an actress; she spoke only when he asked her a direct question. Although she tried to remain distant and aloof, it was hard.

To work out her frustration, she spent hours riding across the island. The sweltering heat of late summer was oppressive. One afternoon, toward dusk, she changed from her riding clothes into her swimsuit.

The pool was blissfully cool when she dove in. She hoped the refreshing water would alleviate the discomfort of the merciless sun and her own restlessness. She swam lazy laps, drawing comfort from the exercise.

She hadn't been in the water ten minutes when John joined her. As he approached the pool, Judy swam to the shallow end, stood up and shook the wet hair from her face. She defied him with her eyes, demanding that he leave and give her some privacy.

He ignored her silent pleas and jumped into the pool. At first he did a series of laps. Somewhat relieved, Judy continued her exercise. When he suddenly appeared beside her, it was a surprise.

"Remember the last time we were in the water together?" he asked, his voice husky and low.

In an effort to get away from him, Judy swam to the deep end and treaded water. She remembered that afternoon on the beach all too well; he'd held her in his arms while the rolling surf plunged them underwater. He'd kissed her and held her body close to his as the powerful surf tossed them about.

Now his presence trapped her. She refused to meet his look.

"You remember, don't you?" he demanded.

"Yes," she cried, and swallowed hard.

His face tightened and he lowered his voice, each syllable more seductive than the last. "So do I, Judy. I remember the way you slid your arms around my neck and buried your face in my chest."

She shook her head in denial.

"You trembled when I kissed you and you clung to me as though I were your life. I remember everything."

Judy closed her eyes. "Don't," she whispered. She desperately wanted him to leave her.

"I'm not going." He saw that her eyes were overly bright and that she was struggling to hold back the tears. "I miss you. I want things to go back to the way they were."

Her chin rose. "They can't," she said, her mouth trembling. "They'll never be the same."

As much as he tried, McFarland couldn't understand what had changed. Why had she all of a sudden asked to return to New York? He'd tried—heaven knew he'd tried—to understand, but she'd made it impossible. In a week, she'd hardly spoken to him. He'd attempted to draw her out, to discover what was troubling her. All she did was look at him with her large, soulful eyes as though she might burst into tears at any moment. After a week, he was losing his patience.

"Why can't they be the same?" he asked.

"I'm your prisoner."

"No, you aren't," he shouted.

"You brought me here as an amusement."

"In the beginning, perhaps, but that's all different now."

"But it isn't," she said flatly. "Nothing is. I'm your prisoner," she repeated.

"But you were happy."

She flinched at the truth. "Yes, for a time I was."

"What changed?"

"The walls," she said in a tormented voice. "I could see the walls of my cell closing in around me."

McFarland had no idea what she was talking about. Walls? Cell? She had more freedom now than she realized. She ruled his heart; he was hers to do with as she wished.

"Judy," he said, trapping her against the bright blue tile of the pool. His face was only inches from hers. "You're talking nonsense."

"To you, maybe. You don't understand."

"I understand this," he said, weaving his fingers into her wet hair. He kissed her then, pressing his body against her own as he hungrily claimed her mouth.

Judy pulled away, and he didn't stop her. But he said, "It was good with us. You can't have forgotten how good."

"Yes, I remember," she wept. Instinctively, her body arched toward him and she slipped her arms tightly around his neck. She was trembling when he kissed her once more and when she arched against him, he nearly lost his grip on the pool's edge.

"I can't let you go," he whispered. He kissed her gently, slowly, again and again until she was weak and clinging in his arms. His body burned with need for her. Raising his head, he looked into her eyes. "I'll give you anything."

Tears scorched a trail down her face. "I only want one thing."

Knowing what she was about to say, McFarland closed his eyes to the pain.

"I want my freedom," she sobbed. Her shoulders shook uncontrollably as she climbed out of the pool. "I want to go home."

Guilt tore at him. He could deal with anything but her pain. Judy was using his conscience against him and in that moment, McFarland thought he hated her.

Then, seeing her tear-streaked face as she reached for the towel, McFarland realized something more—he hated himself twice as much.

Her tears didn't diminish, even when Judy returned to her room. She was shocked by the power John had to bend her will to his. How easily he'd manipulated her. She had to admit that his kisses were even more potent than her desire to go home to her family. Within minutes she'd been willing to give him anything he wanted.

When McFarland returned to his office, his mood was dark. He was short-tempered with anyone who had the misfortune of being within earshot. It was as though he wanted to punish the world for trying to take away the only woman he'd ever cared about.

"Mr. McFarland," Avery said, late that same afternoon. He stood in the doorway, not daring to approach his employer's desk.

"What is it?" McFarland barked. "I haven't got all day."

"It's Ms. Lovin, sir."

The pencil McFarland was holding snapped in half.

"She's staying, Avery, and there's not a damn thing you can say that'll change my mind."

"But her family..."

"What about them?"

"They've personally appealed for your mercy. It seems the Lovin boy is getting married and requests his sister's presence at the wedding."

"They appealed for mercy! I hope you told them I have none." McFarland shuffled through some papers, paying unnecessary attention to them.

"The family's requesting some indication of when you plan to release Ms. Lovin. The wedding can be delayed at...at your convenience."

"Mine." He snickered loudly. "I hope you told them I don't plan to release her." He couldn't explain to Avery that he was *afraid* to release her. Afraid to lose her. Afraid she wouldn't come back.

"You won't let her off the island even to attend her brother's wedding?"

"No."

"But, sir..."

"That will be all, Avery."

McFarland's assistant took a deep breath, as though gathering his courage before speaking.

"Listen, Avery," McFarland said, unwilling to listen to anyone's opinion regarding Judy. His mind was made up. "Feel free to submit your resignation again. Only next time I may not be so willing to give it back."

That evening, McFarland sat alone in the library. During the years he'd been on the island, he'd spent countless nights in this room. Now it felt as cold and unwelcoming as an unmarked grave. When he couldn't tolerate it any longer, he rose and stepped outside, heading toward the stables. A beer with Sam would relax him. He was halfway there when he saw Judy, silhouetted in the moonlight, sitting on the patio by the pool. Her head was slightly bowed, the soft folds of her summer dress pleated around her. The pale light of the moon shone like a halo around her.

The scene affected him more than all her pleas. He remembered standing on the ridge, watching her play with the island children on the beach below. He recalled how her eyes would light up just before his mouth met hers; he recalled how she clung to him. With vivid clarity, he remembered the fall from the horse and how he would've given everything he owned not to see her hurt, not to lose her. Now, he was losing her anyway.

His presence must have disturbed her, because she turned and her eyes found his. McFarland's stomach knotted at the doubt and uncertainty he saw in her gaze. He yearned with everything in him to ease her pain, but if he did he would only increase his own. He needed her. The beast who'd once claimed he needed no one was dependent upon a woman. *This woman.*

The sudden thunder and lightning barely registered in McFarland's mind. The drenching rain soaked him in minutes, and still he didn't move.

Judy came to him, her gaze concerned.

"Go inside," he rasped.

Her face was bloodless. "Not without you."

He nearly laughed. It shouldn't matter to her what became of him; she was the one who wanted to walk out of his life.

"John." She urged him again a moment later.

"I find your solicitude unconvincing."

The flatness of his voice sent a chill through her veins. Judy hesitated.

He saw that she was as drenched as he was. "Go inside," he murmured. "I'll be there in a few minutes."

"If you stay out here, you'll catch a chill."

Raw emotion fueled his anger and he shouted loudly enough to be heard over the furious clap of thunder. "Leave me!"

Her eyes welled with tears.

McFarland couldn't *bear* to see her cry. He stepped close and cupped her face. His heart ached with all the emotion he felt for her. He could *make* her stay, force her to live on the island and ignore her desire to leave. In time she'd forget her family, he told himself, accept her position on St. Steven's and in his life. He would give her everything a woman would possibly want; everything he owned would be hers.

In that moment, McFarland knew that everything he possessed, all his wealth, all that he was, would never be enough for Judy. He dropped his hands and turned toward the house.

When they reached the front door, John opened it for her. Judy paused and looked up at him. Her own distress hardly compared to the misery she witnessed in his eyes.

"John," she whispered brokenly. Even now his unhappiness greatly affected her. Even now she loved him. "I—"

His face tightened as a dark mask descended over his features, a mask she recognized. He'd worn it often in the first weeks after her arrival. She'd forgotten how cold and cruel he could look, how ruthless he could be.

"Don't say it," he interrupted harshly. "Don't say a single thing. Not a word." He turned and abruptly left her standing alone.

* * *

Princess was saddled and ready for Judy early the next morning. She hadn't slept well and looked forward to the rigorous exercise.

"Morning, Sam," she said, without much enthusiasm.

The groom ignored her, holding a gelding's hoof in his lap and running a file across the underside.

"Sam?"

"Morning," he grunted, not looking at her.

"Is something wrong?" Sam had been her ally and friend from the beginning.

"Wrong?" he repeated. "What could be wrong?"

"I don't know."

"For nearly two weeks now, this place has been like a battlefield."

Judy opened her mouth to deny it.

"But does ol' Sam question it? No." He lifted his head to glare at her. "I figured whatever was wrong would right itself in time. Looks like I was wrong."

"I wish it was that simple," Judy murmured, stroking Princess's neck.

Sam continued to file the gelding's hoof. "McFarland bites my head off and you walk around looking like you spent half the night crying your eyes out. You get any paler, and someone could mistake you for a ghost!"

Judy raised her hands to her cheeks, embarrassed.

Sam lowered the horse's leg to the ground and slowly straightened. "McFarland been shouting at you again?"

"No."

"Has he been unfair?"

"That's not what this is about."

"Did he get after you for something you didn't do?"

"No."

Hands on his hips, Sam took a step toward her. "Do you love him or not?"

Judy felt the blood rush through her veins.

"Well?" he demanded.

"Yes," she answered, her voice shaking uncontrollably.

"I thought so."

She pushed back her hair. "Loving someone doesn't fix everything."

"Then do whatever you have to do to make it right."

Judy swallowed down the hard lump that had formed in her throat. Sam made everything sound so…uncomplicated.

"For heaven's sake, woman, put an end to this infernal bickering. And do it soon, while there's still a man or woman who's willing to work for John McFarland."

Judy rode for hours. When she returned, a maid announced that McFarland wished to see her at her earliest convenience. With her heart pounding, Judy rushed upstairs for a quick shower.

By the time she appeared in John's office Avery seemed greatly relieved to see her.

"You're to go right in," he instructed.

"Thank you, Avery," she said as he opened the door.

John was writing, his head bent, and although she was fairly sure he knew she was there, he chose to ignore her.

After the longest minute of her life, he looked up at her and gestured for her to take a seat. His expression was cool and distant.

Judy shivered as she sat down. "I've been in communication with New York this morning," he said evenly.

She nodded, not knowing what he was leading up to. He could be referring to her family, but he hadn't said as much.

"The launch will leave the island at five tomorrow morning. However, the helicopter is at your disposal."

Judy blinked. "Are you saying I'm free to go?"

"That's exactly what I'm saying."

It took a moment for the full realization to hit her. She sighed as the burden was lifted from her shoulders. "John—"

He interrupted her. "From what I understand, you'll be home in plenty of time for your brother's wedding."

Her smile was tremulous. "Thank you."

He nodded abruptly. "Is tomorrow soon enough, or would you prefer to leave now?"

"Tomorrow is fine."

He returned to his paperwork.

"John…"

"If you'll excuse me, I have work to do," he said pointedly.

Judy stood, clasping her fingers tightly in front of her. "I'll never forget you, John McFarland, or this island."

He continued with his work as though she hadn't spoken.

"If I don't see you again…"

John glanced at his watch and while she was speaking, reached for his phone.

Judy blinked back stinging tears of anger and embarrassment.

"Goodbye, John," she said softly, and with great dignity, turned and left his office.

That evening Judy ate alone. The dining-room table had never seemed so big or the room so empty. She'd spent the afternoon preparing for her departure. Her suitcase was packed, her room bare of the things that had marked it as hers. She'd visited the children one last time and stopped at the stables to feed Princess and Midnight. Sam had grumbled disapprovingly when he heard she was leaving and when she hugged him goodbye, the gruff old man's eyes glistened.

After all the excitement, Judy had expected to sleep that evening. To her surprise, she couldn't.

At midnight, she made her way down the stairs for a glass of milk. She noticed light from under the library door and cracked it open to investigate. She found John sitting at the oak desk, a half-full whiskey bottle in one hand and a shot glass in the other.

He raised his head to study her when she entered the room, and his eyes narrowed. "What are you doing here?"

The words were slurred. Judy shook her head, hardly able to believe what she was seeing. In all the weeks that she'd been on the island, John had never abused alcohol. "You're drunk."

He lifted the bottle in mocking salute. "You're darn right I am."

"Oh, John." She nervously tucked her hair behind her ears, feeling wretched.

"You think too highly of yourself if you assume I did this because you're leaving."

"I…"

He refilled his glass, the whiskey sloshing over the sides. He downed the contents in one swallow and glared at her. "You were a nuisance."

Judy didn't respond.

"I should've got rid of you weeks ago."

Ten excellent reasons to walk away presented themselves. Judy ignored each one. For some perverse reason she wanted to hear what he had to say.

"You're such a goody-goody."

She clasped her fingers more tightly together.

"I could've had you several times. You know that, don't you? You were willing enough." His eyes challenged her to defy him. "But I didn't take what you so generously offered." His short laugh was without humor. He leaned forward and glared at her. "You know why? I like my women hot and spicy. You're sweet, but you'd soon grow tasteless."

Judy's face burned with humiliation; each word was like a lash across her back.

His eyes were cold. "Why are you still standing there?"

Unable to answer him, Judy shook her head.

"Get out!" he roared. "Out of my house! Out of my life!"

Part of Judy yearned to wrap her arms around him and absorb his anger and his pain. But she didn't move, didn't take a step forward.

"Go on," he shouted. "Get out of here before I do something we'll both regret."

"Goodbye, John," she whispered. She closed the massive doors when she left and flinched at the unexpected sound of breaking glass.

"Goodbye, Beauty."

The words were so faint that Judy wasn't sure she'd heard them.

Judy sat in her room, waiting for the sun to rise. She hadn't slept after the confrontation in the library; she hadn't even tried.

At four, the maid came to wake her and was surprised to find her already up. "Mr. Anderson will escort you to the dock," the girl informed her.

"Thank you."

Avery was waiting for Judy at the bottom of the stairs.

He took the suitcase from her hand and gave her a sympathetic smile. Judy paused and glanced in the direction of the library.

"Take care of him for me, will you?" she asked.

Avery cleared his throat and looked doubtful. "I'll do my best."

The launch was at the dock. Judy hugged John's assistant and Sam, who arrived at the last minute, looking flustered and upset.

Only when the boat had sped away did Judy turn back to the island. In the distance she saw a third figure standing separate from the others.

John McFarland watched the only woman he'd ever loved vanish from his life. In releasing her, he had made the ultimate sacrifice. It was probably the one completely unselfish act of his lonely life.

Ten

The sound was what astonished Judy most. Street noise: buses, taxis, traffic, shouts, raised voices, laughter, televisions, radios. The clamor was less irritating than it was distracting. The island had taught her to appreciate the wonders of silence.

But this was Manhattan, not St. Steven's Island, Judy had to repeatedly remind herself. The first few days after her arrival home, she'd felt as though she'd returned to another planet. The life that had once been familiar and comfortable felt strangely out of sync—and appallingly loud. In time, she knew she'd adjust, just as she'd adapted to life on the island.

"It's McFarland, isn't it?" her father asked her over breakfast the first week she was home.

"John?"

Charles Lovin's features were tight with anxiety. The months apart had taken their toll on him. It showed in the way his eyes followed her, his gaze sad and troubled. "Mc-Farland treated you abominably, didn't he?"

"Of course not," Judy answered, dismissing her father's fears with a generous smile. "John McFarland was the perfect gentleman."

"From the beginning?"

Judy lowered her eyes to her plate as a twinge of loneliness brought tears to her eyes. "In his own way, yes. He's an unusual person."

"You think I don't know that? I died a thousand deaths worrying about you alone with that…that beast."

"I wasn't alone with John and, Father, really, he isn't a beast."

Charles Lovin's instant denial faded in Judy's ears. She pretended to be listening while her father listed John's many faults in a loud, haranguing voice. Her thoughts were a thousand miles away on a Caribbean island where orchids grew in abundance and children laughed and a man ruled his own kingdom.

"Judy, are you listening to me? Judy?"

"I'm sorry," she said contritely, looking at her father. "What were you saying?"

Father and son exchanged meaningful glances.

"I'm sure you can appreciate that Dad and I were concerned about you," David said, studying his sister.

"Naturally. I would've been worried myself had the circumstances been reversed," Judy murmured, feeling wretched. She wanted to defend John, but both her father and her brother were filled with bitterness toward him.

"He never spoke to us personally," David continued. "I can't begin to tell you how frustrated Dad and I were. We must've contacted McFarland a hundred times and never got past that assistant of his. By the way, what's this Anderson fellow like?"

"Avery?"

"Yes. I tell you, he's an expert at sidestepping questions. No matter how much Dad and I hounded him, we never got a straight answer."

At the memory of Avery Anderson, Judy brightened and spent the next five minutes describing John's assistant. "He really is a funny little man. So polite and—"

"Polite!" Her father nearly choked on his coffee. "The next thing I know, you'll be telling me McFarland's a saint."

Judy blushed at the memory of the times he could have made love to her, and hadn't. "In some ways he *was* a saint."

Her announcement was followed by a stunned silence.

"Any man who pulls the kind of stunts John McFarland does will burn in hell," Charles Lovin stated emphatically.

"Father!"

"I mean it. That man is a demon."

Judy pushed her plate aside and managed not to defend John. "And just what did he do that was so terrible?"

"Why, he…he nearly destroyed our business."

"It's thriving now. You told me so yourself."

"Now!" Charles Lovin spat. "But McFarland drove us to the brink of disaster, then took delight in toying with us."

"He told me once that he held you in high regard," Judy informed him.

"Then Lord help us if he ever wants to be my friend!"

With great difficulty, Judy kept her own counsel. Neither her father nor her brother understood John the way she did. In their position, she'd probably feel differently, but that didn't change her opinion of him, her love for him.

"Does he do this sort of thing often?" David asked, as he sliced his ham.

Judy blinked, not understanding.

"Were there other women on the island?" he elaborated.

"A few. But I was the only one he…" She paused and searched for the right word.

"You were the only woman he blackmailed into coming?" her father finished for her.

"The only one he sent for," Judy corrected calmly.

"That man is a menace to society," Charles muttered angrily as he sipped his coffee.

Judy couldn't tolerate their insults any longer. She sighed and shook her head. "I hate to disappoint you both, but John McFarland is kind and good. He treated me with respect the entire time I was on the island."

"He held you like a prisoner of war."

"He released me when I asked," she told them, stretching the truth only a bit.

"He did?"

"Of course." She dabbed the corner of her mouth with her napkin, ignoring the way both men were staring at her.

"He held you for three months, Judy," David said, watching her keenly. "You mean to say in all that time you never asked to leave?"

"That's right."

Again father and son exchanged looks.

"I don't expect you to understand," she told them lamely. "The island is a tropical paradise. I didn't think of asking to leave until…until the end."

The dining room grew silent.

Her father hugged Judy before she left. "It's good to have you home, Beauty."

"It's good to be home, Dad."

In her bedroom, Judy ran her fingers over the brocade-covered headboard and experienced none of the homecoming sensations she'd expected. She loved this room; it was part of her youth, part of her existence before she'd met John McFarland.

Sitting on her bed, Judy felt a poignant sense of loss. She'd changed on the island. Because of John, she'd learned what it was to be a woman and no matter how much she might have wished otherwise, she couldn't go back to being the frightened girl who'd left New York.

A letdown was only natural, Judy tried to reason with herself. When she'd been on the island, home had seemed ideal. Everything was perfect in New York. There were no problems, no difficulties, no heartache. To her dismay, she'd discovered that reality falls far short of memory....

A polite knock at the door diverted her attention from her troubled thoughts. "Come in."

Marie Ashley, David's fiancée, walked into the room. "Are you ready?"

"I've been ready for weeks," Judy said, rising from the bed. She slipped on a pair of comfortable shoes. "I plan to shop till I drop."

"Me, too," Marie said, her eyes shining. "David and I need so many things. Oh, Judy, we're going to be so happy." She hugged her arms around her middle and sighed with ecstasy. "Did he tell you that I broke into tears when he proposed? I couldn't even answer him. Poor David, I'm sure he didn't know what to make of me, blubbering and carrying on like that."

"I imagine he got the message when you threw your arms around his neck and started kissing him."

Marie's hands flew to her hips. "He told you!"

"Ten times the first day I was home," Judy told her cheerfully. "I don't know who's more excited, you or my brother."

"Me," Marie said unequivocally.

Laughing, they hurried down the stairs to the sports car Marie had parked out front.

The day was a busy one. True to their word, both women shopped until their feet ached and they couldn't carry another package. They ended up back at the Lovin family home, bringing take-out Chinese food for dinner.

Judy deposited her shopping bags in the polished entryway. "Bently," she called, "we're home."

A quick grin cracked the butler's stiff facade as he regarded the pair of them. He already treated Marie like a family member. "Several wedding gifts arrived this afternoon," he informed them primly.

"Here?" Marie asked, surprised.

"I can assure you, Miss Ashley, I did not haul them from your family's home."

"Where are they, Bently?" Judy asked, sharing a smile with Marie.

"In the library."

"Come on," Marie said eagerly, "let's go check out the loot."

Judy followed her soon-to-be sister-in-law into the book-lined room.

"I took the liberty of unwrapping them for you," Bently said.

Judy and Marie paused in the doorway and gasped at the rich display of paintings and sculptures. Judy's hand flew to her heart. Each piece was lovingly familiar; they were the things her father had sold in a desperate attempt to save the shipping line. The ones he'd surrendered piece by piece, prolonging the agony.

"All this?" Marie breathed. "Who? Who would possibly give us so much?"

Judy knew the answer even before Bently spoke.

"The card says John McFarland."

Judy's eyes drifted shut. John, her John.

"Why, he's the man—" Marie stopped short. "Judy?" Her voice was low and hesitant. "Are you all right?"

Judy opened her eyes. "Of course. Why shouldn't I be?"

"You look like you're about to faint."

"It's from lack of nourishment," Judy explained, her voice shaking. "You dragged me through half the department stores in Manhattan and didn't feed me lunch. What do you expect?"

"I want you to tell me everything. Now sit down."

Judy did because she wasn't convinced she could remain upright for much longer.

"Bently, bring us some coffee, please."

"Right away, Miss Ashley."

Despite her misery, Judy smiled, finding a new respect for her brother's fiancée. "I swear, within a year you'll be the one running the family business."

"I'll have my hands full managing David," Marie returned matter-of-factly.

The coffee arrived and Marie poured, handing Judy the first cup. "You don't need to say much," she began. "It's obvious to me that you love him."

Judy dropped her gaze. "I do. Unfortunately, my family hates him. They think he's some kind of monster."

"But you know better?"

"I do, Marie. He frightened me in the beginning—he can be terrifying. Believe me, I know he's arrogant and stubborn, but as the weeks passed, I discovered that underneath he's a man like every other man. One with hurts and doubts and fears. I learned how kind and generous he can be."

"But, Judy, he forced you to live on that island."

"It's beautiful there. Paradise."

"David and your father thought he was mistreating you."

"Never. Not intentionally. Once I had a riding accident—my fault, actually, although John seemed to blame himself and—"

Marie gasped.

"I didn't let my family know," Judy said. "They would only have worried and I couldn't see any point in increasing their anxiety."

"What happened?"

"I fell—it doesn't matter. What does matter is that John was so wonderful to me. I've never seen anyone more concerned. He spent hours taking care of me. I think he slept in my room for at least two nights. Every time I woke up, he was there. I… I didn't know any man could be so gentle."

Marie smiled faintly. "What are you planning to do now?"

Judy held the coffee cup with both hands. "I…don't know."

"Do you want to go back to the island?"

Judy hung her head and whispered, "Yes. Nothing's the same without John. I loved St. Steven's, but more important, I love John."

"Oh, Judy, your father…"

"I know." She managed to keep her voice steady. "I think he'd rather die than see me go back to the island. John will always be the beast in his eyes."

"Give him time," Marie suggested. "Look what happened with David and me."

Judy wasn't sure she understood. "I know David hasn't seen anyone but you for a couple of years."

"Five years, Judy. I waited five long years for that man."

Judy had no idea the romance between them had been going on all that time.

"Because of the financial problems with the business, David told me it could be years before he'd be in a position to marry me or anyone. He said it was useless for me to wait."

"How painful for you."

"Oh, it gets worse. He broke off our relationship and suggested I marry someone else. When I refused, he insisted I start seeing other men. He made a point of introducing me to his friends and when that didn't work…" Her eyes were dull with pain.

"What happened?"

"I wouldn't give up on him. I loved him too much. If he didn't want to marry me, then I wasn't getting married. There's never been anyone else for me. Only David."

"What did he do?"

Marie's smile revealed a great sadness. "He said some cruel things in an effort to keep me from what he called wasting my life."

Judy recalled her last night on the island and the horrible things John had said to her. He loved her; she was sure of it. But he'd never asked her to stay, never *told* her he loved her. Still, she knew he did…

"Of course, all his insults didn't work," Marie continued. "I knew what he was doing. But he couldn't have gotten rid of me to save his soul."

"I take it he tried."

Marie's mouth quivered. "Oh, yes, for months. Inventive schemes, too, I might add, but I'm more stubborn than he took into account."

Judy gripped her friend's hand. "I hope he knows how lucky he is."

"Are you kidding? I plan to remind him every day for the next fifty years. Now," she said, taking a huge breath, "it's your turn, Judy Lovin, to prove to a man that you mean business."

Judy's gaze rested on their clasped hands. "The night before I left the island, I found John...drinking. He told me he was glad to see me go."

"What did you say?"

"Nothing."

"Good."

"Good?"

"Right. He didn't mean it."

"I know. He was hurting."

Marie smiled. "The guilt's probably driving him crazy about now."

Judy studied her brother's fiancée. "What makes you say that?"

Marie gestured toward the array of wedding gifts that filled the library. "Look around you."

"But—"

"No buts, girl," Marie interrupted. "You're going back to the island. And when you do he'll be so happy to see you there won't be a single doubt."

Judy went pale.

"It's what you want, isn't it?"

"Yes, but Father and David..."

"Just who are you planning to spend the rest of your life with, anyway? Do you really believe they'll appreciate your sacrifice? Do you think my family was overjoyed with me hanging around year after year?" Marie asked. "Good grief, no! They were convinced that unless I married David, I was going to become a permanent fixture at the old homestead."

Judy laughed, despite her misery.

"My dad was practically bringing home strangers off the street to introduce to me. I'm telling you, between David and my father, I turned down two neurosurgeons, a dentist, three attorneys and a construction tycoon."

The thought was so ridiculous that Judy couldn't stop laughing. Soon Marie joined her and they kept it up until their sides hurt and tears rolled down their faces.

That one talk with her future sister-in-law gave Judy all the fortitude she needed to face an army of Charles Lovins. She chose her moment well—the reception following David and Marie's wedding.

"Father," she said, standing beside him in the receiving line. "I have something to tell you."

He shook hands with a family friend before turning to his daughter. "Yes, Beauty?"

"I love John McFarland."

She expected a bellow of outrage, anger…something other than his acceptance and love. "I suspected as much. Are you going back to him?"

Tears brimmed in Judy's eyes. "Yes."

"When?" His own voice sounded choked.

"Soon."

"He'll marry you?"

Judy chuckled and winked at her sister-in-law. "He'd better."

Charles Lovin arched his eyebrows. "Why's that?"

"I'm not taking no for an answer. Marie and I have a bet on which one of us is going to present you with your first grandchild."

The older man's eyes sparkled with unshed tears. "Then

what are you doing sticking around here?" He hugged her fiercely. "Be very, very happy."

"I know I will. You'll come visit?"

"If he'll allow it."

Her arms tightened around him. "He will, I promise."

The launch slowed to a crawl as it approached the dock of St. Steven's Island. Two formidable security guards were waiting to intercept the unannounced intruders.

"Ms. Lovin?"

"Hello, Wilson," Judy said, handing him her luggage. "Is Mr. McFarland available?"

The guard looked uncertain. "I believe he is. Does he know you're coming?"

"No."

He winced at that, but didn't hesitate to help her climb out of the boat.

"Will you see to it that my things are delivered to my room?" Judy asked.

"Right away."

"Thank you, Wilson."

By the time Judy arrived at the house, there was a small army of McFarland employees following her, all talking excitedly.

Sam arrived, breathless from the stables. "Hot dog," he cried and slapped his knee. "It's about time you got here."

"I was only gone two weeks."

"That's about thirteen days too long!"

"How has he been?"

Sam rolled his eyes. "Impossible!"

Judy glanced around to see that several of the other employees were nodding their heads, agreeing with Sam's assessment.

"He's fired me three times in the last week alone," Wilson volunteered.

"Moi aussi," the chef added, ceremoniously crossing his arms over his chest, greatly insulted. "He had ze nerve to suggest I return to cooking school."

"Everything will be better now that Ms. Lovin's here," Sam assured the irate staff. "Next time you leave, though," he warned Judy, "we'll all be on that boat with you."

Ms. Reinholt, who'd stayed to work at the new medical clinic, gave a decisive nod.

"I won't be leaving," Judy told them confidently.

A small cheer arose and when she entered the house, she was met by a red-faced Avery.

"Ms. Lovin!" He looked stunned, flustered, then relieved. "Oh, thank God you're back."

"Where is he?" she asked, resisting the urge to hug her friend.

"The library." He pointed in the direction of the closed doors as though he expected her to have forgotten. "I tried to take care of him like you wanted," Avery said, his words coming out in a rush. "Only, Mr. McFarland, well, he didn't take kindly to my concern."

"I can imagine," Judy said, grateful for such loyal friends.

Summoning her courage, she stood in front of the library doors. She found it fitting that he would be there. The last time she'd confronted him had been in the same room. Only this time, she planned to do all the talking.

She didn't knock, but opened the doors and stepped inside.

"I said I wasn't to be disturbed!" John shouted.

Judy's heart constricted at the sight he made, hunched behind a desk. He looked hard, his blue eyes devoid of any emotion except anger and regret. She noted the lines of fatigue around his eyes and the flatness of his mouth.

"John, it's me," she said softly, loving him so much that only strength of will prevented her from walking into his arms.

His head snapped up. His eyes went wide with questioning disbelief and he half rose from his chair. "Beauty." He froze as though he couldn't decide what to do.

"Don't, John."

"Don't?" he repeated, puzzled.

"Don't ask me to leave. I won't, you know."

McFarland heard the catch in her voice and sank back into the leather chair. How well she knew him; the words had dangled on the tip of his tongue. He'd been about to demand that she go right back where she came from. It wasn't what he wanted, but he had to protect her from himself.

Judy moved farther into the room. "David's wedding was beautiful, and ours is going to be just as special."

"Ours?" he mocked.

"Yes, ours! You're marrying me, John McFarland."

"You're sure taking a lot for granted."

"Perhaps."

"Judy, no." He wiped his face and wondered if he was dreaming. He wasn't. "Don't do this. You're making it difficult to send you away."

She met his eyes boldly. "I plan on making it impossible."

He said nothing for the longest moment. "Judy, there's someone better for you in New York. Some man who'll give you the kind of life you deserve. Some man your father will approve of. He's right—I am a beast."

She planted her hands on his desktop, remembering

everything Marie had gone through for David. "I only want *you*."

"Forcing you to come here, to live on the island, was a mistake."

His face revealed nothing, but she felt the powerful undertow of his emotions.

"It's not a mistake for me to love you, John."

He flinched as though she'd struck him.

"I'm not good enough for you," he told her in a hard, implacable voice. "The things I did to your family…the things I did to you."

"Coming to this island was right for me. *You're* right for me. I love you. All I ask is that you love me in return."

Again he flinched, and his jaw tensed. He reached out to stroke her cheek. "I've loved you from the moment you showed me how you'd tamed Midnight."

Her gaze holding his, Judy walked around the desk. McFarland stood.

She slipped her arms around his neck and leaned into him. "Oh, John, life doesn't make sense without you. I had to leave you to learn that. There's no one else for me, no other place I want to be but here."

"Judy." His fingers plowed through her hair as he slanted his mouth over hers. He kissed her again and again, as though it would take a hundred years to make up for these past two weeks.

"I live in a tropical paradise and it was winter without you," he breathed into her hair.

"It's summer now," she whispered.

"Yes," he said, his voice raw. His hand was gentle on her hair. "I love you, Beauty. But I don't know why you'd want to marry a beast."

"I have my reasons," she said as she lovingly pushed

him back into his chair. "There's a small wager I need to tell you about."

"Oh?" He pulled her into his lap and she leaned forward and whispered it in his ear.

The sound of McFarland's laughter drifted through the library doors and the seven who'd gathered there sighed contentedly.

Winter had left the island, never to return.

From that moment, the people of St. Steven's liked to tell how the Beast was gone forever.

Beauty had tamed him.

* * * * *

Get 4 FREE REWARDS!

We'll send you 2 FREE Books plus 2 FREE Mystery Gifts.

FREE
Value Over
$20

Both the **Romance** and **Suspense** collections feature compelling novels written by many of today's bestselling authors.

YES! Please send me 2 FREE novels from the Essential Romance or Essential Suspense Collection and my 2 FREE gifts (gifts are worth about $10 retail). After receiving them, if I don't wish to receive any more books, I can return the shipping statement marked "cancel." If I don't cancel, I will receive 4 brand-new novels every month and be billed just $7.24 each in the U.S. or $7.49 each in Canada. That's a savings of up to 28% off the cover price. It's quite a bargain! Shipping and handling is just 50¢ per book in the U.S. and $1.25 per book in Canada.* I understand that accepting the 2 free books and gifts places me under no obligation to buy anything. I can always return a shipment and cancel at any time. The free books and gifts are mine to keep no matter what I decide.

Choose one: ☐ **Essential Romance**　　　　　☐ **Essential Suspense**
　　　　　　　　　(194/394 MDN GQ6M)　　　　　　(191/391 MDN GQ6M)

Name (please print)

Address　　　　　　　　　　　　　　　　　　　　　　　　　　　Apt. #

City　　　　　　　　　　　State/Province　　　　　　　　　Zip/Postal Code

Email: Please check this box ☐ if you would like to receive newsletters and promotional emails from Harlequin Enterprises ULC and its affiliates. You can unsubscribe anytime.

Mail to the **Harlequin Reader Service:**
IN U.S.A.: P.O. Box 1341, Buffalo, NY 14240-8531
IN CANADA: P.O. Box 603, Fort Erie, Ontario L2A 5X3

Want to try 2 free books from another series! Call 1-800-873-8635 or visit www.ReaderService.com.

*Terms and prices subject to change without notice. Prices do not include sales taxes, which will be charged (if applicable) based on your state or country of residence. Canadian residents will be charged applicable taxes. Offer not valid in Quebec. This offer is limited to one order per household. Books received may not be as shown. Not valid for current subscribers to the Essential Romance or Essential Suspense Collection. All orders subject to approval. Credit or debit balances in a customer's account(s) may be offset by any other outstanding balance owed by or to the customer. Please allow 4 to 6 weeks for delivery. Offer available while quantities last.

Your Privacy—Your information is being collected by Harlequin Enterprises ULC, operating as Harlequin Reader Service. For a complete summary of the information we collect, how we use this information and to whom it is disclosed, please visit our privacy notice located at corporate.harlequin.com/privacy-notice. From time to time we may also exchange your personal information with reputable third parties. If you wish to opt out of this sharing of your personal information, please visit readerservice.com/consumerchoice or call 1-800-873-8635. **Notice to California Residents**—Under California law, you have specific rights to control and access your data. For more information on these rights and how to exercise them, visit corporate.harlequin.com/california-privacy.

STRS21MAXR